ISBN 978-1-332-53076-2
PIBN 10221606

1 MONTH OF FREE READING

at

www.ForgottenBooks.com

By purchasing this book you are eligible for one month membership to ForgottenBooks.com, giving you unlimited access to our entire collection of over 700,000 titles via our web site and mobile apps.

To claim your free month visit:

www.forgottenbooks.com/free221606

Similar Books Are Available from
www.forgottenbooks.com

THE

MERCHANT OF ANTWERP.

A TALE FROM THE FLEMISH OF

HENDRICK CONSCIENCE.

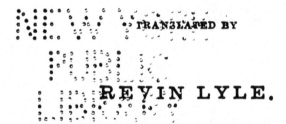

TRANSLATED BY

REVIN LYLE.

BALTIMORE:

KELLY, PIET AND COMPANY,

174 W. Baltimore Street.

1872.

THE

MERCHANT OF ANTWERP.

CHAPTER I.

A LOUD whistle echoed through the station of Malines, and the train, which had just arrived from Brussels, started again on its way to Antwerp. The engine attached to thirty cars trembled beneath the great weight, but soon overcame the resistance of its burden, and dashed across the country with the rapidity of lightning.

Notwithstanding the loud noise of the locomotive, the sound of many voices could be heard.

The last car but one was filled with travelers, who had been on a pleasure party to Brussels, and whom fortune had favored at an archery meeting.

All of them wore badges upon the breast ; many of them still held their bows in their hands, while others proudly displayed the prizes they had won—a coffee pot, a cream jug, or a pitcher.

Their unexpected victory, and the beer they had drunk had made them almost mad in their wild joy. They sang and shouted without intermission, and clamorously related the heroic feats of the meeting.

A single traveler, seated in a corner of the car, appeared not to belong to their company.

He was a young man, very handsomely dressed in black, whose appearance denoted, if not wealth, at least great personal care. His fine cloth coat fitted his figure without a crease; his cravat was tied with art, and his glossy gloves covered fingers which heavy work seemed never to have hardened.

As he kept his eyes down, and occasionally smiled, some of the gay archers were inclined to amuse themselves at the expense of the young dreamer; but when he raised his head and looked at his traveling companions, his countenance seemed to make a deep impression upon them, and, without knowing why, all appeared to feel a respectful sympathy for the unknown.

The features of the young man were regular; a bright color tinged his cheeks, and his black hair curled luxuriantly round his finely formed head; but what particularly impressed the archers was something strange in his large blue eyes, a look full of fire, of pride, and of self-reliance, but at the same time so gentle, so unaffected, so kind, that he inspired every one with confidence and esteem.

The archers recommenced singing with new energy, and the young man, buried in thought, had again bowed his head, when the train stopped at the station of Malines.

The gay band noisily left the carriage, the whistle sounded, and the train again started on its way.

A smile lighted the face of the young man, and he looked around him as though surprised at his sudden isolation.

He lifted up his head, drew from his pocket a purse, and took from it a package of bank bills, which he counted and turned over several times, evidently with no other object than the pleasure of touching the treasure; a light sparkled in his large eyes, and from time to time a cry of joy escaped him.

After having replaced the purse in his pocket, he rested his head on his hand, as if he would concentrate his thoughts upon a single object. Doubtless, what he saw, or what he thought he saw in vacancy, filled his soul with joy; for his eyes were opened wide and his face was radiant.

At last, returning to more material thoughts, but which, nevertheless, seemed to be in direct connection with his happy dreams, he commenced counting on his fingers, and murmuring the word *coffee*, accompanied by such names as St. Domingo, Brazil, Bahia, and Maracaibo. Then he raised his head and gave a sigh of relief, as though he were satisfied with his conclusions.

There was something remarkable in the actions of the young man; his movements were quick and decided, yet quiet and dignified. He seemed to pause between each gesture as if reflecting upon the thought before him. This gave him a reserved and intelligent manner, while the energy of his movements indicated a brave and passionate heart.

He roused himself at last from his reverie and walked towards the door. He looked out at the fields, and seemed to trace the course of the smoke, which, like a huge serpent, enveloped the cars; but, in truth, he saw nothing, for his thoughts were far away with things of the past, or, perhaps, on what was still hidden in the mysteries of the future.

After some moments he again took out his purse, glanced at it, and put it back into his pocket without opening it. He slowly bowed his head, and remained for long time buried in thought, when, suddenly, he raised his arms towards heaven, his eyes beamed with hope, and he uttered, as though in prayer, the name of " Felicité."

The sound of this name, which seemed to escape from his lips involuntarily, brought a blush to his cheeks. He appeared to reproach himself with some reflection, and shook his head in dissatisfaction, when the loud whistle of the engine announced their arrival at Conlech.

They stopped but a moment, and the train was on the point of starting for Antwerp, when the door of the carriage was opened, and a man jumped upon the platform.

"Ah! how do you do, friend Francis," cried the young man to his new traveling companion.

The latter, evidently provoked at the meeting, did not reply, and stepped backward with the intention of seeking another place, but as the train had already started, he was pushed back into the carriage by the guard, and found himself forced to occupy a place in the society of him who had so pleasantly wished him "Good day."

The last traveler was also a young man, of a good countenance, with light hair, and genteelly dressed, though with less elegance than his companion. The latter, astonished at the angry expression and silence of the new-comer, looked at him a moment, and laughingly exclaimed :

"Ah, my dear Francis, surely I am deceived. You appear angry with me. It cannot be. Anyhow I am glad to meet you. Where have you been ? I have not seen you for three weeks."

"Let me alone!" muttered the other, with an expression of anger.

"I who intended to go and seek you on Monday? For you no longer come to our office."

"I would rather lose the chance of making a good speculation than to find myself in the presence of a false friend. God only knows if I will retain my senses," exclaimed the ast comer.

" Why, what have you done ?" asked the young man, with surprise, but without anger. " *I* a false friend ! Take care, Francis, there is some mistake here. I know nothing about it. Besides, no one condemns a good friend without seeking some explanation."

The self-control of the young man seemed to exasperate the other; he turned pale, and his lips trembled, while he murmured the word " hypocrite."

His companion, wounded by this insult, slowly raised his head, and glanced at him with flashing eyes; but restraining himself with an effort, said :

" Do you call me a hypocrite ? What blindness has come over you ? Come, Francis, let us be men. If we are to be enemies it shall only be after a full explanation. For my part, I do not believe I have anything to reproach myself with."

" Is it not true, Raphael, that the daughter of Spelt, the grocer, is a beautiful girl ?" asked Francis, with irony.

" Certainly she is a beautiful girl," replied Raphael.

" And amiable ? " enquired Francis.

" Very amiable."

" And he who wins her as a wife will be very happy ?" continued Francis.

" Without doubt," answered Raphael, " she has much intelligence and feeling."

Francis, while listening to this praise from the lips of his companion, uttered a cry of rage, and with a tone of contempt, said : " Her father has plenty of money; Lucy will be a good match. Such a marriage would give to a clerk the means of entering into business on his own account. It would be worth while for such a cause to betray a friend, and to embitter his whole life. Is it not so, Mr. Raphael Banks ? "

1*

"I do not understand you, you are mad," replied Raphael, with impatience.

"I will become mad, perhaps; but it will not be without being first revenged," replied Francis, despondingly.

"My parents and Lucy's were friends; she has played with me thousands of times when we were children. We were brought up together to be one day united in marriage. Our love was mutual, and grew stronger day by day. I became a traveling clerk; I entered into commerce; I traveled, I worked, I have made enough to give my wife an honorable position in the world; and at the moment I expected to attain the object of my life, my best friend comes to destroy all my happiness. He sneaks into the house, flatters and caresses her father, usurps my place, without reflecting that by this treason he gives a mortal wound to his best friend. But never mind; it shall not pass quietly. Terrible things will happen before my misfortune is consummated."

A quiet smile parted Raphael's lips.

"I see you are in trouble, Francis," said he. "I have cause to be angry at your bitter words, but you are a good fellow, and I feel sorry for your mistake. You are possessed with the most unaccountable impression of me. I do not see the least appearance of reason in your accusation."

"Can you tell me you do not love Lucy?" asked Francis.

"I have a high esteem for her," replied Raphael, "but I do not love her."

"Yet if her father should come to you and offer you her hand you would eagerly accept it, would you not?" continued Francis.

"No, Francis, I would refuse it."

"What! refuse such a beautiful girl, so intelligent, so good, and with a handsome fortune!" exclaimed Francis.

" Were she much more beautiful, and her father pos-sessed of ten times more money, I would still refuse her," said Raphael.

There was a moment's silence, and Francis appeared to be convinced he had accused his friend falsely.

"Is what you tell me really true?" he stammered, with a joyful light in his eyes.

"Do you not know I am honest and true, Francis?" asked Raphael. "Have you confidence in my word of honor? Well, then, I declare your suspicions have no foundation, and you have allowed yourself to be troubled by false appearances. I give you my hand upon it."

Francis warmly pressed the hand of his friend, and exclaimed: "Thank you, my dear Banks; you have relieved me from a terrible trouble. Grief and despair have possessed me for three weeks. Forgive the bitter words I addressed to you; forgive the wanderings of my mind. Jealousy blinded me; but, be assured, it was not my fault. It appeared to me everything was against me."

Raphael Banks took a seat beside his friend, and said to him, smiling: "Come, Francis, tell me what made you suspect me, for I do not understand one word of all this affair."

"Well, I will explain. You know Mr. Spelt has entered from time to time into business speculations. By my advice he lately bought a lot of Java coffee, in the hope of making a nice little sum. But, instead of that, he has lost. This is a sad thorn in the flesh to him, and he cannot forgive me. I have fallen into disgrace, and will perhaps see my Lucy married to another. It is enough to drive one mad. Would you believe it, Raphael, yesterday I found three gray hairs!"

"Impossible," exclaimed Raphael; "you are not yet twenty-six,"

"It is true, nevertheless," replied Francis; "jealousy will make a man grow old in a few weeks."

"But, Francis, your explanation leaves me still in ignorance. What have I to do with it?"

"I will tell you. Whether Mr. Spelt does it to torment me, or whether he really thinks it, I do not know, but he seems to have made up his mind that you, you, Raphael Banks, are to become Lucy's husband."

"I marry Lucy Spelt?" exclaimed Raphael. "What an idea!"

"Yes, you, my friend," replied Francis. "It is now three weeks since he has forbidden me to enter the house; but Lucy comes to my mother and relates her troubles. Her father talks of no one but you. He praises your temperance, your intelligence, your excellent business capacity, your elegant dress; yes, even your black hair and large eyes. Moreover, he endeavors to make Lucy understand that you will be a good husband for her, and yesterday he informed her that he intended to speak to you of the marriage. Do you know what he said of me? That I am a fool, a democrat, and shall never have his daughter's hand as long as he lives. You must admit that I had apparent reason for being angry with you, Raphael—and stop! With my hand on my heart, I tell you, I am not yet quite satisfied."

"Hold, hold," said Raphael, laughing, "you know you are wrong. I do not intend to marry so soon, my friend, and, in any case, it will not be Lucy. To such a marriage there is an insuperable objection."

"What objection?" asked Francis.

"It is an affair of the heart," replied his companion.

"You love another?" exclaimed Francis, with delight. "Well, Lucy has suspected it. She says one of her friends always speaks of you in such high terms."

" Can it be possible—Felicité ? " murmured Raphael.

The blood mounted to his temples, and while endeavoring to overcome his emotion he remained silent.

Francis, satisfied that he had discovered the secret of his friend, said to him :

" You are troubled ; forgive me."

" What nonsense ! " replied Raphael. You forget that Felicité is my employer's daughter, and I am only a poor clerk."

" Chief clerk, Raphael."

" Does that lessen the difference between us ? Moreover the young lady is only seventeen. She is still an innocent child," said Raphael.

" An innocent child," muttered his friend to himself.

" You understand me, Francis ; respect, gratitude—"

" My poor friend, I pity you," exclaimed Francis.

" Why ? " asked Banks, in alarm. " Then you really believe I—"

" I am sorry, Raphael," interrupted Francis, " to have, unintentionally, lifted the veil which, probably, concealed the secret of your heart. Perhaps you did not know it yourself. However it may be, let me give you a word of advice. Perhaps my marriage with Lucy may still be doubtful ; but, no matter, I am your friend. You have permitted yourself to fall in love with Felicité Verboord. This affection will cause you much trouble. Open your eyes before it is too late, and do not embark on a sea which promises nothing but shoals and dangers. Felicité's father is rich ; you possess nothing."

" I have ten thousand francs," replied Raphael

" You have—since when ? " cried Francis.

" When I arrived in Brussels a distant cousin had just died and left me her heir," explained Banks.

"It is only a small sum," said Francis.

"Yet it will enable me to begin business on my own account."

"And what then?" asked Francis.

"What then—who can look into the future? Who can say that I will not become rich as many others have done? Until then no woman shall hear one word of love from my lips; whatever feelings I may have in my breast, no one shall know it."

His friend shook his head with an expression of astonishment, and murmured:

"Poor Banks! I hope your dream may be realized, but I know the suffering of being in love, and I pity you. Then it is true: Felicité!"

Raphael took his friend's hand, and said in an agitated voice:

"Believe what you like, you are in a great measure mistaken; but, whatever may happen, remember, Francis, the slightest hint respecting this will be an injury to my employer and to Miss Felicité. I beg you then by all you hold dear, never say a word at my house which could cause a suspicion of such a thought."

"Be assured I will not," replied Francis. "From this moment my mouth shall be closed, and I will try to forget that Mr. Verboord has a charming daughter. But, Raphael, is the wound then really as incurable that you ——?"

"Let us speak of something else, I beg you," interrupted Raphael.

"Do you wish it? So be it; I no longer know anything." After some moments of perfect silence, Banks said absently:

"There is nothing doing in coffee, at present. What is your opinion? Do you think it will advance?"

" The market has been very dull for a few days. Nobody wishes to sell. The news from America indicate a rise, yet the market in London is even duller than ours."

" There are vague rumors," said Raphael, " that some large banking houses have commenced a large speculation in coffee. If this news be true, we will soon see a change of price. I pity the victims, for there are always some who suffer in a commercial crisis."

" Your employer, Raphael, has a large quantity of coffee in his warehouses; let him be careful."

" That is true," said Banks. " Yet those who are able to await the end of the storm often get the most profits. But the train is stopping: we are at Antwerp. How short the journey has seemed to me!"

"And to me also," said Francis, " a pleasant talk——."

The train stopped and the two friends got out of the carriage. When they had left the station, the travelling clerk said:

" I must say adieu, Raphael; I thank you sincerely for having comforted me. I have to attend to some business in the suburbs. You can render me a great service, but I do not like to speak to you about it."

" Why not? Do you doubt my willingness?"

" Lucy's father sometimes calls you in as you are passing, does he not?"

" Yes, he has done so lately," replied Raphael.

" That was one reason I was so unhappy," said Francis. "And if he still invites you in, will you go?"

" I will tell him I have not time," answered Raphael.

"Are you sure?" inquired Francis.

" Yes, Francis, and in a way that will make him understand that I do not like to be stopped in passing his house."

" But he will seek you in your own house, or at your

office," said Francis. "When he has a thing in his head, he will not give it up. Raphael, if you wish to be generous to your unhappy friend——"

"That is just what I wish to," said Raphael.

"I beg you will try to persuade Mr. Spelt to let me marry Lucy. You are so eloquent, and he has such confidence in you."

"Be satisfied, Francis, said Raphael, "I will try."

"Give me your hand, you are a good fellow, and a true friend. Monday, I will be at your office, as heretofore, to show my samples to your employer. Good bye!"

Raphael walked towards the gate. Many persons were walking outside of the city, for it had been very warm during the day, and at the hour when the sun is nearly in the west, the peasantry were able to enjoy the evening air upon the ramparts.

The young man passed through the crowd, and walked into a lonely street upon his right. He walked slowly, in deep thought; he shook his head with an expression of anxiety; but he soon threw off his sad thoughts, a smile parted his lips and he proudly raised his head.

He had arrived at the Street of the Emperor, and fixed his eyes upon a large house in the distance; it was evidently the residence of a merchant; for at the side of the front entrance there was a large black door before which was tanding a wagon loaded with boxes.

Raphael Banks quickened his pace, and hastened towards the men engaged in unloading, when a man came out of a neighboring house, and stopped him, saying familiarly:

"Ah! my dear Mr. Raphael, so you have returned? Do come in for a moment."

"Excuse me, Mr. Spelt, I have not time," replied Raphael.

" Ah, but I will not let you go. Your business can wait a few moments : besides, Mr. Verboord is not there. Do come in. Whether you wish it or not, Raphael, you must come with me. What I have to say is very important to us both."

" You do not wish to force me, Mr. Spelt ? "

" I beg your pardon, but I do."

" What can you want with me ? " asked Raphael impatiently.

" Stop, stop, my young friend, don't get angry, it will do no good ; I need your advice and you cannot refuse me."

Raphael remembered his promise to his friend, and thinking this might be a favorable opportunity to fulfill it, yielded to Mr. Spelt's entreaties.

" Excuse me," he murmured, " my haste to be at the office is my only reason for refusing. Please do not detain me long.

The grocer conducted Raphael through the store into a handsome room.

" I am entirely alone," he said ; " Lucy and the servant have gone out. This was my reason for insisting upon your coming in. The matter about which I wish to talk to you must be discussed by ourselves alone. Sit down, my friend ; I will get a bottle of my best old wine."

" Do not do so, Mr. Spelt, I cannot drink now."

" Not if our conversation should have a pleasant ending ? " asked the grocer.

" In no case, sir," replied Raphael.

" Ah, we will see."

" If you will only tell me what you wish to see me about," said Raphael.

" Well, sit down, and you shall know. Does not your

2

heart beat rapidly ? If you could only guess what I am going to ask you! You ought to know, that is you could know. Yes, I know, I am not telling you, but your precipitation disturbs my ideas. Bah, let us go straight to the point. This is the question. I wish to have my daughter Lucy married. She is still young, and might wait, but we never know what fancies may possess a young girl. I would like to have it settled at once. I wish to find her a good husband, a young man who is steady, who understands business, and can appear to advantage in society. In a word, a handsome man, witty and yet dignified, with a good prospect before him. He could not fail to love Lucy, but I would not care if he had money or not. Do you not know such a husband for my daughter ?"

And the grocer looked at Raphael with a mischievous smile, and added:

" You are very modest, my friend. It is a virtue which becomes young people; but if I urge you to be sincere. Come, speak frankly ; I am sure you know such a person.

" Yes," answered Raphael, " I do know such a one."

" Don't be afraid to name him," cried Mr. Spelt, rubbing his hands in delight.

" Francis Walput," said Raphael.

" Francis Walput ! " cried the astonished grocer.

" Certainly, sir; it is his portrait you have just drawn."

" Not at all, there is no resemblance."

" It is true you have not mentioned all his virtues," said Raphael.

" It is a mistake. You have not said what you think, Raphael. In an affair of the heart, a young man is always bashful."

" It is not so, Mr. Spelt. I am convinced that Francis Walput is the only man who can make Miss Lucy happy.

"Then, my dear Raphael, if I gave him my daughter in marriage, you would approve?"

"I would rejoice for your sake, for your daughter, and for my friend Walput; for I am sure neither of you would ever regret the marriage."

Mr. Spelt crossed his arms on his breast, and looked at the young man with doubt and astonishment.

"You do not speak frankly," he said, shaking his head. "I insist upon your expressing your true sentiments. But supposing, for a moment, that I am deceived, why should you give me bad advice?"

"Bad advice!" exclaimed Raphael.

"Yes, your friend Walput is a fool who has not the least idea of business. He does not even know how to behave in society. Besides, his political opinions do not agree with mine, and lastly he has caused me to lose several thousand francs. I wish to hear no more of the stupid youth; he shall never, never be my daughter's husband."

Raphael saw that the right moment had arrived for fulfilling his promise. The unjust accusations against his friend had pained him, and with much warmth, he exclaimed:

"What can make you so unjust in this matter to one who respects and loves you? Francis Walput stupid! Why everybody praises his brilliant mind, and fine business capacity. Is there any reason to think the world mistaken? Walput already is at the head of a good business. Is not that a proof of his ability? I know him well, and I am convinced that he has a better chance than most men of acquiring in time a handsome fortune. Another point you ought to consider is, that he possesses the esteem and confidence of the mercantile community. If he were ignorant and incompetent, would he be so generally respected and loved?"

The grocer shook his head, but did not reply.

" As to the political opinions of Francis Walput," continued the young man, " he loves his country and her rights as we all do, but the duties of his business have not given him time to enter into politics. Ah! Mr. Spelt, you know as well as I do, his heart is good and generous, his energy untiring, and his character unsullied. Besides he is an agreeable man, wanting in nothing which is pleasing to a woman, and which can make her happy. Your daughter and he have been attached from childhood, and you for a long time encouraged their affection. Be kind and have pity upon two young people, who are now plunged in grief and anxiety. Why make them suffer needlessly, when you are satisfied that Walput is a good man and deserves your entire confidence ?"

" You advise me then ?"—stammered the grocer, absorbed in his own thoughts.

" I advise you to let them marry without delay, and if you longer refuse your consent, you are in danger of committing an indiscretion as a father, and perhaps a bad action as a man."

Raphael had spoken with so much fervor, that the grocer felt completely at a loss, and muttered to himself:

" How could I have so deceived myself? He does not seem to suspect what I wish to say to him! Walput is not a bad match, he has already made some good speculations. For want of a better—It is strange, notwithstanding—"

" I must now leave you, Mr. Spelt," said the young man.

" Is this frankly your advice, without their being anything you seek to conceal ?" asked the grocer. " You wish me to permit Francis Walput to marry Lucy ?"

" I would be most grateful to you, sir, to permit me to

think that I had been able to hasten this happy marriage. Let me go now. I must go to the office, and it is already night."

"I will no longer detain you," replied the grocer.

Notwithstanding, in the store he again stopped Banks, and said to him:

"Now, come, Raphael, put your hand on your heart, and tell me do you not feel some regret?"

"For what?"

"For the advice you have just given me."

"None, whatever."

"Some persons have made me believe that you had an affection for my daughter. Besides, you always greet her with a marked cordiality."

"I have a high esteem for her," replied Banks, "and she deserves it; but as for her affection, as you understand it, none at all."

"How coldly you speak of her. I believe if I were to offer you my daughter in marriage, you would refuse her."

"I would refuse," answered Raphael.

"It cannot be possible," exclaimed Mr. Spelt. "She is a beautiful girl; she will have a handsome settlement, for she is my only heir. What I offer you, is an agreeable woman and the means of commencing business on a very large scale, in a word, happiness and fortune."

"I know it, sir, and I feel very grateful for your generous offer; but, notwithstanding, I must refuse it"

"Well, you are in love with some one else, or your conduct is inexplicable!" exclaimed Mr. Spelt, pressing his hand to his forehead.

Raphael bowed politely, and quickly left the store.

A few steps further on, he rapped at the door of the

2*

house, before which had stood the loaded wagon. At this moment, the street was empty and dark.

" Ah, good evening, Mr. Banks," said the servant who opened the door. " What kind of a journey have you had ?"

" Very pleasant, thank you, Theresa," replied the young man entering the hall " Are the clerks still at the office ? "

" They have just left."

" Is Mr. Verboord at home ? "

" No, he is at the Philotaxe."

" And Mrs. Verboord, where is she ? "

" Mrs. Verboord is still at Brasschaet with Miss Felicité. They are having a delightful time; they will remain till Monday at the country house. It is a pity you came in so late from your journey. Mr. Verboord would doubtless have asked you to accompany him to-morrow to Brasschaet. You know to-morrow is Mrs. Verboord's birthday ? They are to have an entertainment at the country house."

" I have still a short half hour to work at the office," said Raphael. " Will you please give me a light, Theresa ?"

" Here is the lamp which belongs to the office. Mr. Verboord will, perhaps, return before you get through."

" Perhaps so; if not I will seek him at the Philotaxe, for I have something important to tell him."

Thus saying, the young man crossed the passage, opened a door and entered the office.

After placing the lamp upon a large desk, he paused in the middle of the room. He evidently was dreaming over what had just happened, and his reflections were not with-out sadness, for he shook his head gravely while murmuring in a low tone the names of Felicité and Francis.

He, however, soon threw aside these sad thoughts and

approached the desk. He took down several large ledgers, compared their contents, wrote down their sums, counted and recounted, and at last closed the books with a smile of satisfaction, saying to himself:

"The second clerk is very exact in his accounts. All is in order. I really believe he could now attend to the entire office business. I shall probably not be here much longer. He can take my place. I am glad for his sake; he deserves it. Now, I have finished. Mr. Verboord has not come. Shall I go to the Philotaxe? Why not? I ought to tell him of my inheritance; he was anxious to hear what would be the result at Brussels. Ah, some one opens the door. It is he." A few moments later, the merchant entered the office.

Mr. Verboord was a man of good height, but very thin. Although not much over fifty, his back was bent, his hair and moustache were grey, nearly white; his forehead displayed deep wrinkles, and his cheeks were hollow. All indicated a man who had much to do and who was often burdened with care. Notwithstanding, there was a calm dignity in the expression of his eyes which showed a superiority, and gave (to his countenance) energy and dignity.

"Still here, Mr. Banks?" he said as he entered. "You wished to satisfy yourself all was right. Your zeal is laudable, my friend; but, after returning so late from a journey, you might have rested till to-morrow."

"To-day is Saturday, sir," replied Raphael "Besides, I had something to tell you, which I know will give you pleasure; for you are very kind to me. I have inherited something."

"Inherited!" exclaimed the merchant. "From your unknown cousin? How much? A few hundred francs?"

"No, no, sir, ten thousand francs!"

" Ah, indeed! Ten thousand francs. A nice fortune for a young man. It is a first-rate capital. Many who are now rich had not as much when they began."

" Yes, sir, and I have it here in my pocket-book."

The merchant reflected a moment in silence, and then replied thoughtfully :

" Ten thousand francs! This will alter your position in the world, my good Raphael. If you know how to make a suitable investment of this capital, you may expect much in the future. We will speak of this later—Raphael, there are no news yet from Charleston."

" I know it, sir."

" This delay begins to give me anxiety," continued Mr. Verboord.

" I see no occasion for that," answered Raphael. " There have been violent storms on the ocean, and but a small matter is necessary to delay the arrival of a ship for a score of days."

" I know that; but on the last shipment of cotton to South Carolina, I gave several notes, which will expire during the course of the following week. If I do not get money from America, how will I honor my name?"

Raphael remained silent and appeared to reflect.

" Perhaps I am wrong," continued the merchant " thus to risk the greatest part of my fortune in a single venture."

The young man shook his head thoughtfully.

" What do you think Raphael? My correspondent wrote to me that the article was in great demand, and urged me to send him without delay, an entire cargo of the best cotton fabrics. It is not usual to refuse to fill the orders of such a house, besides it was very profitable to me. Yet I am not satisfied."

" Excuse me, sir," said Banks, " but I do not understand your anxiety. Your correspondent is at the head of an old and reliable firm. You have often told me that this house has been honorably known for fifty years, and has never even been shaken, when hundreds of American commercial houses have been ruined in a general bankruptcy. For the love of heaven, sir, fear nothing from this matter."

"No, Raphael, there is nothing to fear in the matter, but if the money does not soon come, I ought to seek some means of redeeming the promises I have made."

"You have such means at your hand."

"You are very suggestive, my good Banks, but I doubt if your advice will easily relieve the present embarassment. Tell me what you mean?"

"You have a large stock of coffee in your warehouse; sell it and get its value."

"I would lose by it," replied Mr. Verboord. "The price will advance during the next week."

"That is possible, sir," said Raphael, "but, the reverse might also happen. The condition of the market appears to me to be fluctuating and dangerous. In any case, I only wish to show you that you have the means of finding in a moment the necessary money, and that you can wait without anxiety of mind the arrival of your American correspondence."

"You are right, Raphael. It is comforting at least. I am rather anxious by nature, you know. Until this time, no business misfortune has ever befallen me, and yet there are days when a secret anxiety possesses me. My nerves are easily agitated, it is a disease which increases with age. Notwithstanding, a few words are sometimes sufficient to dispel this fear. Come, my friend, the servant has made my tea; you will drink a cup with me, and we will

seriously talk over your future. You know I have a deep
affection for you and only wish to see you succeed."

The young man followed his employer, and sat down to
table with him.

When the tea had been poured out, and the servant had
left the room, the merchant resumed :

" So, my friend, you possess ten thousand francs ? I
need not advise you to be economical ; I am quite sure you
intend to put this money into business."

" Certainly, sir," replied Banks.

"I could easily say to you," continued Mr. Verboord,
" place your money in my house, and you shall have your
share of the general profits ; but a young man like you
ought to try his own strength, and make for himself a position in the world. I have unbounded confidence in your
intelligence and industry ; and, indeed, if a young man ever
had a chance of making a fortune, it is you, Raphael. I
would, therefore, advise that with this ten thousand francs
you commence business on your own account, quietly, prudently, and, above all, with principle. Do you think my
advice good ?"

" Ah, sir," exclaimed Raphael, " how can I ever thank
you for the interest you deign to take in my success ! Yes,
I have resolved to attempt this kind of business, prudently,
as you say, but with courage and energy. For you must
know a strange passion possesses me. I wish to be rich in
a short time, in a few years; and if I do not succeed—
But I will succeed, at least to a certain extent. It is not
only a hope, it is a faith, a kind of certainty. Confidence
in one's self is a source of courage, and perhaps of under-
standing, in matters of business ; but when one does
stumble in the path he falls from a height. There is but
one thing which troubles me, one thing which pains me!"

sighed the young man. " I must give up my position as clerk. I can still remain here some time, but in the end I must leave your office. If I could only have passed my life here, in your service, in your house!"

" It must be otherwise, my friend," replied the merchant. " Besides, the second clerk, taught by your example, is energetic and capable."

" If I had only been able to do something to show my gratitude for your kindnesses," said Banks, sadly. "But if I cannot pay your generosity by an unlimited devotion, believe that Raphael Banks will bless until the day of his death him who rescued him from misery, and treated him with paternal kindness."

" Pshaw, my dear Banks," laughed Mr. Verboord, " you exaggerate the little I've done for you. I took you into my office, and then I made you chief clerk because you deserved it, and I was interested in you. If I have felt for you a warmer friendship than one usually has for his clerks, it has been because you are an exemplary young man, intelligent, handsome, honest, and grateful. Truly, I wish Heaven had given me a son, with your character, appearance, and intelligence."

Raphael, deeply moved by these words, exclaimed :

" Oh, sir, this is too much."

" Not so, my son ; you forget your former position."

" I will remember it to the end of my life," replied Banks. " I was the only support of my old mother. The German commercial house, in which I was then fourth clerk, removed to Cologne, and I lost my place. My mother became sick. I sought employment for months in the different offices, and found it impossible to get a situation any-where. Then came debts ; my mother wanted necessaries ; I became discouraged, and saw only humiliation and misery

before me. It was then that my situation became known
to you. You took pity on my distress. You admitted me
into your office; you gave me more than I had ever earned,
you cared for my mother. And when God, alas, called her
to Himself, you soothed her last agonies. I can see her
still on the day of her death; she knew there was no longer
hope, and still she smiled, and was joyful. A rich lady
spoke words of comfort to her, and an angel, a child, a
young girl, loaded her with favors and caresses. It was you,
sir, who sent these angels of consolation to my mother.
From kindness to me, and compassion for a poor sick
woman, you sent your wife and child to the house of your
clerk. Oh, may God refuse me every happiness in this
world if I ever forget it!"

Raphael appeared much agitated, his eyes shone with an
unusual light. Mr. Verboord, deeply touched by the sound
of his voice, had bowed his head. There was a moment of
silence.

"You exaggerate, my friend," Mr. Verboord at last said.
"That which caused me to so highly esteem you then was
your deep love for your mother. My wife and daughter
still visit those who need assistance and consolation. Do
not let us speak any more of those things. They excite my
nerves. Let us return to the subject of our conversation.
You intend to commence business immediately?"

"I will still remain with you," replied Raphael, "for a
month, six weeks, or perhaps longer, until the second clerk
becomes familiar with his duties, and I can leave without
inconvenience. In the meantime, if the opportunity presents
itself I can do some little business."

"Do you wish to become rich in a few years?" said Mr.
Verboord. "It is a dangerous idea. The beginning is
always difficult. I know something about it, Raphael.

Like you, I entered the race with only a small capital. I worked during several years without much advancement. Then suddenly I had a considerable capital at my disposal; marriage brought me relief. I married the daughter of a rich lace maker; and my position in the world, my credit as a merchant were assured. You, who are a handsome man, Raphael, have greater chances than others to make a good marriage. Make a few good speculations, gain the confidence of the public, and then seek for a woman with a sufficient dower."

The young man looked at the merchant in silence, with an expression of astonishment and anxiety.

"Ah, ah, how incredulously you look at me," said Verboord, with a burst of laughter. "Do you wish a wife like that? I do not think it would be difficult for you to find one immediately. There is the grocer, Spelt; every time he sees me he speaks of you with the highest praise, and asks me things which a man only seeks to know when he has serious ideas about a person. You appear angry, my dear Banks."

"Lucy Spelt? Never! never!" murmured the young man, in a trembling voice.

"I am only jesting," said Mr. Verboord. "The grocer is not as rich as he thinks himself; and really if you wait a few years until you have a business of your own, you will have a right to look much higher."

The young man's face brightened, and a smile lighted his eyes.

"I say it because I think it," continued the merchant. "You are young and have time to wait; your face is handsome and intelligent, you have good manners, and are eloquent. Suppose you are successful, and your capital increases, could not a man such as you aspire to the hand

3

of a rich heiress, even if she belonged to the highest commercial circle? What do you think?"

Raphael was delighted at this prophecy. He smiled in a strange manner, and appeared not to hear what Mr. Verboord asked him.

"You smile at such a future," replied the latter, pleasantly. "Your ambition is great, my son, but you are right; in this matter you do not underrate your own value. Be of good courage. Who knows what the future may have in reserve?"

Raphael still did not reply. The merchant looked at him with surprise, yet kindly. The clock struck eleven.

"Eleven o'clock!" cried Mr. Verboord; "I ought to be in bed. We will speak more calmly of your affairs to-morrow. My advice will be useful to you, Raphael, at least at the beginning."

He rose up, and Banks followed his example, but instead of going out, stopped abruptly and seemed to hesitate.

"You have something on your mind; there is still something you wish to say to me, is there not?" inquired the merchant.

"Yes, sir. Mrs. and Miss Verboord are not at home. I wish to ask you to tell them to-morrow of my good fortune."

"Where is my head!" cried Mr. Verboord. "Sit down a moment. I was about to commit a great mistake. My wife and daughter charged me expressly to invite you to come to-morrow to Brasschaet. Besides it is also my wish. To-morrow we will have a fête at the country house; it is St. Lawrence's day, and my wife's birth-day. Do you know we intend presenting her with some beautiful gifts?"

"Yes, sir," said Banks, with diffidence. "Do not take my boldness amiss if I also ask your permission to present a gift to Mrs. Verboord."

"You! a present to my wife?" cried the astonished merchant. "Does your inheritance already burn your hands? Impossible!"

"No, no, sir," replied Raphael. "I saw this week at Mr. Van Geeri's some beautiful flowers, and I thought, if you would permit it, I would like to offer them to Mrs. Verboord on her birth-day."

"Some flowers? That is another thing. You do not need my permission for that, Raphael. My wife is not very fond of flowers; Felicité, on the contrary, is foolishly so. Your present, therefore, will be welcome, especially to my daughter. I think the news of your inheritance will rejoice my wife more than anything else; and if I were in your place I would not tell her the happy news until the time comes to offer our presents. The love which you showed for your sick mother has awakened with her a strong affection and esteem for you."

"Oh, Mrs. Verboord is not less kind and generous than yourself," exclaimed the young man.

"Well, say nothing till the time comes for wishing her joy. She does not know you have been to Brussels."

"I shall do as you desire, sir."

"Raphael, you must start to-morrow in the diligence. Tell them that I will only come in time for dinner. I wish to wait for the arrival of the eleven o'clock mail."

"Let me stay, I beg you, sir," said Banks. "You do not take enough rest. Spare your health."

"No, there are some matters I ought to attend to, and persons I ought to see. To-morrow at Brasschaet I will show you the plans of the change I wish to make in the country house—that is to say, the building I wish to add to it. At present there is but one hunting pavilion, which is not enough. I hope to give up business some day, and pass my old days in quiet at Brasschaet. This is why I wish to prepare an agreeable retreat, something like a small modern chateau. You will give me your advice; you have artistic taste. For my part I know nothing about it; business fills my brain."

He rested his hand on the shoulder of Banks, who had now risen, and said to him, as they walked towards the door:

"Now, good night, happy mortal! Sleep soundly, and do not dream too much of the fortune you are going to make, or of the beautiful, rich, and gentle wife who smiles upon you in the future."

The young man was so much moved that he could not utter an intelligible good-night, and found himself in the street before he knew it. He stopped as though lost in the darkness, pressed his forehead with both hands, and exclaimed aloud:

"Oh, my God! is it possible? 'The beautiful, rich, and gentle wife which smiles upon me in the future.' I am dreaming—Oh, my poor head! Business—future—yes, yes, and then, happiness—happiness—"

He sprang forward as if intoxicated, and disappeared in the shadows.

CHAPTER II.

THE stage coach from Antwerp to Holland stopped only for a moment at the "Swan" tavern at Brasschaet, and immediately resumed its course.

Raphael Banks left the highway, and followed a cross path into the country.

He was dressed with even more elegance and care than on the previous day; and his white gloves and white cravat indicated that he was going to attend some grand fête.

A great joy sparkled in his eyes; a smile full of enthusiasm shone on his face, while he drew in long breaths of the spring breeze, which brought to him the sweet perfume of the fir trees and the distant heaths.

It was a glorious day in May. Nature, young like himself, breathed only joy, gratitude, and happiness. The sunlight sported in a thousand different colors between the leaves of the trees. These bright and sparkling beams were in accord with the thoughts of the young man, which were joyous and soothing. The songs of the birds concealed in the bushes filled the air. He understood very well what they sang, for the same songs and same wishes existed in his own beating heart. The flowers opened their chalices to the gracious light of spring, the butterflies chased one another through the air, all seemed to reflect his heart, to express his emotions and his hopes.

Raphael paused in admiration, and gazed with loving

3*

looks on the beautiful scene. He resumed his journey, rubbing his hands and smiling at his own thoughts, as though he only saw joy and happiness in the future.

After having followed the path for some time he looked towards a house, which was half concealed behind the trees around it, but whose white cornice appeared above an iron grating. Some rustic houses scattered around, and a little chapel near the road, announced the hamlet of Brasschaet. The neat white house, slightly elevated, seemed to be only a hunting lodge, for it was evidently not large enough to be the residence of a wealthy family.

Raphael Banks, having wiped the dust from his clothes and shoes, advanced towards the gate, which was open, and entered the court-yard.

A young servant girl who came out of the house, exclaimed with astonishment:

"Are you alone, Mr. Banks? Has anything happened? Will not Mr. Verboord be here before dinner?"

"Yes, Mary, before noon; dinner is ordered for two, is it not? Mr. Verboord has something to attend to in the city."

"We are to have a grand dinner. There is a fête to-day. Doubtless you know it, sir, for our young lady has been to the road at least a dozen times already to see if you were not coming."

"To see if I were not coming?" stammered the young man, much moved, and with difficulty concealing his emotion.

"That is to say," replied the servant, "Miss Felicité was watching the road to see if her father was not coming; but she expected him to bring you."

Raphael, to turn the conversation, looked towards the house, and gravely asked:

" Is Mrs. Verboord within, Mary ? "

" No, sir, she returned from church with my young lady and they rested here before the gate for half an hour, hoping Mr. Verboord would come, then tired of waiting they went into the garden, by the back door, to walk on the heath."

" Will you do me a favor, Mary ?   A man will bring a covered basket of flowers here.   Let him put it in the shade under the shed.   Then take off the cover and sprinkle the flowers lightly."

" I understand," cried Mary, " it is a present from you to Mrs. Verboord.   Fear nothing I will take good care of it."

" Which way did Mrs. Verboord go ? "

" I have already told you, on the heaths, by the back garden door.   You will easily find them.   But if you wish, I will go in search of her, and announce your arrival."

" No, thank you, Mary ; I do not wish to interrupt her walk, I will seek her myself."

He crossed the garden, then some thin fields of rye, and soon reached a crooked path which wound between some young fir trees.   Further on, he came to a cleared spot, all purple with the flowers of the heath, thence the path led into a thick woods.

He was astonished not to see Mrs. Verboord and her daughter, although he looked for them on all sides and listened for the least noise ; but at last after leaving a high thicket, he saw Mrs. Verboord on the heath and Felicité, who was talking, by her side.

A deep sigh, or a suppressed cry escaped from Raphael's breast, and he hastened forward like a man possessed by an irresistible impulse ; but a feeling of respect, perhaps the voice of duty, suddenly restrained him.   He walked more slowly and made a great effort to assume a calm and quiet expression.

The good news of his unexpected inheritance was on his lips; but he remembered his promise to Mr. Verboord, and he determined to conceal his new happiness until the proper time. His eyes did not leave Felicité. Notwithstanding his efforts to command his emotion, his eyes sparkled and his heart beat rapidly. The slender form of Felicité, her light curls moved by the soft breath of the spring breeze, her white robe which rested like a transparent cloud upon the carpet of purple heath flowers, all this filled him with admiration and plunged him into a kind of ecstasy.

But suddenly the smile disappeared from his lips and his face became serious, for Felicité had turned round and had pronounced his name. He saw the two ladies advance towards him with evident pleasure, and he observed, almost trembling with joy, that Felicité drew her mother impatiently by the arm to go to him more quickly.

Miss Verboord was a pretty girl with dark blue eyes and remarkably good features. Although she had the form of a woman, her cheeks were covered with the velvet down of youth, her smile was open and naive, and her step had all the elasticity natural to youth.

When she saw Raphael Banks she uttered a cry of joy, and her sweet face beamed with an expression of unfeigned happiness, while a smile as bright as a child's parted her lips.

Her mother, instead of being astonished at these expressions of friendship for the clerk, looked at her daughter with pride and seemed to think:

"How charming my Felicité is when an unexpected pleasure causes her blue eyes to shine so brightly!"

Mrs. Verboord was not handsome; small-pox had left deep marks upon her cheeks, and yet there was a striking resemblance between her and her daughter. This caused her to love her daughter still more dearly. How could it have been otherwise? In Felicité she saw herself again, not only as she now was, but as she might have been had not the terrible disease destroyed her beauty. Since the birth of Felicité she had not left her for a moment, and it was only within two months that they had resolved to introduce the young girl occasionally into the world.

This secluded life and the unbounded love of her mother had given to Felicité, although endowed with both feeling and intelligence, the appearance of an artless child, without experience.

"Ah! Raphael, there you are! How glad I am!" cried the young girl. "How much pleasure we will now have! I know who will be astonished—and you know too, don't you? Ah, but we must not talk of it; all will be well——"

The clerk, overcome with emotion, dared not trust himself to reply. He bowed to Mrs. Verboord and her daughter, and murmured some words of respectful salutation.

"We are happy to see you, Mr. Banks," said the mother of Felicité. "I was beginning to fear that some unexpected business had prevented my husband from coming to Brasschaet. I must thank him for remembering his promise to invite you to spend Sunday with us."

"I am overcome, madam, at your kindness to me," murmured Raphael. "How shall I thank you for the honor you do me?"

"Not at all, Mr. Banks; on the contrary we are your debtors, we are quite selfish in our joy at your arrival.

The solitary life of the country has not many attractions for me, because I have always lived in the city; but when I listen to any one who, like you, adores the country, I seem also to become sensible to the smallest beauties of nature. As to Felicité, that is easily understood; although she loves her mother devotedly, the conversation of an old woman must appear monotonous. The poor child ardently desires the presence of a young heart which enjoys life as truly as herself."

While Mrs. Verboord addressed these friendly words to Raphael, Felicité had drawn back a step behind her mother, and was making curious signs to the young man. She touched her ears and her arms as though she were putting jewels on them, she pressed the collar on her shoulders, threw her hands above her head and opened her mouth as if loudly applauding something. All these gestures explained in advance what was to be done at the fête; how presents were to be made to her mother consisting of ear-rings, bracelets, and a collar of lace; how they would triumphantly cry: "Long live Laurence!" and how much Mrs. Verboord would be surprised and happy.

The face of Felicté, beaming with the light of her artless joy, was of a touching beauty; her eyes were so soft and rested so familiarly upon Banks, that the young man no longer listened to Mrs. Verboord. He was wild with happiness, and yet his heart was oppressed. He felt that he must summon all his strength to conceal what was passing in his heart, and this violent effort almost proved unfortunate.

" Ah, but what is the matter? You are not listening to me," cried Mrs. Verboord, turning round in astonishment. " It seems to me Felicité is making mysterious signs to you. What is there between you two that I cannot know?"

Raphael became crimson, and stammered some unintelligible words, as though he felt really guilty.

Poor Banks! Ordinarily he was a frank and courageous man; but in the presence of this innocent girl he became timid and sensitive as a child, and the slightest word made him tremble.

Mrs. Verboord had pity upon his embarrassment.

"Do not take my words seriously, my friend; I was jesting," she said "Felicité was foolish, and I am quite sure you do not understand any of her strange gestures. Come, my child, let us go in and embrace your father, he will think us indifferent."

"I forgot to tell you, madam, that my employer is still in the city," interrupted Raphael. "He has some business matters to finish this morning, and he will not be at Brasschaet until dinner."

"Indeed, not for two hours!" said the lady, sighing. "Poor Mr. Verboord! He is always full of cares. Although I have little love for a country life, I have urged him to buy property here in the hope that it would be a diversion for him. Whenever I can persuade him to come to Brasschaet, he feels compelled in a couple of hours to return to the city. I only pray he may not lose his health by constant thought and calculations."

"Oh, but to-day he will remain very late in the evening," cried Felicité. "He has promised me, and you may be sure he will keep his word, mamma."

"Well, since we are not hurried, we will continue our walk on the heath and in the woods," said Mrs. Verboord. "Mr. Banks will accompany us, and will give us the news of Antwerp, since we left."

They slowly continued their walk across the heath. The mysterious signs, which Felicité still continued to make, frequently prevented the young man from replying properly to the questions of Mrs. Verboord. The eyes of Raphael sparkled with a strange brightness; he wore upon his face an expression of intense happiness and enthusiasm, and at times he unconsciously regarded Mrs. Verboord and her daughter with a look, which seemed to have no connection with the conversation, or even with the artless expressions of joy from the young girl.

"You know something, Raphael, which you do not wish or dare not tell us," said Mrs. Verboord, with a smile which seemed to say she guessed his secret.

"Yes, yes, he is hiding something from us," cried Felicité; "but he is quite right, mamma, not to tell you. You will know it soon enough."

"Believe me, I know nothing," replied the young man with embarrassment.

Felicité came close to his side, and looking into his eyes, said with a childish irony:

"Stop, stop, Mr. Banks, you know nothing? Look in my eyes for a moment! Ah, ah, it is something he will tell me within an hour, to me alone."

Raphael trembled under this long look, and turned his head away in deep emotion.

"You deceive yourself, Miss Verboord," he stammered. "What should I conceal from you?"

"Come, come, do not dissemble, Raphael; it is useless," she replied "If you knew nothing extraordinary, why should you thus smile to yourself? Why does your face beam with such a mysterious joy?"

"Indeed, there is something unusual about you; I, too, have observed it," said Mrs. Verboord.

The young man knew not what to reply; and yet his heart was so full that he felt compelled to give expression to his feelings. He summoned all his courage, and said, with a voice which he endeavored to control, but which still trembled with joy:

"Yes, madam, I am excited and happy; but there is nothing surprising in my joy. To be seated during the whole month before a desk, to be shut up between four walls, and then suddenly to be summoned to the country through the kindness of one's employer, and to be able to do what one likes in the fresh air, like a bird suddenly set at liberty; to see oneself surrounded by the grandeur of nature, to gaze upon an unlimited horizon; to breathe the air laden with the perfume of the heath; to hear only songs of joy; to behold the verdure of the trees and the flowers; and besides this, to be favored with proofs of friendship and esteem from the wife and daughter of my benefactor, by the angels of charity who comforted my mother in her last hours. Is not all this enough to fill my soul with joy and gratitude, and to lift it up to God who has made this glorious world, and my generous benefactors?"

The voice of Raphael had gradually become clear and sonorous. This eulogy upon the scene around him afforded the means of expressing his emotion without betraying its cause; and he really possessed a sincere admiration for the beauties of nature.

Felicité regarded him with astonishment. She had given more attention to the sound of his voice than to the sense of his words.

"Mamma, how eloquent Raphael is," she murmured. "One would think he was singing."

"It is a pleasure to hear you speak of the beauties of nature," said Mrs. Verboord. "You have a poetical soul, Mr. Banks. Poets and artists do not see things like other men. You must not be offended, but I think there is a lit-

tle exaggeration in your enthusiasm.   For example, you
praise the horizon of the heaths.   It seems to me grey, sad,
and monotonous."

" You are right, madam," smilingly replied Raphael,
who had by this time lost all his embarrassment.   " Yes,
the distant horizon is grey and cloudy ; but let me call your
attention to one fact : it is without limit, like the sea.   When
our sight is thus lost on all sides in a heaven without end,
it awakens in our heart a feeling of grandeur, of power, of
immensity.   Why it is so I cannot explain ; but it is as if
our life became more intense, as if our mind awakened to
higher thoughts.   Perhaps, madam, it is a confused idea of
the sublimity of the infinite."

" I understand you, sir.   It is neither the color nor form
of things which affects you ; they are only beautiful to you
as they affect your soul; that is to say, according to the
nature of the thoughts they awaken in your mind."

" Yes, madam, I could not have explained myself so
well," replied Raphael.

" You are, doubtless, for the same reason an admirer of
the heaths.   Notwithstanding, to me they seem very monotonous."

" Truly, madam; but the monotony and continual silence
of so vast an expanse make a deep impression upon the
soul.   If we contemplate the innumerable existences which
are here developed, and are constantly renewed without the
intervention of man, can we fail to feel impressed with a
mysterious awe, as though we felt clearly and perceptibly
the presence of God in the midst of this free and virgin
nature ? "

" There is some truth in what you say.   There have been
moments when such thoughts have come to me.   You will
end, Mr. Banks, in making me love the heaths."

" I do not think you are right, Raphael," exclaimed Felicité, in a tone of reproach. " You only admire what is grand and exciting, and you pay no attention to smaller things ; but, tell me, what is there more beautiful than the flowers? more enchanting than the song of the nightingale ? "

" Oh, Miss Verboord, you misunderstand my opinions.' replied the young man. " There is nothing in nature, however small, which has not its beauty, and whose contemplation may not become a source of joy. As to the flowers, which you love, be assured they possess in me an ardent admirer."

" Ah, ah," suddenly exclaimed Felicité. " After my father builds the château, he will soon arrange the grounds. He will have gardens for me. I will have all kinds of flowers in these, and you shall tell me the names, Raphael, for you know their names, do you not ? "

" Only of some ; but your desire is sufficient to induce me to learn the names of those of which I am ignorant. I often walk in Van Geerl's garden, and with a little attention I can become familiar with the names of many plants."

" Stay," said Mrs. Verboord, " you remind me, Felicité, that I wish to talk to Mr. Banks about the construction of the little château, to hear what he may say, for it is certain we know nothing. Raphael, has Mr. Verboord shown you the plan of the building ? "

" No, madam, but he intends showing it to me to-day upon the spot."

" If you intended building a small château here for your own use, how would you have the front ? " asked Mrs. Verboord.

The young man seemed to be thinking, but did not answer.

" You ought to know ; you are almost an artist ? " added Mrs. Verboord.

"How would I have the front ?   Mr. Verboord told me that the front would not be large.   In that case, I would have it very simple, elegant, fine, almost plain, with ornaments only around the doors and windows."

" Do you hear, Felicité ? " exclaimed Mrs. Verboord. " Your father spoke of Greek columns at the door, and what he described appeared to me more like the entrance to a museum.   It would be too heavy for a small country-house."

" Yes ; but, mamma, if papa wishes it so, that ought to be enough."

" Certainly, my child, he is the only master.   But he has much confidence in the good taste of Mr. Banks.   The interior of the building does not please me much more."

Felicité, who was not much interested in this conversation, and who was perhaps vexed in seeing her mother altogether absorb the young man's attention, stepped aside and stopped for a few moments.   She gathered here and there a flower, and stripped it of its leaves with agitation ; but she soon grew weary of her isolation, and her looks were fixed on Raphael with an expression of impatience.

The latter, astonished at the disappearance of the young girl, turned his head.   She again made signs to him to interrupt this conversation, so little interesting to her, and to stop behind to try to exchange some words in secret with her.

Raphael Banks was much excited ; all these proofs of friendship and of sympathy filled him with joy, and caused him to dream of happiness in the future.   Yet he pretended not to understand the signs of the girl, and turned his head to reply to some new question from Mrs. Verboord.

Felicité ran forward, stopped her mother, and said to her, with a smile :

" Dear mamma, you have been talking a long time to Raphael; may I also say a word to him ? "

" Why not, my child ? "

" Yes; but all alone with him. It is something you shall know after awhile, mamma, but which you cannot know now."

" Very well, confide your secret to Raphael," said the mother, laughing.

" Come, come," cried Felicité, seizing the young man by the arm.

But Raphael, embarrassed and timid, regarded Mrs. Verboord with a questioning look.

" Be indulgent to a childish caprice, Mr. Banks," she replied. " Do as she wishes. Her secret, be assured, is not very terrible."

The two young people advanced some steps along the path. When they were far enough from the old lady not to be heard by her, Felicité burst out laughing, and said, with animation :

" Raphael, there is to be a fête to-day, a delightful and joyous fête. My mother knows nothing about it, and she does not suspect why I am so gay and happy. How astonished she will be ! We have bought all sorts of pretty things for her. My father's present to her is a pair of diamond ear-rings; my present is a carved gold bracelet, and a handsome set of lace. Besides, I have a song full of sentiment for the piano; it is called, *The Fête of a much loved Mother*. When she finds herself loaded with all these presents, when our congratulations resound in her ears, and, above all, when I sing the touching words of my song, my mother will weep with feelings of delight; and we, we will

4*

laugh and dance for joy. I wish the time were come, I am dying of impatience. But what is the matter, Raphael? You seem very grave. I have so ardently desired your presence that you might share my joy!"

"Ah, I am too happy," murmured the embarrassed young man, "your kind attentions and friendship."

"But you must laugh and be gay to-day. Now, I have just thought of something. You will be there with empty hands like a stranger; that cannot be. I will give you the gold bracelet, and you will give it to my mother as a present from yourself."

"Thank you, Miss Felicité, but I have a present."

"You have? For my mother? What is it?"

"A basket of flowers."

"Handsome flowers?"

"The handsomest I could find in the large nursery of Mr. Van Geerl."

"Ah, that is well; how surprised my mother will be! Your present will perhaps give her more pleasure than ours; for she certainly does not expect it. I have forgotten something, yet that is not true, for it is what I wished to speak to you of. You know how to sing; do not deny it, for you took part in the Choral Society at the Concordia."

"But I do not know much about music," replied Raphael.

"It is not necessary for you to be a finished musician. You have a fine voice, and that is sufficient. In the piece which I am to sing there is a strain, only two verses, which ought be repeated by a male voice; something like an echo or reply. Come, Raphael, the thought that we will sing together in honor of my dear mother fills me with joy."

Raphael looked down on the ground. The friendly words of the young girl had deeply moved him, and he no longer dared to look at the bright blue eyes, in whose depths there seemed to mingle, with their expression of innocence, a more serious feeling.

"You cannot refuse," continued Felicité. "What you will have to sing is very easy. You have only to repeat, in a lower tone than mine, these words;" and she sang, in a low voice:

"Mother, dearest mother,
May you long live to bless me!"

"Will you do this for me, Raphael?"

"Never, never, Miss Verboord, I would not dare!" stammered Raphael, much surprised.

"Why not?" inquired Felicité.

"I cannot tell you exactly. It would not be respectful to speak to Mrs. Verboord as if she were my mother."

"What strange fancy is this?" cried the young girl; "it is so in the song; every one knows very well you speak in my name. Ah, ah, poor Raphael! He is always timid." And she commenced to laugh at him, to teaze the young man without pity, and to clap her hands.

Mrs. Verboord, who was only about a dozen steps behind them, gazed smilingly upon her daughter, and seemed to take pleasure in seeing her so joyous. Doubtless she knew the secret which Felicité wished to tell Banks. She had not the slightest misgiving. Raphael was always reserved, respectful, and even remarkably cold.

At this moment she saw the young man coming towards her, and Felicité following him, laughing immoderately.

"What amuses my daughter so much, Mr. Banks?" she asked.

"Something of no great importance, madam," he replied. "Miss Verboord is very gay to-day, and, indeed, it is not without"—

"Be quiet, Raphael," cried the young girl, putting her finger on her lip. "It is our secret; you must not betray it."

"Come away, I wish to know nothing," replied Mrs. Verboord. "As you have confided your secret to Mr. Banks, I will talk a little more with him of the plan for our little château.

"No, no, mamma, not of that. I have still much to say to Raphael; but this time you may listen to me if you like. You know, moreover, that I wish to tell him about the party at Mr. Dorneval's."

She stepped between her mother and the young man, slightly pushing her aside, and said to him in a lower tone:

"Ah, you don't know, Raphael, how much pleasure I had. My head was turned. It was the night before we left for Brasschaet, and I have not seen you since. I have often wished for you to come that I might tell you all about it. You know the rich merchant who lives in the Great Square?"

"Certainly, I know Mr. Dorneval very well."

"The party was at his house. They had fine music and we danced. It was splendid! I was all in white, and wore a crown of daisies which shone like a circle of stars round my head. There were a great many elegantly dressed, and agreeable young people. Everybody told me I was charming; my ears still burn with all the praises and compliments I received. Truly, I felt as if I were in Paradise! Why are you looking down with such a serious expression, Raphael? Do my words annoy you?"

"No, Miss Verboord," murmured Banks with a half-concealed sadness, "I picture you to myself surrounded by all these people, and I can almost imagine I hear all their words to you."

" That is impossible, Raphael. There was one person who hardly left my side during the evening : a handsome young man, agreeable, graceful, and with large black eyes like yours. He said a thousand pretty things to me which I received as meaning nothing ; but, at last, he asked me very seriously if I would consent to become his wife, if my parents permitted. At this strange question I burst out laughing. Seeing me so much amused, he became grave and did not address another word to me ; but he looked so sadly at me from a distance, that I felt inclined to pity him. Even now when I recall his sad face, I accuse myself of having pained him by my laughter. But, only think of it, Raphael, to speak to me so suddenly of marriage. I am much too young. Why do you not answer me ? You pay no attention to what I am saying. That is very rude."

" Who is this young man ? " inquired Banks, in a voice which sounded like a long sigh.

" Who is he ? You know him. It was Alfred, Mr. Dorneval's oldest son. What are you saying to yourself? Why do you hang your head so strangely ? "

Banks was buried in unhappy thoughts and remained quiet. He could hardly breathe, and his heart beat with agitation. The image of Alfred Dorneval was constantly before his eyes ; this young man, who belonged to one of the richest and most influential families in Antwerp, seemed to have made a deep impression upon the mind of Felicité. Since that evening she had thought continually of him. Perhaps she already loved him—and he had spoken to her of marriage ! What a dark cloud suddenly descended between Raphael and his bright dreams ! Felicité did not understand his emotion, and was about to ask him another question when her mother exclaimed :

" Felicité, Felicité, there comes your father."

The young girl, without waiting for her mother or Raphael who followed her, ran like a deer across the heath to meet her father, and threw herself upon his breast with an exclamation of joy. She kissed him several times and said :

" Ah, thank heaven, you have come. Your prolonged absence made me anxious. Now I am happy. All is ready ; mamma knows nothing. We will have so much pleasure ! "

" Yes, yes, much pleasure," repeated Mr. Verboord. " You are in the age of pleasures and you ought to enjoy them, my daughter, for later, later—Is Mr. Banks here? "

" Certainly, he is there with mamma. But papa, you look sad ! For my sake forget your business for a little while ! I have dreamed for a long time of this happy day, and I have been so rejoiced in thinking you would share our gaiety. And here you are full of care and thought ; come, come, papa, drive away these gloomy feelings."

" You are mistaken, my child," said the merchant with a smile, which he endeavored to make cheerful. " I am happy and contented in mind ; but I cannot dance and frolic like a young girl."

" Is it really true, papa, that you are happy and in a good humor ? "

" Very true."

" Oh, then I am satisfied."

At this moment her mother and Raphael joined them After embracing his wife and daughter, the merchant commenced to speak of indifferent things. Mrs. Verboord repeated to him what Raphael had said about the plans of the château, and she entered into long explanations. At first Mr. Verboord listened with some attention to what she said ; but soon his thoughts turned in another direction.

Raphael, who was absorbed in his own gloomy reflections, replied absently every time Mrs. Verboord appealed to him

This strange conduct had already drawn from Felicité more than one reproach, when the merchant suddenly said:

"Laurence, it is nearly dinner time. Will you go and see if it will soon be ready. I have some business matters to talk over with Mr. Banks, and I wish to be alone with him for a moment. Felicité, you will follow your mother."

This order seemed to pain the girl.

"Papa," she exclaimed, "I hardly have the happiness of seeing you, when you send me away to talk of business. You do not keep your word."

"I do not send you away, my child, I only ask you to leave me for a moment alone with Mr. Banks. You are too good and reasonable not to satisfy my desire."

Felicité bent her head without replying, and followed her mother, who had already turned back.

Mr. Verboord looked at his clerk and said:

"You are sad, Raphael. Perhaps you have already heard the bad news."

"The bad news?" repeated the young man. "No sir; but I read in your face that something troubled you."

"Yes, truly, I am alarmed. I met Mr. Dorneval this morning; he expressed himself as very glad to see me, and showed me a telegram from London, which says it is supposed there will be a great fall in coffee to-morrow. This depression had already been felt during the last two days; but a very great fall was expected. If Mr. Dorneval's information prove correct, I am threatened with a great loss. What do you advise me to do? What would you do in my place?"

Banks replied, after a few moments reflection,

"In your place, Mr. Verboord, this is what I would do. I would wait till to-morrow. If the market was still tolerably good, and if I could, without much loss, find a purchaser, I would sell my coffee ; but if the price was considerably lower I would keep my coffee and wait for it to rise."

" And suppose the fall continues ? "

" It is a chance, sir, I know. Commerce is full of risks."

" Then you think it will return to its usual price within a week ? "

" I would be willing to predict it, sir. From your own words, and from the general sentiment, I infer that the expected fall be caused by a coalition of large English houses. When the price has fallen quite low, they will raise it, in order to sell at a large profit what they have bought ; if this be so, those who keep their coffee will have their part of the gain."

Mr. Verboord pressed his hand to his head and sighed deeply.

" But, my dear Banks," he said, " I have not the time to wait. Suppose your views are correct, whole months may pass before a rise takes place. I must have this week some large, very large amounts at my disposal. And then not to have the receipts from America ! "

" They may come to-morrow, sir. Perhaps, too, the expected fall in coffee may not be known to-morrow. Then you can sell.

" Good heavens ! " cried Mr. Verboord, with feverish agitation, " these suppositions give me but an indefinite hope. I know, my dear Raphael, I am very much discouraged and frightened. The presentiment of a great misfortune possesses me. I do not know why it is, but such is the case. It is impossible for me to remain at Brass-chaet. Letters may come; telegrams may arrive from London and Amsterdam. I cannot rest here a moment. I have ordered the coachman to get the horses ready; I will return to Antwerp immediately; but how shall I tell my wife, and above all, Felicité?"

A look of joyful surprise shone in Raphael's eyes. What Felicité had said to him had wounded his heart. He felt that he would not be able at the fêtes to conceal his grief and to feign gaiety. And how would he be able to explain his strange melancholy. He, therefore, with secret joy, seized the occasion to leave a place, where to-day, at least, he could find neither repose nor pleasure.

"Mr. Verboord," he said, "I beg you to give me a new proof of your kindness. If you leave, Miss Felicité will weep. She has for so long a time joyfully anticipated this festival. Mrs. Verboord will be no less grieved. The diligence will pass through the village in an hour. Let me go to Antwerp."

"No my friend, that cannot be," replied Mr. Verboord.

"I beg you, sir, enjoy the pleasures of this bright day in peace!" continued Raphael.

"But your departure, Raphael, will not relieve my anxiety. What will you do at Antwerp?"

"If letters or news come, sir, I will receive and open them, as you usually permit me to do in your absence. If there should be anything important in the despatches, I will take a carriage and bring them to you. In this way, you can remain quietly here till late in the evening, or even till to-morrow; for if I do not come, you will know there is nothing to cause you anxiety."

The merchant shook his head in silence.

5

"Perhaps I may be able to do you a service," continued the young man. "If I should find a purchaser, sir, would you permit me to sell the coffee at yesterday's price?"

"To-day is Sunday, Raphael."

"That is true, and I have but a faint hope, but who knows! I am lucky."

"Certainly, I would sell the coffee at that price; but there is no use to think of it, my friend, in the face of bad news."

"And then, sir, there is to be an entertainment to-night at the Great Harmony. I will meet brokers and travelling clerks there, and I will try to learn from them the general opinion. In this way, to-morrow morning, at office hour, we will know the state of affairs, and knowing the cause, will be able to decide what must be done."

Mr. Verboord reflected for a short time, then, taking the hand of his clerk, said to him:

"Raphael, you are a true and faithful young man. Truly my daughter would weep at my unexpected departure, and my poor wife would be disconsolate. I therefore agree to your returning to Antwerp and doing as you have arranged. But I may trust to your coming to Brasschaet if you hear the least news of importance?"

"You may be sure of it, sir."

"Come, then; I do not know how long the ladies may still detain you, and you must not miss the diligence."

The merchant, followed by his clerk, hastened to cross the heath, towards the house; but, after they had walked awhile in silence, he gradually slackened his pace, and bowed his head upon his breast. At the end of the last fir tree, he said to Raphael, in an excited tone:

"It is surprising, my friend, how these gloomy ideas possess and torment me! I fear being utterly ruined, poor, and miserable."

"But, my dear sir, what foundation is there for these unhappy forebodings?" cried Banks.

"No foundation, I know. Ah, it is terrible! To have worked all my life like a slave without a moment's repose; after being happy enough to amass a considerable fortune for my child; and then, in my old age, to tremble lest a single misfortune may rob me of it all! But, as you say, there is no reason for such ideas, at least not now."

While speaking, he had again hastened onwards till they reached the garden. There he paused, and said to his clerk:

"Where are your flowers, Raphael? Have you already given them to Felicité or her mother?"

"No, sir," replied the young man; "they are under the shed beside the stable."

"I will give them in your name to Mrs. Verboord. Have you spoken of your inheritance? Not yet. Well, I will communicate the good news at the proper time. But we must not talk any longer, or you will not get off in time. Be careful not to let them suspect the cause of your unexpected departure."

They approached the house and saw Felicité seated on a bench by her mother's side.

The young girl jumped up quickly, and ran joyfully to meet her father. She took his hand, drew it aside, and said to him:

"Ah, thank fortune! your business is finished at last. Now you will enter into the joy of this happy day. Papa, I beg you to find a chance to get mamma away for a few minutes. I am going to the piano with Raphael to teach him the tune of a song. Do not notice anything. Here, mamma."

"I am sorry, my child, to give you pain," said the merchant, "but business is inexorable in its demands. Mr. Banks will not dine with us; he must leave at once for Antwerp."

Felicité started back and uttered a cry.

"How! what!" she cried; "Raphael going away? Oh, dear papa! why do you frighten me needlessly?"

"No, no, it cannot be; he is teasing us," said Mrs. Verboord. "Dinner is being served."

"It is true, I much regret it; but there is nothing to be done," said the merchant. "Raphael must go at once or he will lose the diligence."

The young girl knew by the sound of her father's voice that there was little hope of making him change his intention. She bent her head down, and said, sadly:

"Alas! I have been so contented all week because Raphael was to spend this day with us! I anticipated so much pleasure, so much happiness! Ah, dear mamma, say a good word for Raphael to remain. If he leaves, I will be unhappy all day."

Banks' heart beat rapidly. The words of the young girl were like balm upon a wound, and he began to accuse himself of being hasty and unjust; but the image of young Dorneval came before his eyes, and he shook his head despondingly.

Mrs. Verboord made an effort to persuade her husband to permit Raphael to remain to dinner, but his severe reply convinced her that she must submit to the necessity.

"Do not stay longer, my friend," whispered the merchant to his clerk. "Depart at once without further explanations. It is the only way to put an end to Felicité's complaints."

Raphael stammered a good-bye, and turned towards the te   When he   ne r y re ched the   t he he rd

Felicité call his name. He turned round and saw the young girl extend her hands to him, with her eyes full of tears. There was something in her look which moved him to the depth of his soul, a sincere regret, a true sorrow for his departure—perhaps the shadow of an unknown love!

The poor young man forgot his employer's advice, and stopped with hesitation, while a smile half parted his lips. But at the same moment he saw the merchant making signs of impatience, and uttering a low cry, he hastily rushed from the garden and disappeared between the trees on the road.

5*

CHAPTER III.

THREE days later Mr. Verboord was seated with his wife and daughter in a room of his town house, at the table where breakfast was served.

The countenance of the merchant betrayed much uneasiness, his cheeks were paler than usual, he had the fixed expression of a man whose thoughts are far away, and about his lips were already drawn deep lines of anxiety.

From time to time he ate a mouthful, evidently not thinking of what he did. Then he opened a portfolio, and read for the tenth time certain important letters; again he made figures upon the envelopes of these letters, and shook his head despondingly at the unfavorable result of his calculations.

Mrs. Verboord looked at her husband with a mingled expression of pity, sadness, and annoyance.

Tears glistened in Felicité's eyes, and she seemed to wish to speak to her father; but each time the words died upon her lips.

During a quarter of an hour complete silence reigned in the room. At last Mrs. Verboord said, in a reproachful tone:

"Verboord, my husband, you do not act rightly by us. Something is troubling you; one might suppose some misfortune had befallen you, and you refuse us any explanation. Of what use are we to you if you deny us the right to comfort you, or at least to share your grief. Come, tell me what troubles you. Confide your anxiety to your wife."

The merchant moved impatiently, yet he replied without anger :

"Laurence, my dear, you importune me in vain. I do not know what you wish me to tell you. It is natural I should think of my business, and you are wrong to try to divert my thoughts."

"It may be that there is no cause for your anxiety," replied Mrs. Verboord; "but can you not understand how much your reticence must pain and alarm us? Yesterday evening, when we returned from Brasschaet, you were as sad as at present; you did not remain with us a moment, you went out immediately; and this morning you are so unhappy that the expression of your face alone is enough to fill us with anxiety. Yet, a few kind and truthful words would relieve our minds."

"Yes, papa, just a word," begged Felicité.

"There are some things you cannot understand," said Mr. Verboord. "You seem to imagine that a merchant can always smile and be gay like other men. What is his life but a constant labor and an eternal calculation. Is he not always struggling with fate, and may he not at any time be unexpectedly overcome in the struggle? Is it strange, when danger is always before his eyes, that he should concentrate all his strength of mind upon the chances of escaping it?"

"Are you really threatened with a great danger?" asked his wife, sighing.

"A merchant is always threatened; but why should you think now that I dread any misfortune? There is none at all. Come, let me think in peace, and take your breakfast, Laurence, without giving yourself needless anxiety."

He turned away his head, and again opened his portfolio, as though he would resume his interrupted calculations.

Felicité rose up, took his hand, and said, in her softest tones:

"Ah, dear papa, I am very unhappy. The day of mamma's fête was not very bright, for then also you were sad and thoughtful. I hoped it would pass away, and you would return to a pleasant mood. This is why I insisted upon mamma's returning to the city. Alas! you have scarcely spoken to me! Yes, for the first time in your life, dear papa, you have not even kissed me! Oh! do let me comfort you."

Mr. Verboord, absorbed in his own thoughts, paid no attention to this innocent prayer. Instead of replying, he struck his forehead, jumped up quickly, and took up his hat.

"Are you going out?" inquired his wife, in surprise.

"Yes, I must go out immediately for a few minutes," he replied. "I have forgotten something, something important. I will be at home in half an hour."

"But you have not finished your breakfast."

"I have no appetite. I will soon be home. Do not be uneasy; there is no reason to fear any misfortune."

Saying these words, he went out hastily.

Felicité commenced weeping bitterly. Her tears increased the anguish of Mrs. Verboord, more alarmed than before by her husband's last words. Why should he have spoken of misfortune? The danger which threatened them must be very great.

She tried for some time to convince her daughter that she was needlessly alarmed; but Felicité, who had not dared to weep in her father's presence, relieved her feelings by her tears, and would not listen to her mother's words of comfort. Filled with anxiety, Mrs. Verboord said to herself

that her husband had no right to conceal from her the cause
of his trouble. It was not from curiosity, but from a sense
of duty that she desired to know it. Had she not a right to
share in and ameliorate her husband's griefs? If he was in
trouble, it was only from love for her and his daughter; for
Mr. Verboord only valued money and position because it
assured him of the welfare of those dearest to him. Could
not those who were the object of his care and solicitude
comfort him and strengthen his courage? That he might
not pain them, he concealed his troubles; but they would
not accept these generous sacrifices, and would exact their
right to know his sorrow.

Mrs. Verboord crossed the room and rang the bell.

"Theresa, go to the office," she said to the servant, who
came in after a few moments, "and tell Mr. Banks I wish
to speak to him."

This name made Felicité look up, and a smile full of hope
mingled with her tears.

Mrs. Verboord was hardly seated before Raphael entered.

The unexpected summons of Mrs. Verboord had agreeably surprised him; for he hoped to see Felicité, and this
hope was sufficient to fill his heart with joy.

When he saw tears upon the cheeks of the young girl he
was filled with pity. She looked at him kindly. He paused
in the middle of the chamber, and bade them good morning.

"Come nearer, Mr. Banks," said Mrs. Verboord,
gravely. "Take this chair, and sit near the table. What
I have to say is important, and I cannot speak freely if you
stand up before me."

The young man took a seat.

"Mr. Banks," she said, "my husband is very sad; he
seems to fear some impending danger, or to grieve over some
misfortune which has already befallen him. Do you know
the cause of his unhappiness?"

Raphael, who was surprised by this unexpected question, hesitated a moment, as though seeking for a reply. At last he murmured:

"You know, madam, that Mr. Verboord has been very nervous for several months. His present depression is the result of it, and makes him appear unhappy."

"That is very unfortunate for Felicité and myself; but it is not what I ask you. We are satisfied that Mr. Verboord has at this time a special cause for anxiety; and he conceals this cause from us that we may not be troubled. We wish to know so that we may comfort him; it is our duty. You doubtless know what troubles him, as you possess his entire confidence. Now, we beg you, my dear sir, to tell us what we so earnestly desire to know."

This entreaty greatly embarrassed Raphael. He said, hesitatingly:

"I beg you to excuse me, madam. What my employer has thought it best to conceal from you, I cannot tell you against his will."

"Then there is something unusual, something important, and you know it?"

"Be kind and generous enough, madam," said the clerk, "not to insist upon my telling you. I think I know why Mr. Verboord has been anxious since his last visit to Brasschaet; but, as he has not spoken to you about it, you will understand that I cannot reveal what he wishes to keep secret."

"Then it is something terrible," cried Mrs. Verboord, in great alarm. "Some misfortune, some disaster threatens my husband, and I cannot know it."

"No, no, madam, he is not threatened with either misfortune or disaster, at least in my opinion," said Raphael, moved with compassion, and almost betrayed into an imprudence by the sad and pleading look with which Felicité looked at him.

"Give us some comfort, my dear Mr. Banks," begged Mrs. Verboord. "Tell us what troubles my husband so much. We will be grateful to you as for the greatest favor."

The young man shook his head with hesitation.

Felicité approached, fixed her eyes full of tears on his, raised her hands towards him, and said in a tone of entreaty :

"Ah, Raphael, be kind! If you persist in your mysterious silence and leave us, I will be very unhappy, and convinced that some great danger threatens my father. You are so good, take pity upon our grief. Relieve my mother; give me the means of offering consolation to my father on his return? Can you refuse me? Must I believe you insensible to my tears; that you have not the least pity for me?"

"Well, madam," said the clerk, deeply moved and completely overcome, "I hope Mr. Verboord will forgive my indiscretion. My excuse will be, that your anxiety will be relieved by what I am going to tell you. You know that my employer has a large quantity of coffee in his warehouse. On Sunday, news were received indicating a great fall in the price, that is why I so suddenly left your country house. From that time the fall has constantly increased; and if we are forced to sell to-day, Mr. Verboord will lose, in consequence, a part of his fortune."

"Good heavens!" exclaimed Mrs. Verboord, "I understand my husband's unhappiness."

"Poor papa," sighed Felicité.

"I assure you, madam, your alarm has no foundation, and I will try to prove it to you. From certain vague rumors during the last fortnight, it is supposed that some of the large commercial houses in London have united to purchase the greater part of the coffee in the different European markets. Of course, to succeed in this, it was necessary to bring down the price of the article. After a while they will force it up to a high figure and thus realize large profits. For small houses this fall is ruinous; indeed, yesterday already two firms of small importance failed in this city; but those who can wait for the right moment, instead of losing, will gain. My employer has no need to sell, he can keep his coffee till the proper time. Therefore, madam, I see no reason for being so unhappy."

The two ladies looked at him doubtfully, as though they had not exactly understood his explanation.

After a moment's reflection, Mrs. Verboord shook her head and said:

"Yes, if the decline really be the result of such a combination, then the price of coffee must rise, I understand it; but are you quite sure of it, Raphael?"

"In commerce, madam, one is never sure of anything; we must always work in calculations, which have more or less foundation. I have examined all the despatches which I have received for some months, and I have watched the changes in the different markets. The stock of coffee in London and Amsterdam is not greater than at this time last year, the crop has been rather less; and the public auction of the Commercial Society has not yet taken place. Therefore, there must be some extraordinary cause for the decline, and in my opinion, it will be found in a coalition of the London houses. Even if I am mistaken, it is certain that the price must rise, for the stock is not equal to the consumption."

"Ah, Raphael, you must tell my father all this," interrupted Felicité, smiling brightly. "He listens to you so willingly, his anxiety will entirely disappear."

"I have made these calculations with your father, Miss Felicité," replied the clerk, "and I have said all I could to comfort him."

"And why does he not believe you?"

"He does believe me, and says my views are correct, but the next moment, he begins to doubt, and gradually falls back to his anxieties. There are times when a man, without knowing it, perhaps, feels disposed to look on the dark side of everything, but this gloomy feeling is transient, and I am quite sure my employer will not long remain in this state."

"If it only should be as you hope!" said Mrs. Verboord. "Surely there is nothing so very terrible to us in the loss of a little money; but to see my husband so distressed, deprives me of all my courage. You speak truly, my friend, do you not? It is not merely to comfort us that you seem so confident?"

"I can give you a proof of my sincerity," replied the young man. "Mr. Verboord has probably told you of my inheritance. This money must be very dear to me as all my future depends upon its preservation. Well, madam, I have used a large part of it in buying some bags of coffee. If my employer's fears should be realized, I would be half ruined by my first speculation. I must, therefore, have great faith that coffee will rise, when I venture to risk the happiness of my life upon it."

Mrs. Verboord assented, and Felicité seemed satisfied with his explanations.

"Now," said Raphael, rising to go, "I must ask your permission to return to the office. Many persons are calling, and as Mr. Verboord is out I must be there to receive them. Be assured, madam, there is no real danger, and you may quietly wait for more favorable circumstances."

6

He turned round and took a few steps towards the door, but the young girl ran to him, and said in a voice filled with emotion :

"Oh! thank you, thank you, Raphael, for the comfort you have given my mother! Speak to my father, and tell him he has no reason to be unhappy. Your gentle and persuasive words will soothe him. As for myself, Raphael, I can never forget your kindness, and I will be always grateful to you."

The young man trembled ; for Felicité, in her gratitude, had pressed his hand. Filled with joy, he left the room murmuring some disconnected words.

In the office several persons were waiting; for the most part brokers and travelling clerks who had come to show samples of different articles, or to ask the price at which Mr. Verboord sold them.

As Raphael had not received any special business orders, he soon satisfied the demands of his visitors, and before long the last one left the office.

The young man gave his directions to the other clerks, and then commenced writing in silence at his own desk. His pen often paused, while a smile parted his lips. He was thinking of Felicité, her gentle look, of her friendly grasp, and his mind wandered away in dreams of a happy future.

For some time, no one came into the office, but at last a young man rushed in laughing and rubbing his hands.

"You seem very happy, friend Walput," said Raphael. "Have you heard any good news?"

"Why do you not know it," joyfully exclaimed the traveling clerk. "There is a sudden rise in coffee. The fall was caused by false reports. Orders have arrived in the market to buy large quantities of coffee. An important rise is reported at Amsterdam. Two farthings on the pound, Raphael! I have come here first to ask if Mr. Verboord wishes to part with his."

"He is not in, Francis," replied the clerk "But I know he would not wish to sell. He would still lose too much, and as the price is now going up he would naturally wish to wait."

"And you will also keep yours, I suppose? You are right. Although on the coffee I sold you day before yesterday, you would make four hundred francs."

"I will sell it to you," exclaimed the young man eagerly.

"Why sell so soon? The price will go up."

"It is my first profit, Francis. I am anxious to realize it. I feel as though I had found a treasure."

"Yes, I remember how much joy I experienced in my first successful speculation, though it was even smaller than this. Then you will sell your coffee at an advance of two farthings? I will take it, consider it sold."

Lowering his voice, he whispered to the clerk : "I have not much time, for there is a great deal to do at the office, but I would like to speak to you in private for a moment."

Raphael left the office, and led the way to one of the doors in the hall.

"Here is my employer's private office," he said, as he opened the door. "We can talk here uninterruptedly. I thought the rise in coffee was not the only reason for your gaiety. If I am not mistaken you did not even want any coffee. I think you wish to talk of Lucy Spelt."

"You are right," replied Francis, "I have important news. I do not know yet if it will terminate favorably ; but, nevertheless, I feel as though some great happiness would be granted me to-day. It is a presentiment, and do what I may to become composed, and moderate my hopes, everything appears to me in rose colors. Ah! what an inestimable service you rendered me by your kind words to Mr. Spelt! Lucy's father yesterday wrote a very kind letter to my mother, telling her he would like to call on her to-day to speak on a matter of importance. It is the first time Mr. Spelt has ever formally announced his coming. What do you think of the news, Raphael?"

The clerk took Francis' hand and replied with sincere sympathy:

"I think the matter is settled and they are going to arrange the marriage settlements. It gives me as much pleasure, Francis, as if I were to be the future bridegroom."

"There is one thing I do not quite understand," murmured Francis. "We may sell the skin of the bear before we kill him! I wonder why Mr. Spelt has not said one word to Lucy of his intention. Do you think he can intend to tell my mother that I must give up all hope?"

"Not at all, Francis. If he wishes to have any private conversation with your mother, it is to arrange the conditions of your marriage. Yes, yes, my friend, all your wishes will be granted, you need not doubt."

"I try to doubt, though really I cannot," joyfully exclaimed Francis. "Ah! to have Lucy Spelt my wife! See, Raphael, I will appropriate you without leave. You are to be my groomsman. And I hope soon you may require the same service."

"Soon!" repeated the clerk with an incredulous smile upon his lips.

"Who knows," cried Francis. "Since day before yesterday, I believe the impossible may become possible. Something Mr. Verboord said to me of you—"

"How, has Mr. Verboord spoken of me to you?" interrupted Raphael, with sudden agitation.

"Yes, and in a manner which made me think. My heart beat with joy for you."

"For the love of heaven, Francis, tell me what he said of me."

"I was in the restaurant near the Exchange when Mr. Verboord came in and sat down at the same table with me. He is very polite to me, you know. We were talking of business matters when I happened to mention having sold some bags of coffee to you. Then Mr. Verboord praised your intelligence and energy up to the skies; he said that some day you were destined to become rich, and no one was more worthy of being happy. In fact, Raphael, there was no quality of the head or heart with which he did not think you endowed, and he spoke of you in such flattering terms, that I seemed to be listening to a father who was praising the virtues of a much loved son. I then understood your hopes, and rejoiced in the thought you would probably escape from the trials of an unhappy attachment."

Raphael's heart beat rapidly while he listened to his friend's words. He remained silent, apparently thinking.

"You see," said Walput, "I will not be the only happy person. This is not bad news, is it, Raphael? Good-bye."

The clerk pressed his hand warmly, walked to the office door with him, and said, with emotion:

"Thanks, many thanks, for your kindness and friendship."

When he was alone, Raphael re-entered the room, and stood still for a moment, with his eyes resting on the ground; but soon he uttered a cry of joy, and his eyes sparkled.

"Four hundred francs," he murmured. "I have gained

6*

four hundred francs! How happy this first gain makes me! If only Felicité knew it! This news would satisfy her and her mother that Mr. Verboord's fears have no foundation."

He left the office and entered the hall, at the end of which he rapped at a door, and opened it on receiving a response.

"Excuse me, ladies," he said, eagerly, "I thought you would be glad to have me bring you good news. There is a sudden rise in the price of coffee."

The two ladies, much surprised, rose up and approached him.

"Thank God," exclaimed Felicité, "for so soon relieving my father of his anxiety."

"Has the price risen all at once to its usual standard?" asked Mrs. Verboord, incredulously.

"Not altogether, madam," replied Raphael; "but it will rise still higher, and my employer will probably be able to sell his at an advantage. I bought coffee at a lower price than his, and I have sold and gained four hundred francs on it."

This news had not the result the clerk expected. A slight smile parted the lips of the elder lady, while Felicité looked at him in astonishment, as though she would ask how such a small gain could cause him so much joy.

"Ah," cried Raphael, "I have commenced business, and God will bless my efforts. I will work and labor so hard that I will force fortune to be favorable to me. This first step decides my whole future life; it points to a brilliant end, and I will attain it whatever obstacles may lie in my path."

"Then it is true that you intend to become a merchant," asked the young girl, in a tone of dissatisfaction. "You, too, will become care-worn and unhappy? Do not do so, you will regret it. It makes me sad even to hear you say it."

"Indeed, my friend," added Mrs. Verboord, "I should think you might choose a happier course."

"But, madam, I feel myself especially called to commerce," replied the young man, "forced into it by an irresistible impulse. If it be true that God has given me mental gifts, it is surely for this; and I would not receive His gifts with ingratitude. I wish to become rich, very rich, and I will be so, be assured."

"Poor Raphael!" sighed Felicité, as if alarmed; "what has happened to him!"

"Be calm, Mr. Banks," said her mother. "Of course we congratulate you on your profit; but four hundred francs are not a fortune."

"Excuse me, madam," he stammered, "I am wrong, and must appear foolish to you; but it gives me a firm faith that fortune will not refuse me her favors. At least, if I should be disappointed, it will not be from want of zeal and energy—and still—but no, I am not mistaken—"

"I see," said Mrs. Verboord, gravely shaking her head, "good advice will be of no avail. You are possessed with the demon of commerce. I admit that these constant speculations and incessant struggles against fate may have something attractive about them to a man; but it does not make the life of a wife and children happy. I would be truly glad, Mr. Banks, to see you enter upon another career."

"I beseech you, Raphael, never be a merchant!" murmured Felicité.

The young man was deeply moved, his heart beat violently. What did Mrs. Verboord's words mean? Why should she be anxious for the future of his wife? What was the feeling which induced Felicité to urge him to give up commerce? Could it be possible that his friend Walput's prediction might be realized? But commerce was the only way to make a fortune.

All these thoughts passed through his brain with the rapidity of lightning. With hesitation, he replied:

"Madam, the most powerful motive of a merchant, the object of all his cares, all his anxiety, is the welfare of his family. What greater proof of love can he give to those who are dear to him than to devote all the energies of his mind, his soul, and his life to their well-being? And when God blesses his efforts, and fortune rewards them, of what use is the money he has gained? To render his wife and children happy, to surround them with luxuries and delicacies, and to be able to say ' behold the fruit of my energy and my love!'"

Felicité's mother looked at the young man in astonishment, and was about to reply, when the door opened, and Mr. Verboord entered.

He appeared entirely changed; his face beamed with joy, and he smiled as he entered. He pretended to be astonished at the presence of his clerk, and paused after advancing a few steps, exclaiming ·

"Well, well, it seems to me you are spending your time very agreeably. I always thought Mr. Banks never left the office in my absence!"

"Mrs. Verboord will make my excuses, sir," said the clerk, bowing to his employer.

He walked towards the door, but the merchant took him by the hand.

"No, stay here," he said; "I wish to speak to you."

"Do not be angry that Raphael has left the office," said Mrs. Verboord. "I sent for him to ask the cause of your distress. It was a happy thought, because he has brought us good news, and has comforted us."

Without seeming to notice this explanation, the merchant approached his daughter, took her head between his hands, and pressed a tender kiss upon her cheeks.

Felicité, surprised by this loving caress, threw herself upon her father's breast.

As soon as he could disengage himself from his daughter's embrace, Mr. Verboord advanced to his wife and took both her hands in his.

"My dear Laurence," he said, "I have given you pain, but you must forgive me. There are now good news, and we may hope the danger is past. I am not angry with Raphael. Perhaps I know what he came to tell you."

"The rise in the price of coffee."

"Ah, my boy," he said, shaking his finger at the clerk, "you have been talking of business matters to women. It is not prudent. Nevertheless, as you have comforted my wife and daughter, I thank you. Happy rascal, who dares to risk his money rashly, and who immediately profits by his imprudence! For if you wish to sell, Raphael, you will gain something already on your coffee."

"I have sold, sir," replied Banks, with a look of suppressed pride.

"Already; it is not possible."

"I have gained four hundred francs, sir."

"But if you had only waited, now that the price is at its highest."

"That is true, sir; but the thought of a first gain bewitched me."

"Tell me, papa," exclaimed Felicité, "don't you think Raphael is wrong to become a merchant?"

"Why, my child?"

"I don't know, papa; it seems to me a sad life, and, truly, if I were free to choose, I would never become the wife of a merchant."

"On the contrary, my dear," said Mr. Verboord, laughing, "I hope you will never marry any one but a merchant."

You only see the reverse of the medal; but, my child, if I had never entered into commercial pursuits, how could I possibly have made a fortune and given you a proper position in the world? Commerce is the only road to wealth."

He put his hand on Raphael's shoulder, and said:

"Here is a young man, Felicité, who will exceed your father perhaps in success, if he is prudent."

"Oh, Mr. Verboord, I thank you a thousand times for the interest you express in me," murmured the clerk, hardly daring to speak, lest he should betray the proud and ambitious belief which filled his heart.

The merchant read in his sparkling eyes that he accepted the prophecy with perfect confidence in its realization.

"Yet, you must not hope for too much," he said; "above all, do not expect too much at once. Commerce has its ups and downs, and it requires much time and patience to acquire a good capital; but have courage, you are young, and even if you should meet with some reverses, in the end I believe you will have a large business. Now I have something to tell you in haste. I will return in two minutes, Laurence."

The merchant led the way into the hall, and then turning to his clerk, said:

"So you know what has been the movement in coffee?"

"Yes, sir; Francis Walput gave me two farthings advance on the pound."

"It has now risen to two and a-half, and is going up. I begin to hope that I will come out of this affair advantageously. I have so much confidence, that if I had any money I could use I would still buy more coffee."

"In two or three days, perhaps, it will have risen to its highest price this season," remarked Raphael. "We can then pay the debts without waiting for the American remittances."

"It is precisely of that I wish to speak to you," interrupted Mr. Verboord. "I have a means at hand. A kind friend, who will not feel the loan of one or two millions, has offered me his services. Although I have not yet told him that his kindness is needed by me, I am quite sure he will immediately agree to all I ask. So, do not worry any more about the matter."

"Are you quite sure the money will be ready?" asked Raphael.

"Certainly I am, when the rich merchant, Dorneval, pressed me to give him an opportunity to oblige me."

"Mr. Dorneval!" exclaimed Raphael, slightly shuddering.

"Well, is there anything astonishing in the name?" asked Mr. Verboord, laughing.

"Nothing, sir," replied Raphael, restraining himself by a great effort; "but if you would only wait till to-morrow. Who knows? You would not, perhaps, have to ask the assistance of another."

"No, I wish to have this case off my mind; and to-day I intend to speak to my friend Dorneval. Go to the office, and if there is any news of importance, let me know."

Raphael took a step forward to obey his employer's order, but, possessed by a strange thought, he turned back, and said :

"Mr. Verboord, I now possess ten thousand four hundred francs; I would be happy to have you use them."

The merchant burst out laughing, and while he looked at his clerk with an expression of friendly irony, exclaimed :

"Well, well, is it possible? He offers me a loan like a large capitalist! Thanks, my boy, for your kind intention, but we have not come to that yet."

CHAPTER IV.

MR. VERBOORD walked to and fro in a large room of a house in the Grand Square. He appeared to be waiting for some one; for he gazed absently at the engravings on the wall, and turned his head towards the door at the sound of the least noise in the vestibule; but his countenance did not betray any deep anxiety.

A gentleman entered hastily, rushed towards the merchant, and took his hand, exclaiming:

"Ah, my good friend Verboord, you must excuse me for keeping you waiting, but the banker Schorul detained me. How happy I am to see you! I intended calling on you to-morrow. You have anticipated me, and I am much obliged to you. We are going to talk over an important matter, are we not?"

"Important and not important," replied Verboord. "Important to me perhaps, but not to you."

"I think I know the object of your welcome visit."

"That is impossible, Mr. Dorneval."

"Impossible? Have you not come to talk to me of a beautiful and charming young lady, who, at my party, dazzled the eyes of all the young men?"

"You are mistaken, Mr. Dorneval."

"In a word," continued Mr. Dornéval, "of your charming daughter, Miss Felicité Verboord?"

"Not at all; I have come to talk to you of business, money, and stocks."

"Ah, indeed; that is another thing," murmured Mr. Dorneval, with a slight shade of disappointment. "Sit down, and I will listen."

"Let me give you a few necessary explanations," commenced Mr. Verboord, "before I tell you why I have come here to-day. My affairs are a little embarrassed."

"Your affairs embarrassed? You astonish me!" interrupted Mr. Dorneval, in much surprise.

"However, that is not what I came to tell you," replied Felicité's father, sighing. "But you shall judge. By the request of my correspondent in Charleston, the house of Christopher Ortado, I sent out nearly a whole cargo of cotton goods. The time in which the payment should have been made has expired."

"And you have not heard from them," said Mr. Dorneval.

"That is true. How did you know it?"

"Because, by the same vessel, I sent out a quantity of silk to the same house, and I also expect payment from them. Navigation has been very difficult lately on the American coast, owing to violent storms. The house of Ortado always meets its engagements promptly."

"Was your consignment large?" asked Mr. Verboord, with some anxiety.

"Very considerable; a large quantity of silk. But go on, my friend."

"The price of the purchase of this cargo of cottons," replied Verboord, "has, of course, left a vacuum in my treasury. It so happens that another part of my capital is invested in a stock of coffee, which I cannot sell now without a sacrifice. I have given some notes which will expire

7

next Monday. If my American remittances should be delayed later than that date——"

"Ah! I understand," interrupted his companion. "You need ready money."

"Only for a few days. I may not need it at all."

"And you do not wish to ask your banker to save your credit."

"That is precisely the case, Mr. Dorneval. Until this time, I have never lost anything; my whole capital is intact; and it is quite safe."

"You have come to me to do you this service? Well! I thank you from the bottom of my heart for this proof of friendship."

"What do you say?" asked Mr. Verboord, looking doubtfully at him.

"Merely that you need not talk so much about it. Send me your note promising to pay me in a month or later as you may wish, and I will have the money ready. My confidence in you is unlimited, and I am delighted to have an opportunity of obliging you; you may use my money freely."

Mr. Verboord was charmed with the kind and generous manner with which Mr. Dorneval granted him the required favor. He took his hand, thanked him warmly and then rose to depart.

"No, sit down a little longer," said Dorneval. "I also wish to speak to you of an affair of misfortune."

"If I could only prove to you how much I appreciate your kind friendship!" murmured Mr. Verboord.

"You can," replied Mr. Dorneval, "and I do not doubt that you will do so. Like you, I think some explanation necessary."

"This is it," he continued. "Mrs. Verboord and your

daughter, Felicité, were at my last party. If I am not mistaken, it was your daughter's first appearance in society. Why have you so long concealed such a treasure, my friend? We must not be selfish about our children. However, the eyes of all the young people were fixed on Miss Felicité during the whole evening. They raved over her artlessness, her grace, and her wit."

"You are too kind, sir, you exaggerate to flatter my paternal pride," said Mr. Verboord, with a gratified smile.

"Not at all; and as a proof of my sincerity I will tell you that Miss Felicité caused my son Alfred, who is as grave as man can be, to fall desperately in love with her. From that time, the poor boy has lost his sleep, made mistakes in my books, and blunders of various kinds, written nonsense in my letters, and is not in a state to do a sum in addition correctly. I really pity him, and begin to fear if this continues, he will be good for nothing the rest of his life. You seem astonished, and I admit you have reason. I have urged him to become better acquainted with Miss Felicité; but he will not listen to me. In business, no man can be more industrious and enterprising than he is; but, in love affairs he is as timid and ignorant as a child of seven years. I thought I would accompany him to your house to-morrow. He is already trembling in the anticipation. As you are here, I will profit by the occasion to ask your opinion about it."

Mr. Verboord waited some time before he answered, and then he murmured with hesitation:

"My opinion about what?"

"About a closer intimacy between our families, perhaps a marriage between my Alfred and your Felicité!"

"Are you serious?" asked Mr. Verboord, incredulously.

"Certainly I am, perfectly serious! A man does not jest about the happiness of his children."

" Will you consent to my coming to your house from time to time with my son ? "

" I am really confused, Mr. Dorneval. What shall I say to you ? Will you really accept my Felicité as your daughter-in-law. Are you willing that my family should be united to yours by ties of blood ? I would never have dared to hope for such an honor, such happiness."

" Do not exaggerate, my good Mr. Verboord," said Mr. Dorneval, cordially pressing his hand. " I know my firm enjoys a high standing, and under these circumstances, I would be happy if a union between us could benefit your affairs. You are a good and honest man for whom I have always had a great esteem ; but, to speak frankly, there is no generosity in the offer I make you. Suppose my fortune is five times greater than yours. I have six children, and you have an only daughter, therefore, you have the advantage over me. Is it not so ? "

" You are so kind as to say so," stammered Mr. Verboord. " Truly your generous offer surprises me ; I can hardly believe I am not dreaming. Ah ! I love Felicité more than my life, more than my fortune. Such a marriage for her would realize all my wishes."

The conversation paused for a moment. Suddenly, Mr. Dorneval exclaimed ·

" Well, my friend, as this marriage seems to please you as well as myself, why should we defer our arrangements ? If I often go with my son to your house, our habits will be changed, and we will lose much precious time. Alfred will continue unhappy and absent-minded, and I fear will neglect the business of my office. Besides, why should he suffer needlessly ? Would it not be better to arrange the marriage immediately ? What do you say to it ? Will you consent ? "

Verboord was much overcome, and only bowed his assent.

"Ah, well! these are my conditions," continued Dorneval. "I will give to my son an interest in my firm on one hundred thousand francs, and a yearly salary of six thousand francs as first clerk in my office. You will also give your daughter the interest of one hundred thousand francs. If in the future our children wish to enter into business on their own account, we will each give them the capital of their income to use as they like. Will you accept these conditions?"

"Without hesitation, with pleasure!" replied Mr. Verboord.

"I have still too much use for my son not to wish he may remain longer with me. He is my first clerk, and takes my place in my absence; he will become my partner. Felicité will live in my house. I will appropriate to her use all the back building, and will furnish it with every luxury suitable for the wife of my eldest son. Be assured Felicité will be loved and cherished as a queen. Besides, Verboord, this will give us an opportunity of meeting every day and becoming better friends. Is it decided? Then you consent, and within a week we will sign the marriage contract."

Mr. Verboord eagerly grasped the hand extended to him, and exclaimed:

"Thank you, thank you. Ah, how happy my darling Felicité will be! How rejoiced her mother will feel at so advantageous a match for her child!"

Dorneval stood up, while Mr. Verboord followed his example.

"By the way," said the former, as though he suddenly

7*

remembered a forgotten point, " you do not doubt that Miss Felicité will be happy to accept my son ? "

" Do not be alarmed. She speaks of your party with so much delight, of the pleasure she enjoyed, and especially of the agreeable manners of your son, that I assure you, I have begun to think, perhaps, a sudden affection had been awakened between the two young people."

" Ah ! so much the better ! My Alfred is a young man who seems born for happiness ; all will go well if you are not mistaken. Felicité is still young——"

" That is true," interrupted Mr. Verboord, " but this is such a desirable and brilliant marriage! Mr. Alfred is young, handsome, agreeable, intelligent, and already well known as a business man. All is combined to make us view this match as a particular favor of fortune. You need not be anxious, Mr. Dorneval, I know my daughter. If the affair were presented to her under a less favorable aspect, it would be sufficient for her to know it to be my wish to cause her to accept."

" You will not be able to give me an answer at the Exchange, I suppose. You will not have time to speak to your daughter, will you ? "

" Perhaps I may. I will go home immediately and announce the pleasant news."

" Any hour, Verboord, I will see you this evening at the Philotaxe. Do not hurry. I will see you either at the Exchange, or this evening ! "

They walked together to the door of the house, and again shook hands.

Mr. Verboord quickly crossed the square, and in a few minutes reached his own house. At the top of the stairs he paused thoughtfully, and while he wiped the perspiration from his brow said to himself:

"I must be calmer. Too great and unexpected a pleasure might make her sick : I must be prudent."

At the same moment, he opened the door of the room, and approaching Felicité, pressed her to his heart without saying a word, while tears filled his eyes. He embraced his wife in the same manner; but whispered a few words in her ear.

Mrs. Verboord started back, and raised her hands to heaven. Her face beamed with delight. Her lips moved, and she was about to speak, but, at a sign from her husband remained silent.

Felicité, much astonished at the joy of her parents, ran to them, and exclaimed :

"For the love of heaven, papa, tell me what has happened. You appear so happy that I am all anxiety to know the cause."

The merchant laughed, and looked into his daughter's eyes.

"May I not know what makes you so happy?" she asked, in a tone of pique.

"You can and you ought to know," replied her father; "but there are some matters which are not explained by a word."

Taking her hand he continued :

"Now, my child, let us be calm. Sit down here beside me; restrain your surprise and delight: you shall know all."

He led her to a chair, sat down before her; and, still keeping her hand in his, said in a half-serious, half-jesting tone.

"Be sincere, Felicité, and answer me frankly. At Mr. Dorneval's party, there were many young gentlemen who were devoted to you, and paid you a thousand compliments.

However indifferent a young girl may be, she always has her favorite among her admirers. Now, then, tell me: which of the young gentlemen at this party seemed to you the most agreeable?"

"What a strange question!" stammered the young girl, in embarrassment. "I have not thought about it, papa."

"I believe you; but think of it a little now."

Felicité was silent; she did not understand her father's object, and looked at him incredulously.

"Well, I will assist you," said Mr. Verboord. "If I am not mistaken, among those present at the party were the s of Mr. Daelmans, the Stevens brothers, the young Van Trichts, and Messrs. Verlaet, Wens, Van Heurel, and Richter. Did either of these appear to you to be the most agreeable?"

The young girl shook her head.

"Then it was some one else; but, who was it? Come, answer me frankly. Which gentleman appeared to you to be the most agreeable, handsome, and distinguished?"

"Ah, well, papa," said the young girl, laughing, "since you seem so anxious to know my opinion on this subject, I will tell you."

"Well, who was it?"

"It was Alfred Dorneval."

An exclamation of joy was uttered by both her parents.

"Ah! I knew it," cried the merchant, pressing his daughter's hand. "Now, listen, Felicité, and I well tell you all; but be calm, do not allow yourself to be overcome. I went to see Mr. Dorneval this morning, to ask a great favor of him, and he granted it most graciously. This matter over, he spoke to me of you and his son Alfred. It appears that since Mr. Alfred met you at the party he has thought of no one else; you made such an impression upon him that he scarcely knows what he is doing, and is in danger of becoming ill."

"Poor young man!" sighed Felicité.

"Alfred has confided his trouble to his father, and asked his permission to marry. Do you understand?"

The eyes of the young girl sparkled with pride; she seemed to understand, but hesitated to express her belief.

"To marry," she repeated; "who with?"

"Ah, ah," cried Verboord, "with her whose charms fascinated him; you, my child."

"How kind of him," she murmured. "Then his great devotion to me was not flattery alone."

"Certainly not; only it has changed into a feeling of pure and deep love. His father, to relieve the anxiety of his son, asked my consent to the marriage, and you may believe I did not hesitate a moment. Felicité, my child, in one month you will be congratulated as ' Mrs. Dorneval.'"

Filled with joy, Mr. Verboord clasped his daughter to his breast, while her mother also embraced her with tears of joy in her eyes.

When the delighted parents had released the young girl from their embraces, she sank into a chair without speaking a word. She was trembling with emotion; a look of pride shone in her eyes, and a half smile parted her lips.

Her parents, seated one on each side, continued to talk to her rapturously of the advantages of this marriage, without giving her time to speak.

"Oh, my dear Felicité, how happy you will be," exclaimed her mother. "You will bear an old and honorable name, and will shine in society among the richest and most distinguished in the city. What an honor!"

"Yes," interrupted her father, "you will have diamonds, a handsome carriage, a regal house; for Mr. Dorneval wishes you to live with him, at least for some time."

" Ah, Felicité; henceforth you will receive the guests at Mr. Dorneval's parties. I can see you already presiding in those magnificent rooms, of which you will be the greatest ornament."

" You will be petted and adored, not alone by your husband, but also by his kind and generous father."

" Your life will be a constant joy, my dear Felicité; the flowers of pleasure will be scattered in your path at each step you take."

" Ah," exclaimed the merchant, " in my old days I will see my daughter the wife of the head of one of the largest mercantile houses in the country."

While they thus sought to make Felicité participate in their delight, she had gradually fallen into a reverie.

" But, my child, you say nothing," said her mother. " Is not such a fate to be envied ?"

" It is too much; I dare not think of it," murmured Felicité.

" You are as happy as we are, are you not ? Come, say so frankly," said her father, laughing.

" Yes, yes, I am happy," she said, hesitatingly; " but, but—"

" But!" repeated Mr. Verboord; " you astonish me."

" But to leave my mother so soon—I am still so young—"

" Is that all ? You will only live a step from here. We will spend every evening together; the two households will form but one."

" Do not think of that," said Mrs. Verboord. " I feel ten years younger at the thought of such a happy marriage."

" Reflect a little, Felicité. Your husband will receive a dower of one hundred thousand francs, and I will also give you the same amount. Besides, Alfred will receive a salary of six thousand francs. From the day of your marriage, therefore, you will have an income of at least sixteen thousand francs. And as the capital will be invested in commerce, I might safely say twenty thousand francs; besides the control of a large house, handsome carriages, and a château, with the handsomest park to be found. Ah! Felicité, you will be as well off as a queen."

The young girl smiled, so as not to lessen the joy of her kind parents; but she was evidently thoughtful and pre-occupied.

"It ought to make you very happy, Felicité," said her father, in a serious voice, " to know that your marriage will give a permanent relief to my anxieties and my nervous complaints. For as soon as the fate of my child is settled I will have no further cause for care. I will hasten to have my country house built at Brasschaet, and I will be able to devote more money to it. Instead of one château, you will have two. I understand your emotion, for marriage is an important event in the life of a young girl, and I will give you time to become calm. But I must now go out; it is the hour of Exchange. I may tell Mr. Dorneval that you are delighted to accept, may I not?"

The merchant was obliged to repeat his question, for Felicité remained as silent as though she had not heard him. She replied at last, without any apparent emotion:

"Dear papa, I will do all you wish."

"Very well; you are a good girl, I know; but of what are you thinking? You are keeping something back."

"No, papa, but I was asking myself what Raphael would say to this sudden news. He will be much surprised, I think."

"The good fellow will be delighted. He always rejoices at the least good fortune which happens to me. I expect the tears will come into his eyes when he learns of this brilliant marriage. You shall see him; I will tell him as I go out that you wish to speak to him. I may come back later and bring the elder Dorneval with me. Anyhow, see that the dinner is presentable; we cannot tell—"

He had already left the room when he uttered the last words.

As he passed the office door he gave his first clerk a sign to come to him; and he, thinking that his employer called him to accompany him to the Exchange, came to him with his hat in his hand.

Mr. Verboord advanced silently towards the door of an inner room and opened it; but thinking they were far enough from the office, he paused on the threshold, and said to Raphael, in a low tone:

" Raphael, I have something to tell you which will give you pleasure."

" Ah, indeed! Has coffee taken another rise?"

" No, no; I am not thinking of coffee, my friend. It is an entirely different affair. Félicité is going to be married."

A nervous chill passed through the frame of the young man; but, although his countenance expressed great astonishment, a strange hope seemed to shine in his eyes.

" Miss Félicité is going to be married?" he murmured.

" Yes; it is a rich and brilliant marriage! Her intended husband is young and handsome; he belongs to one of the largest business firms in the city. His father is worth millions. You seem astonished. How you do look at me. You would like to know who is to be my son-in-law. I have no time now, but go into the parlor, Félicité is waiting for you; she wishes to tell you herself the name of her future husband. She is very happy."

Whilst speaking he had stepped back, and now having finished, he turned round and walked quickly towards the front door.

Raphael remained as immovable as if he had been struck by lightning. He did not utter the least sound, and the expression of his face did not change for some moments; but he soon came to himself, entered the inner office, and mechanically shut the door.

There he threw himself into a chair, and pressed his head between his hands, as if he could no longer bear the pressure upon his brain.

At last, however, his heart beat less rapidly, and the truth impressed itself upon his mind; he arose, looked vacantly about him, and murmured to himself:

"A rich and brilliant marriage! Her future husband belongs to one of the largest business houses in the city! His father possesses millions, and she is very happy! She wishes herself to tell me the name of her future husband! Oh! I feared it! Alfred Dorneval! All my happy dreams, all my joyful emotions, all this sweet hope were only folly, pride—ingratitude perhaps; and her smile, the look of her eyes, the words of her father, all were but an illusion. I, poor fool, thought fortune was preparing such a happy future for me, while she was only laughing at my presumption! Good heavens! if I were guilty, truly I have been cruelly punished. My heart is bleeding, my soul is torn with anguish, despair, and shame, all is dark—my future is a deep precipice, where I see nothing but sorrow; but she is happy!"

This bitter thought made him jump up, while he still murmured:

"Happy!—contented!—but did I dream? Were my eyes altogether mistaken?"

He struck his brow with his hand, then continued, with deeper despair:

"No, no; the proud servant who dared to lift his eyes to

8

his master's daughter has received the reward his vanity deserved. I am a miserable clerk. Alas! why have I forgotten it? Felicité the wife of Alfred Dorneval! What joyful news! There will be great rejoicings, the whole city will give parties, the bride will be covered with flowers, wishes for her happiness will echo on all sides. She will live in a state of perfect bliss, while I languish in grief, die forgotten, and go down to the grave with the secret of my mistaken and ambitious love."

After a moment's silent thought he resumed, in a more resigned tone:

"To die! But is not all dead in me? What is commerce, fortune, the future to me now? For whom or for what shall I live? Alone in the world, without hope, without courage, without an object. Oh, my God! why didst Thou not at least leave me my poor mother, that I might love and work for some one!"

This last thought caused him to burst into tears. But he soon uttered a cry of alarm.

"Good heavens," he exclaimed, "tears on my cheeks! They are waiting for me in the office, may come to call me. Oh, no, I must not betray my culpable weakness. It would be a cruel injury to her and to her father. He is my benefactor; I am a man. Let me hide this unhappy secret in the deepest recess of my tortured soul. Let me fly from here—some one is coming!"

He opened the door and walked towards the street without turning round; then he went from right to left like some one who was blindly seeking for the road; then he rushed suddenly in a direction which, if he followed it, would lead him to the ramparts of the city.

He felt compelled to seek a more open space where he could be alone. After having walked forward for some minutes he turned to the right into St. Ann's street, and left the city by the Borgerhout gate.

Not far from the railroad depot he turned back on the ramparts, without observing that in the direction of the station a man was running towards him making signs. This man followed him to the rampart, and when he had reached him threw himself upon his breast with an exclamation of joy.

"Oh, my dear Banks," he cried, "how happy I am to meet you! My mother has had a conversation with Mr. Spelt. Lucy is to be my wife, all is settled, the wedding is to be in six weeks. A thousand thanks, my friend, for your kind assistance. Mr. Spelt says you are the means of my happiness. You spoke to him so highly of me! What is the matter? Are you in trouble?"

He stepped back in astonishment.

"You are pale, your eyes are red, you have been weeping; what does it mean?"

"Ask me nothing," said Banks, sighing; "my heart is broken, my soul is dead; all is over with me."

"Do not speak in enigmas, Raphael; I am trembling with anxiety."

"I beseech you leave me, I must be alone, or I shall go mad."

"Has any misfortune befallen your employer?"

The clerk shook his head.

"Have you made an unfortunate speculation and lost your inheritance?"

"No, Francis."

"Or lost your place with Mr. Verboord?"

"Not so."

"Then, tell me, for the love of heaven, what makes you so unhappy, that I may assist you, or, at least, comfort you."

" Comfort me? That is impossible. The dagger which has pierced my heart has wounded me fatally. All hope is lost."

" But the sympathy of a friend—"

" There are some secrets which a man carries with him to the tomb," said Raphael.

The travelling clerk was silent for a moment; while an almost imperceptible smile parted his lips.

" Ah! I begin to suspect," he exclaimed. " This violent grief, this deep despair! I know by experience the unfortunate complaint. But, my friend, is it necessary to believe that happiness is lost because a dark cloud appears in the heavens? Your disease will be cured by the first ray of sunlight! Come, confide your grief to me. Why conceal from me what I have known a long time? Felicité, is it not?"

" She is going to be married," said Raphael, sighing.

" Good heavens! To be married? To whom?"

" Alfred Dorneval."

" Is it really true? Is the marriage arranged?"

" Decidedly."

The travelling clerk grew pale; he took Banks by the arm, and said to him:

" Now I understand your grief. It is a terrible trial to be suddenly deprived of hope. But, perhaps, you are mistaken. This marriage may be only talked of. The least thing may prevent it taking place. Then you will have needlessly suffered this great sorrow."

" Felicité is happy: she anticipates the marriage with delight," replied the clerk, bitterly.

" Happy, is she? She is young, innocent, and pure. A first love is not so soon forgotten."

" Ah! be quiet, you break my heart," said the young

man. "I deceived myself. Pride blinded me. In her sweet smile, and friendly pressure of the hand, I thought I recognized proofs of affection; the extreme kindness of her parents seemed to encourage me. Alas! she did not even suspect my ambitious hopes. She is going to be married; a marriage which will kill me—her father came to tell me of it under the impression I would be delighted to hear it. And she, Felicité, wishes herself to tell me the name of her future husband, that I may participate in her joy and triumph! Poor fool! I dreamed of love, of happiness, of a future; I saw in the distance a paradise awaiting me—I have awakened, my soul bleeding, despair in my heart, and the grave open at my feet!"

Francis Walput led his friend to a bench and forced him to sit down.

"Come, Raphael," he said, "try to be calm, and let us talk like men. Suppose this marriage does take place; however deep a wound may be, it heals at last. You are young, you will be comforted, and the time will come, when you will no longer think of this trial."

"Never, never!" said Raphael harshly, "It is not possible for me ever again to enjoy either rest, hope, or happiness. It is my life which has been taken from me."

"These are ideas which arise from your despair, Raphael. Time, new affections, the cares of business will cure the sickness of your soul."

"There is no room in my heart for another love; I hate business. It was for her I wished to become rich, that she might never regret her love for me, that I might repay her for what she might sacrifice for me. Who have I to work for now? For myself? For what end? I have no longer either ambition or strength. All the world is indifferent to

8*

me. There is nothing left for me but to go away and pine and die far from her."

"What!" exclaimed Walput, "you would leave Antwerp? What folly! No, no, to-morrow you will have strength to conquer your grief and will give up such an idea."

"Be reasonable in your turn, my friend," said Raphael. "I would not be able to see Mr. Alfred Dorneval enter my employer's house without jealousy. Would I not be forced to count the days as they passed, before he led Felicité to the altar? Could I possibly assist till the last in the preparations for my misfortune, and listen to the daily rejoicings over the event which causes me to hate life? Would not my heart be constantly wounded? Could it be expected from any man?"

Walput shook his head despondingly. "Poor Banks!" said he, sighing, "whatever cause you may have for unhappiness, you look at the affair more darkly than necessary. Although to-day you will not listen to any consolation, to-morrow you will take a calmer and more cheerful view of your condition. As to your plan of leaving Antwerp, I am quite sure you will not carry it out."

"But I will be compelled to carry it out," replied Raphael. "Mr. Verboord has acted generously by me, his wife attended my mother on her death-bed. If a foolish mistake has made me forget my debt of gratitude, I will now remember what I owe my benefactors. Who can tell if Alfred Dorneval may not come to live in Mr. Verboord's house after his marriage? He would then be my superior and give me orders. And even should I give up my position as clerk, would I not meet her every day in a handsome carriage seated beside him who has taken the light from my life? No, some day I would betray what I had dared to hope, and it would be a cruel return to those who have a claim upon my gratitude."

The travelling clerk looked at his watch and said kindly :

"The exchange is already open, and I must go. Come with me, Raphael; you ought to take some dinner and then it will be time to go to your office."

"I am not going to return to the office," replied Banks.

"Why, have you given up the place ?"

"No, but it is the same thing."

"Still I cannot leave you alone in such a state of mind, Raphael. Come, be a man. Come to the city with me, I will go to your room with you, and after I return from the Exchange, will call for you. We will then walk about, and talk till you feel calmer. I will tell Mr. Verboord you have a severe headache, and wish permission to remain at home. So that your absence to-day will not surprise any-one."

The clerk did not answer.

"Do you wish to make me late at the Exchange?" asked Walput. "So be it. Mr. Spelt who expects to meet me there may take it as he likes, I will not leave you."

Raphael arose.

"It is all the same to me," he said. "I do not wish to be the means of involving you in difficulties. Let us go, I am ready."

They turned round behind a grove of lilacs, and entered the main path. The clerk walked with his head bowed. Walput stopped suddenly, and said to him ·

"We have time enough, Raphael; in less than a quarter of an hour I will be through at the Exchange. I am in a state of indignation."

"Against me ?" asked Banks, in surprise.

" No, against Felicité and her parents. Their conduct towards you is cruel and very much to be blamed. Only think of it, to receive a young man into their family as handsome and sensible as you are, to allow him to talk unreservedly to their daughter ; to seek opportunities apparently to inspire him with hope ; and then because a rich man offers his hand, they sacrifice their unhappy victim to their ambition, and break his heart without the least pity ! If I were in your place, I would revenge myself by profound contempt."

This outburst of Walput was only a feigned indignation, by which he wished to arouse a feeling of vexation and anger in the wounded heart of his friend, believing it would be the best weapon against his despair.

Raphael looked at him and smiled sadly as he replied :

" She is still an artless child, Francis ; she has never suspected that I felt for her, or hoped to receive from her anything but friendship. The kindness of her parents has made them blind. They have not noticed what was passing in my heart. With whom can I be angry ? Who is to blame ? Who has anything to regret, excepting myself alone ?"

Francis renewed his efforts ; but Raphaël, absorbed in his sad thoughts, did not seem to listen, and fixed his eyes upon the ground. While they were walking in the narrow road, they did not observe driving rapidly behind them, a barouche to which were attached two full blooded English horses.

As they did not hear the noise of the wheels on the soft turf, the driver called to them to get out of the road.

They sprang aside, and as the carriage passed them like lightning, enveloping them in dust, they heard the word "scoundrels," uttered in a sneering tone.

"Alfred Dorneval!" exclaimed the travelling clerk, angrily.

"Behold my prediction," cried Raphael, shuddering. "There you can see the future; such is to be my fate, while she will be seated beside him. No, no, let me go, and place the world between us!"

Walput took his friend's hand and murmured: "Come, come, my poor friend. He may return; let us go on!"

Thus speaking, the two young men turned into another path and disappeared behind the bushes.

CHAPTER V.

UITE early the next day, Felicité was standing near her chamber window, her head bowed upon her breast and her eyes resting on the ground. She was buried in deep thought, and for some time remained as motionless as a statue, without the slightest movement to betray what was passing in her mind. Mrs. Verboord, who had entered the room a moment before, looked at the young girl, smiled, and shook her head, as if she guessed the cause of her daughter's absence of mind.

She approached the window, saying:

"Come, my child, you cannot——"

Felicité started and began to tremble, but when she recognized her mother, a slight blush colored her cheeks, and she said, sighing:

"Oh, dear mamma, is it you! How you frightened me!"

Her mother looked at her in astonishment.

"Why should you be alarmed, my child," she asked. "What frightens you?"

"I don't know, mamma," said the young girl, sadly. "I was thinking deeply, your voice startled me, and I felt as frightened as though some danger threatened me."

"What does that mean?" cried Mrs. Verboord, laughing; "one would suppose you to be in grief."

" Ah, mamma," said Felicité, " I am tired and excited ; a strange sadness oppresses me."

" Sit down, my child ; I will soon comfort you. Perhaps you have not slept, and the night has been wearisome."

' I was dreaming, mamma, continually dreaming.''

" Of course, it was very natural ; you were dreaming of your happy marriage. In imagination you assisted in the preparations for the wedding, tried on your elegant dresses and jewels, and perhaps have pictured yourself at the altar with your betrothed."

" Yes, mamma," sighed the young girl, " I believe I dreamed of all that. I saw you, my father, Mr. Dorneval, and many other persons, but I have only a confused and vague recollection of them."

" My child, it is only fatigue which makes you sad this morning. I am quite sure your dreams were pleasant and agreeable."

" No, mamma, I must have wept and trembled in my dreams ; for I awoke much frightened, and even now I feel a depression and anxiety which I cannot overcome."

" But, what did you dream ? "

" I do not remember, something frightful, I know. Yet it seems to me that a strange voice murmured all night long in my ear, ' Give up this marriage ; it will make you unhappy.' "

" What nonsense, how childish," cried Mrs. Verboord. " You know the meaning of dreams must always be reversed. Therefore, this would indicate that you are to be very happy. How could it be doubted for a moment ? "

" My feelings are strange and unaccountable, mother. This marriage gives you and my father so much pleasure, and seems so advantageous for me ; yet it alarms me."

" We all know the fancies of a young girl," replied Mrs.

Verboord. " Listen to me, Felicité. Before my marriage
I had had time to know and appreciate your father's character at its true value. He loved me, and I felt the deepest affection for him. My greatest desire was to be united
to him for life; yet when my father told me I must marry
him I was so surprised by the news that I began to tremble
like a leaf. I went to my room and wept the whole day. I
was happy, still I was frightened, and wept. It is the
same case with you."

Felicité sighed.

" It is easily understood," continued Mrs. Verboord.
" A young girl is brought up at her mother's side in childish innocence, loving, joyous, careless, and with no responsibility. She understands that for most of us marriage is a
necessity in life, and she sighs for the time when the husband of her choice will give her a name and position in the
world. But, when the desired moment arrives, she looks
with regret on all she leaves behind: the innocent joy of
childhood, her girlish independence, the house where she
was born, her dearly loved parents. Besides, the unknown
future frightens her; the new duties of wife and mother
which she accepts, the life of personal responsibility, and
many other reflections of this kind trouble her mind. But,
Felicité, it is so with all the world. It does not prevent us
from being happy, and from thanking God for His kindness
to us."

The young girl did not appear fully convinced.

" Do you not believe me?" asked Mrs. Verboord.
" Wait a little and you will see."

" What you tell me is doubtless true," replied Felicité.
" Still, with me it is not quite the same thing. You, dear
mamma, had had time to know my father well, and had
long desired to marry him. Yesterday I was but a child

who had never thought of such important things. Mr. Dorneval is, doubtless, a very amiable young man; but I have only seen him once—"

" It is enough, as those few moments awakened in your hearts a reciprocal affection."

Felicité shook her head negatively.

" What ridiculous whim is this?" cried Mrs. Verboord, reproachfully. " Why conceal that you were pleased with the manifestations of Alfred's love ?"

" I thought so yesterday, mamma," murmured Felicité.

" And now ? "

" Now, it seems to me I will never be able to love him. I do not know why it is so, but when I think of it my heart aches."

Mrs. Verboord looked at her daughter almost angrily.

" Oh, dear mamma, do not be angry with me. These are foolish ideas, and I know I am wrong. They will pass away. But may I ask a favor of you ? "

" Well, speak."

" Must I really leave my dear mother and father so soon ? This painful separation is doubtless the cause of my sadness and my alarm. Ah ! I beg you, mamma, to use your influence with my father to have the marriage delayed a little. Do not be angry at my request ; but if it can only be postponed a few months, or even a few weeks, however short a time, that I may become accustomed to the thought of leaving you."

Mrs. Verboord was gratified at this proof of filial love, and answered kindly :

" As you so earnestly desire it, my child, I will advise your father not to hasten the marriage too much. Yet I know he will regret any delay. Did he not say he had asked and received a great favor from Mr. Dorneval ? Sup-

9

pose Alfred's father insists upon it ? Your father would not wish, and perhaps could not refuse him. You would not like to give your father trouble, would you, Felicité ?"

" No, mamma."

" Suppose he insists ? "

" Then I will submit, and do what he wishes."

" Without complaining ? " asked Mrs. Verboord.

" Without complaining, mamma; but do try to get a delay."

" I will do all I can, my child. Be comforted now, and drive away your anxious thoughts. Take your embroidery, it will divert your mind."

" Mamma," said the young girl, " when I came down stairs I had determined to go to church. I feel the necessity of prayer. It will calm and comfort me."

" Go to church, Felicité. Prayer is truly the only means of bringing peace to troubled hearts."

The young girl threw a shawl around her shoulders, took her prayer book, and started to go out, when a sudden thought detained her.

" Mamma," she said, " is Mr. Banks in the office ? "

" I do not know," replied Mrs. Verboord. " The office is not open, it is too early."

" Was he very sick, mamma ? "

" No; a headache is nothing; one does not often feel it the next day. If, however, he should not come to the office, we will send to inquire how he is."

" Send soon, please, mamma," said Felicité, as she went out.

When she was on the street near the residence of Mr. Spelt, Lucy, dressed to go out, appeared on the door-step. The grocer's daughter ran to her friend, and smiling, said:

" Oh, Felicité, how glad I am to meet you ! We were

together at boarding school, and have always continued friends. I know you will be glad to hear of my happiness. You do not know it! I am going to be married to Francis Walput. What do you say to that?"

"I also am going to be married," replied Felicité.

"You, too, going to be married! Ah, what good news! How happy our good friend Banks ought to be! I am sure he is almost crazy."

"My father says he was so surprised and pleased that he could not say a word."

"Then it is joy that has made him sick?"

"Do you know he is sick?" asked Felicité, in surprise. "My father invited him to see us, but he did not come. He was taken with a sudden headache, and sent his friend, Mr. Walput, to tell my father."

"I know all about that," replied Lucy, "for it was the cause of my father becoming so angry that it nearly broke off my engagement. It was arranged that Francis Walput should come to tea at our house with his mother. My father had directed the best things, and his oldest wine, to be brought out. At the Exchange, Walput came up to him and told him it would be impossible for him to come, as his friend, Raphael Banks, was very sick and needed his care."

"Good heavens! is Raphael seriously ill?" cried Felicité, much alarmed.

"No; it is the effect of his emotion. Do not be unhappy, my friend; he will be better to-day. At first my father was very angry with Francis, because our little party had to be put off; but, as he has a great esteem for Mr. Banks, he has forgiven it, and invited our company for day after to-morrow."

"I do not understand," said Felicité, thoughtfully, "why Raphael should be so troubled."

"What! at such a marriage! When a man loves secretly for years, without daring to speak, almost without hope, then suddenly hears the father of his beloved say to him: 'Be happy, I will give you the hand of my only daughter!' has he not reason to rejoice?"

Felicité looked at her friend in astonishment. She was silent for a moment, then asked:

"But, Lucy, of whom are you speaking?"

"Of whom should I speak but of Mr. Banks?"

The poor girl hung her head to conceal the color which suffused her face,

"What does this mean?" cried Lucy, in surprise.

"I have only seen my future husband once!" sighed Felicité.

"Are you not going to marry Raphael?"

"No, Lucy; I am engaged to Alfred Dorneval, the son of the rich merchant in the Great Square."

"Am I dreaming or awake?" murmured Lucy, starting back in surprise. "Alfred Dorneval! Oh, now I understand poor Raphael's illness. He will certainly die."

"He will die?" repeated Felicité. "No, no, Lucy, not if my marriage gives him so much pleasure."

"Let us rest a little while in the Square," said Lucy. "I am so astonished I cannot go on. Alfred Dorneval! It is not possible!"

She led her friend to the least frequented side of the Square, and asked her, in an agitated voice:

"Is this marriage decidedly arranged?"

"Yes."

"How quietly you answer, Felicité."

"My parents think me happy. How can I oppose them?"

"So you can give Raphael his death blow without

regret? He who has loved you so devotedly, thought only of you, hoped only for you, wished to live for you alone!"

"For the love of heaven, Lucy, do not tell me such things," stammered Felicité, much excited. "You make me shudder. I know very well that Raphael has friendly feelings for me, and tries to be agreeable to me; but what you imagine—No, no, you are certainly mistaken."

"Can it be possible?" exclaimed Lucy. "Must you be told that Raphael loves you with all the strength of his soul? Have you never observed it? Then you do not love him at all; unhappy young man! Well, listen to me; I can prove it to you. My father was so infatuated with Raphael, with his handsome and noble face, his intelligence, and fine manners, that he decided I should marry Mr. Banks. You are surprised, are you not? It is true, nevertheless. My father invited Raphael to our house, and positively offered him my hand. Raphael has no fortune, but your father and mine both think that he has every chance of becoming rich if he had a capital in the first place. In accepting my hand he would get this capital. Besides, without flattering myself, I am not the ugliest person in the world, so that such a marriage ought to have been an unexpected happiness for him. Yet he refused it."

"He refused!" exclaimed Felicité, sighing.

"Yes, and do you know why? He told his friend Francis, who, by the way, had already guessed it, that there existed in his heart an affection for another so deep, he would refuse all the riches of the earth rather than be unfaithful to it. Who does he love? Have not your eyes told you a hundred times? Besides, there is no mistake about it; he confessed it to Francis Walput."

Felicité was deeply moved. She could scarcely believe

9*

her ears. Yet this revelation did not pain her, for, while she was buried in thought, a slight smile parted her lips.

"Poor Banks," continued Lucy, sadly, "who so generously secured my happiness and his friend Walput's, what is reserved for him henceforth in this world? A life of sadness and despair, doubtless a short life; for he will pine away and die of grief. Felicité, you may yet save him. Your parents love you so much! They would not be able to resist your tears and entreaties. Oh, how I long to save him from this terrible blow, and return him the kindness he so disinterestedly rendered us. You are silent, Felicité. Have you no feeling for his sufferings?"

At this moment an old woman ran across the Square, and threw herself on Lucy's breast.

"Ah, my dear niece, I hear you are going to marry one you have loved a long time. I know him; he is a fine young man, of good family, and with a high reputation: that is enough. His mother was my friend long ago. Your father sent me news of it yesterday, and I came by the first train. Come to the house with me; I have so many things to tell you!"

"I am coming, I am coming, my dear aunt," murmured Lucy, in embarrassment.

"Stay, what is the matter with this young lady?" cried the old lady. "So young, and yet to be in trouble!"

Lucy took her aunt by the arm and led her to the other side of the Square. She then returned to Felicité, but perceiving she wished to be silent, merely gave her a sign and disappeared with her aunt.

Mr. Verboord's daughter continued her walk with unsteady steps, entirely absorbed in her sad thoughts. She knew not what to think; she feared to attach any faith to what she had just heard; but the light gradually broke in upon her mind, and when she entered the church her tears were flowing. However, the sanctity of the place gave her strength to overcome the outward signs of her emotion. She knelt upon a cushion, opened her prayer book, and tried to pray.

Yet, in spite of all her efforts to raise her thoughts to Heaven, she could not prevent herself from thinking of what Lucy had told her. From time to time the tolling of the little bell at the altar aroused her from her reveries, and then she tried to follow the prayers of the priest; but the words of her friend continued to re-echo in her ear.

Then her youth passed slowly before her eyes, as if painted on canvass. She recalled, with strange distinctness, every day, every hour that Raphael had spent in her presence, his smallest word, his slightest smile, the trembling of his voice, and the sparkling of his eyes. Yes, it was really true; the unhappy young man had concealed it; and now she was going to be married! The simple announcement of this marriage had made him sick! He would perhaps die because he had loved her.

The young girl shuddered, and summoned all her strength to avoid bursting into tears. What frightened her yet more, was a voice within her breast which cried·"And you also love him, Felicité!" but she smothered the voice and forced herself to believe it was only a fancy of her agitated mind. Yet it seemed to haunt her like a bad dream.

At last the young girl was forced to admit, with a sigh of anguish, that it was only an expression of the sad truth.

The repeated sounds of the bell announced that the priest was celebrating the Holy Communion.

Felicité bent her head, and crossed herself; but, although

she truly and earnestly raised her heart to God, a human
face intruded upon her devotions, and when the priest left
the altar, she prayed to God to have mercy upon poor
Raphael and to protect him.

Felicité arose and left the church. In the street she
walked with her head bowed down. It seemed to her that
the looks of the passers-by would make her blush with
shame; and she feared each one would read in her face the
cause of her emotion. Everything frightened her, houses
and men. She felt she could find neither consolation nor
rest excepting on the bosom of her good mother.

But she did not find her mother in the dining-room.
She threw herself upon a chair, put her hands before her
eyes, and wept bitterly.

She remained thus a long time to relieve the anguish of
her heart, until a gentle voice said to her:

" Are you weeping, Felicité?"

The young girl drew her mother to her heart, and said,
sighing:

"Oh! dear mamma, help me, comfort me! Your poor
child is very unhappy."

"Unhappy!" repeated Mrs. Verboord, much astonished
at Felicité's tone of despair. " You have forgotten what
I said to you this morning. It will not continue. Every
young girl who is going to be married is agitated and
frightened."

" No, mamma, it is not that. A secret, a dreadful secret
which has been told me—"

" Trust me with this secret, which is so important," said
her mother.

Felicité opened her mouth to speak; but hesitated and
muttered something unintelligible.

"Well, my child, I am listening," said Mrs. Verboord,
with an incredulous smile.

"I am afraid, mamma; see how I tremble. Ah! I fear you will scold me, but believe me that before to-day I knew nothing of it. You are so kind to me !"

"But explain yourself, Felicité; what you say is an enigma to me."

The young girl was silent for an instant as if trying to summon strength and courage, then she replied in a firmer voice:

"I am innocent; you are my mother, and if I could not pour out my grief on your compassionate breast, where would I seek for consolation? Mamma, it will surprise you, perhaps grieve you also. Raphael has become suddenly ill; it is because—because Raphael—grief—sorrow—

"Well, what is it? What of Raphael?"

"He loves me, mamma."

Mrs. Verboord burst out laughing, but the beseeching look and clasped hands of Felicité awakened her pity.

"My child, some one has made you believe that in jest," she said quietly.

"Oh, mamma, do not laugh," said Felicité, solemnly. "By your love for your only child, I beg you to believe it is true."

Mrs. Verboord, who was beginning to doubt, turned pale. She took her daughter's hand and said:

"Some one has deceived you, Felicité. Tell me who told you this?"

"Lucy Spelt."

"How is it that Lucy knows it?"

"Her father wished her to marry Raphael, and Raphael refused because he loved another, and he admitted to his friend Walput that it was I—whom he loved."

"What wonderful things are you telling me?" cried Mrs. Verboord. "Raphael must have lost all—But I neither can nor will believe it. It is an old woman's tale."

"When my father told him yesterday I was going to be married he became suddenly ill, so ill that Francis Walput had to stay with him all day!"

There were some moments of silence, during which Mrs. Verboord seemed much excited and indignant. By a great effort she restrained her feelings, sat down beside her daughter, and said severely:

"No, my mind refuses to believe in such ill-conduct Raphael, whom we believed to be so devoted and grateful, whose serious mind and respectful demeanor inspired us with unlimited confidence in him; Raphael to have forgotten so entirely what we have done for him! Not only to dare to lift his eyes to the only daughter of his benefactor, but to speak to other people of his foolish hopes! He, to wound us so, when we have shown him only kindness! It cannot be; with such a heart as his, he has not become ungrateful in a day."

The young girl, her eyes filled with tears, sought pardon for Raphael and murmured in a scarcely intelligible voice:

"Oh, mamma, do not be so severe upon him!"

Mrs. Verboord, into whose mind there appeared to enter a suspicion, shook her head with a smile, and said

"But, suppose you are not deceived. What have you to do with Raphael's error, my child? It is his own fault if he has prepared for himself a bitter deception; we have no right to trouble ourselves about it. You will marry; Mr. Banks will leave our house, and in a short time he will not think of his mistake, excepting to regret having so far forgotten his duty."

"No, no, mamma," sobbed the young girl, bursting into tears, "grief has made him sick, despair will kill him. Oh, this thought frightens me. He, such a good, noble-hearted young man, to die from having loved me too well! What a horrible future! I would never have peace on earth; his face would haunt my dreams, I would see him pale and unhappy, accusing me of being the cause of his premature death! Mamma, mamma, do not let him die!"

Mrs. Verboord felt disposed to reproach her daughter, for there was something in her words which wounded her mother's heart. But she was touched by Felicité's bitter tears and excessive anguish, and restrained her indignation. Besides, she was afraid of deceiving herself, though she wished to doubt.

"Oh, my child!" she said. "God grant my suspicions may be only foolish fears! You are sorry Mr. Banks is unhappy at the time you are going to be so happy. It is natural, as until now he has always shown himself devoted and kind to your parents; respectful and useful to you. I can understand that you feel sensible of the pain your marriage will cause him. But, my dear Felicité, your pity is only friendship, is it not?"

The young girl blushed to her ears, and let her head fall upon her breast.

"Speak, speak, Felicité!" cried Mrs. Verboord, with anguish. "Do not leave me in this terrible uncertainty. You do not feel anything but friendship for Mr. Banks, do you? If he has forgotten what he owes his benefactors, you, at least, have not allowed your heart to be touched by a secret love? Come, tell me frankly, I command you!"

"Mamma, mamma, forgive me!" sighed the young girl trembling.

"Forgive you? For what! Good heavens!"

"I believe I love Raphael."

"No, no, it is not true! You are mistaken, your imagination deceives you!"

"I have confessed it to God himself, in church, mamma."

"It is incredible! How long has my child been deceiving me?"

"Deceive, my mother! Felicité deceive you! Oh, what a cruel reproach! Yesterday I knew not the meaning of the word love, and I did not believe I loved any one but you and my father. But my marriage, the complete change in my life, my frightful dreams last night, his sickness, his despair, all have combined to awaken the fatal knowledge in my breast."

The last words of the young girl had soothed the alarm and indignation of Mrs. Verboord. She did not doubt the truth of Felicité's explanation, for the innocent child had always been truthful, and the confession itself was a convincing proof of her sincerity. After a moment's silence, she said quietly to her daughter, who still continued to weep:

"Felicité, my child, drive these thoughts from your mind. Be calm; return to reason, to conscience, to your duty. Think of your good father. Who can tell if he will not become sick from grief, nervous as he already is?"

"Oh, I beseech you do not tell him, mamma!"

"Can you conceal from him an emotion which causes you to weep at the happiest moment of your life?"

"My father need not know what troubles me; but from you, mamma, I could not have a secret even if I were guilty."

"Thank you, Felicité, for your love for me. Then I may hope you will not grieve your father; that from respect and love for him, you will overcome your sorrow, and appear happy when he speaks to you of your marriage? Ah, if you do not do so, he will certainly be sick."

" You promised, mamma, to try to delay the marriage."

" Yes, I will try."

" And I will try to become accustomed to the thought of our separation."

" And to forget your error?"

" And to forget Raphael," sobbed the young girl.

A heavy step was heard in the hall.

" Good Heavens! I hear your father!" exclaimed Mrs. Verboord, in a suppressed voice. " He must not see you so pale, and your eyes filled with tears Come to your chamber till you overcome your emotion."

She took her daughter by the arm and left the room with her by a side door.

While Mrs. Verboord was occupied in comforting her daughter, the merchant was seated in his private office before a table covered with books and papers. He had also three or four newspapers before him. He held one in his hand, and fixed his eyes upon the third page, where the prices and conditions of the markets throughout Europe were quoted. The news appeared favorable, for he smiled and shook his head with apparent satisfaction. When he had finished the page he was reading, he looked at his watch and murmured :

" Ten o'clock already! I must not forget that I promised Mr. Dorneval to call on him at his house this morning to arrange definitely the conditions of the marriage contract. I ought to go and dress. I must hurry and not keep him waiting."

As he arose, some one rapped at the door.

" Ah! my dear Banks," he cried, " you are better. I am delighted ; for if you had continued ill when we were so joyful here, it would have pained me very much. But you still seem very sick, my poor Raphael. How pale you

10

"I do not understand you," he murmured "We agreed, I believe, that you should leave the office in a month or six weeks, when you were to begin business on your own account. What, then, is the meaning of your request?"

"I beg you, sir, to grant my immediate dismission."

"Do you wish to leave me to-day?"

" This afternoon, sir, I wish to examine the books and papers, and explain everything to the second clerk, that my absence may not occasion the least inconvenience."

" My poor Banks," cried Mr. Verboord, " you are sicker than you believe—your hollow voice, your strange look; you need repose, be assured. I cannot keep you in my office against your will; you are perfectly free, but do not let us speak of that now. Return home; then, when you are quite well, we will talk of it."

" It is impossible, sir," said the young man, stopping the merchant with a gesture of entreaty.

" How impossible?" replied the latter. " I do not know why it is, Raphael, but your strange language frightens me. What prevents you from taking necessary repose before deciding on so important an affair?"

" Because I have come to say good-bye to you. I am going to take a long voyage, and do not know if I will again see my benefactors."

" Are you going to leave the country?"

" Yes, I will leave Europe."

" Stay, Raphael, believe me, you still have fever, and your brain is a little excited."

" No, sir, you are mistaken. I am not sick, and my mind is perfectly clear. I knew very well this unexpected news would surprise you; but I could not leave my country without bidding you ' adieu,' and thanking you again for your kindness."

" You can leave Antwerp every week, almost every day, for the four corners of the world. Your impatience, at least, is inexplicable. Tell me why you are so hurried that a few days seem too long a delay?"

" A particular circumstance," replied Raphael. " An old friend, a classmate, whom I would like very much to accompany, is going with me. I have thought of this arrangement all night, and have firmly decided to carry it out. Business is too slow here for my impatient spirit. I wish to try my fortune in America."

Although there was something forced in the cool energy of the clerk, the merchant began to think himself mistaken. He took the young man by the hand, made him sit down, and said to him:

"Now let us talk quietly of your strange determination. Do you really wish to go to America?"

"Yes, sir."

"To enter into business? Have you reflected fully upon all the possible contingencies of such a decision?"

"I have thought over them all."

"It is not possible. Listen a moment, Raphael. Do you know how things are managed in America. There every one is eager to make a fortune quickly. It is a constant struggle to make money, without rest, without intermission, every one against the other; and in this crowd of avaricious people, every means is employed to succeed; each one tries to crush and deceive his rival; they rise and fall, become bankrupt twenty times, and, without caring in the least for the victims who suffer by them, continue this wild struggle without pity. You have ten thousand francs. Before you touch American soil a good part of this will have disappeared. You will then find yourself in a strange country without means to undertake anything important. You will be immediately surrounded with all kinds of people, who, while offering you the most friendly services, have no other end than to become masters of the little money you possess. Your kind and trusting disposition will expose you to deception of all sorts. In a short time you will probably lose all; and you will then, far from your country and friends, have to ask for a clerkship in some office, to save yourself from want."

Mr. Verboord had intentionally exaggerated this picture of commerce in America to make an impression upon the mind of the young man. When he had finished he looked at him with a questioning glance.

"I have thought of all that," said Raphael, indifferently. "This struggle, this combat is the life I desire. They do not all fail who seek their fortune in America. There are others also who in a short time acquire great riches."

"But how many return to Europe without a cent, disheartened, disappointed, and sick in body and mind? Does not fortune smile upon you sufficiently in Belgium, that you wish to put the sea between you and your dear country? Your first speculation brought you a good profit. I will be happy to help you and sustain you by my acts and advice, especially now that the marriage of Felicité will relieve me of all care. Ah, my friend, it is very foolish to run after a shadow, when you have the object of your desires at your hand. Stop, I tell you if you carry out your plan I will be very sad; I will follow you in imagination and believe you to be unhappy. No, no, stay in Antwerp; I will promise you speedy success. Will you not give up your foolish resolution?"

Raphael was deeply moved; yet he continued calm, and said:

"Your kindness, sir, is unlimited. If I could discharge my debt to you I would not hesitate an instant; yet I cannot give up my voyage to America. I beg you to let me bid you adieu."

"Ah!" cried Mr. Verboord, rising, "I do not understand you at all. You persist in going against my advice.

10*

We shall see! Come with me, you shall soon talk dif-
ferently."

He led the young man by the hand into the hall, and
moved towards another door.

There Raphael drew back, and inquired:

" What are you going to do, sir?"

" What am I going to do? Lead you into the dining-
room."

"'I beseech you let me go!" cried the clerk, in suppressed tones.

" Well, what does this mean?" asked Mr. Verboord,
much astonished. " Would you go without bidding adieu
to my wife and daughter?"

" No, no, sir, it is not that," stammered Raphael. " You
are right. Do not notice my agitation. I will follow you."

As he spoke, he trembled from head to foot, and was as
pale as death.

He gave a sigh of relief when he saw Mrs. Verboord was
alone.

" Where is Felicité?" asked Mr. Verboord.

" She is a little indisposed," replied Mrs. Verboord, fix-
ing her eyes on Raphael. " She had a severe headache and
has gone to lie down; but it is not of any importance."

Mr. Verboord glanced at the clock, and said:

"I must dress to call on Mr. Dorneval. I am late.
Look at Mr. Banks, Laurence. Would you believe it, a
fancy has suddenly seized him to go to America. I leave
you to persuade him to give up this foolish idea. He is
obstinate for the first time in his life. If he dares to resist
your advice, call Felicité; she will soon overcome his
resistance. When I come down I will ask our young
dreamer to accompany me. I will not be long. Do not
forget, Raphael, that we are all good friends, and love you
sincerely."

With these words he left the room.

Mrs. Verboord at first looked severely at the young man; but the sorrow she read upon his face touched her, and caused her to pity him. The news of Raphael's project of quitting Antwerp immediately confirmed her in the belief that he was incapable of forgetting his duties, and of actually proposing.

"Is it really true that you are going to America?" she asked.

"It is true, madam," replied the young man. "Accept the respectful adieux of him whom you have so generously protected. The remembrance of your goodness and kindness will never leave me. In whatever place I may be, believe me, I will pray for you, and ask God to give you a long and happy life. Ah, I beseech you, do not seek to change my resolution; it will pain me so much not to be able to follow your advice."

"Do you fear I would wish to detain you?" asked Mrs. Verboord. "On the contrary, your departure proves to me that I was not mistaken in you. Your resolution is praise-worthy, and I approve of it."

Raphael blushed, grew pale, and trembled as he looked at Mrs. Verboord.

"Yes, I am aware, though, perhaps, you may doubt it, that you have allowed an impossible hope to arise in your heart. I ought, as a mother, to reproach you; but since you know your duty, and generously sacrifice yourself for the good of those who have always desired your welfare, I can only pity you. Go, sir, try in a long voyage to forget your mistake. We will think of you with pity for your grief and gratitude for your devotion."

The young man, deeply moved, looked down on the floor, and remained silent.

Mrs. Verboord resumed, in compassionate tones:

"Do not lose courage, Raphael; fortune will, no doubt, smile upon you in industrious America. If, however, you should be unsuccessful, always remember you have friends in Antwerp who only wish to see you happy."

"Thank you, thank you, with all my heart," murmured the young man.

"That which pains you now," continued Mrs. Verboord, in a more friendly tone, "is a feeling which you may think incurable, but which will grow less very quickly, and in time disappear altogether. In a few months you will even have forgotten that—"

Raphael, overcome by sudden emotion, raised his head, and said, sighing, while his eyes flashed:

"Forget! Oh, no, no, never! The tomb alone—"

"Do not continue, sir," interrupted Mrs. Verboord, with an imperative gesture. "This folly will be cured. Hide in the deepest recess of your heart a secret that you must not tell to any one. Above all, do not let Mr. Verboord suspect anything; it would cause him too much sorrow."

There was again silence.

"When will you leave?" she asked.

"To-morrow, or the day after, I do not know, madam," replied Raphael. "As soon as it is possible."

"To-morrow, day after to-morrow," she repeated, with astonishment. "No, no, that must not be. It would, perhaps, destroy the effect of your generous intention. My husband, your friends, would ask how it happened that your unexpected departure and another important piece of news were announced at the same time. Come, Raphael, show that there is no sacrifice too great for you to make to guard us from danger or to spare us a grief. Remain some time yet, if only for a few weeks. I beg of you do not refuse. The peace of my husband, the honor of a person who is dearer to me than life, are in the balance. Will you not delay your voyage till you can leave without awakening suspicion?"

"I will try to grant your request, madam," replied Raphael, with a heavy sigh. "But it will depend upon other circumstances, on my strength or my weakness May God give me power to resist the inexorable impulse which possesses me!"

"There is Mr. Verboord coming down," said Mrs. Verboord, "By all we have been able to do for you, Raphael, conceal the cause of your departure from him!"

The merchant entered smiling, and exclaimed:

"Well, you have succeeded, I hope."

"In part, at least," replied Mrs. Verboord.

"I will finish the task, Laurence. Come, my boy, you must accompany me to the Great Square. I will give you so many reasons on the way that you will have nothing more to say. You must stay in Antwerp, my dear Banks, at least till after the wedding. In the mean time many things may happen, and the ideas of young people turn from white to black. Ah, I will teach you to leave your country so suddenly!"

While speaking he led the young man to the door.

Mrs. Verboord had risen and followed him. She took Raphael's hand, pressed it tenderly, and said:

"Courage, sir, courage; be strong in doing your duty."

"Thank you, thank you; may God bless you, madam," murmured Banks, with tears in his eyes, as he followed the merchant from the room.

CHAPTER VI.

YOU seem so depressed, my dear Felicité," said Mrs. Verboord to her daughter, who was seated, silent and thoughtful, at the table. "Try to change this sad expression of face. You saw how anxious your father was when he came in last eve. I trembled with fear. If he had discovered or even suspected anything! Your father is coming down. If he finds you so pensive, he will seek to learn the cause of your sadness. I beg of you, my child, do not give him any reason to question you."

"Do not fear, mamma," said the young girl. "I feel quite strong."

"Make a great effort, my child, to recover your usual manner. It is very necessary, as Mr. Dorneval and his son Alfred are coming to dine with us to-day. If you do not overcome your feelings, how will you be able to receive your future husband properly? I can understand that this first visit from Mr. Alfred frightens you. It would alarm you under ordinary circumstances; but, I beg of you, Felicité, do not forget that your father's peace and happiness may depend upon your courage."

"Do not be anxious, mamma, if night has soothed my feelings, the cloud will have entirely disappeared before mid-day; and I will be able to conceal the anguish which fills my heart."

"What do I hear?" cried Mrs. Verboord in a reproachful tone. "Your heart filled with anguish! Ah! Felicité, is it thus you submit to duty? Notwithstanding your promises, you still permit a fatal passion to possess you!"

"It is not that, mamma," said Felicité, sighing. "My feeling is only pity. Poor Raphael is sick!"

"Not so, my child, it is a fancy of your imagination. You allow yourself to be needlessly anxious. Raphael understands that he has allowed himself to be led away by a false hope, and he has taken a brave and wise resolution. In a fortnight he will sail for America. What an example his submission to duty ought to be to you, Felicité. He has found comfort and strength in resignation."

"Alas! my father, yesterday, without knowing it, gave him a mortal wound."

"You have dreamed that, Felicité."

"Mamma, do you not remember my father's words on his return yesterday evening. Did he not say that he had told Raphael of Mr. Dorneval's visit. Did not papa tell him also that he would like to invite him to dinner but that it was not proper now?"

"Well! is not that natural?" interrupted Mrs. Verboord.

"What an humiliation!" sighed Felicité.

"Humiliation! Not at all. The affair which was to be arranged rendered the presence of other people impossible."

A sad expression, and a slightly ironical smile passed over the face of the young girl.

"My father said," she replied, "that he would have him under some pretext called in at the dessert, to drink a glass of wine to my happy marriage. Do you not believe, mamma, that Raphael's proud and sensitive heart was broken by such a thing. To admit him, like a servant, in the presence of Mr. Alfred to drink to his own humiliation—perhaps, to his approaching death!"

" But he will not come," said Mrs. Verboord.

" No, mamma, he will not come; but he has received the cruel blow, and his heart bleeds deeply."

" Félicité, Félicité, you have promised not to think of him. You are weaker than yesterday."

The young girl bowed her head.

" Dear mamma, you are mistaken," she murmured. "I will forget him. I am now strong enough to conceal the feeling, which you truly have called a fatal passion; but a feeling of pity will bring his image before my eyes against my will."

Mrs. Verboord shook her head sadly. She looked at her daughter for a moment in silence, then replied :

" My poor Félicité, you suffer, I know! I understand your grief, my child. But conquer your emotions, struggle with your thoughts, let the consciousness of duty strengthen you against the passion of your heart. Oh, smother a feeling which will throw a continual mourning over your life, which will render you unhappy, and also your father, mother, and husband. No, you cannot take the sacred vows of marriage, until you overcome your weakness. I will ask for and obtain a delay, by some means or other. But to-day, Félicité, to-day you must summon all your strength to conceal that the marriage frightens you. May I hope that love and gratitude to your father will enable you to do so ? "

" Believe me, mamma, you will be satisfied with me," replied the young girl, firmly.

" Well, show that you wish and are able to fulfil your promise. I hear your father coming. Do not let him see your sadness."

Mr. Verboord entered. Anxiety and care could be read upon his features. His wife wished him good-morning. Felicité welcomed him in a low voice, and tried to smile.

But the merchant, doubtless, saw there was something constrained in their salutations. He concealed his own anxiety, and said in a light tone without sitting down:

"I do not know how it is, but you are both incomprehensible to me. You, my daughter, to-day are to meet, as his betrothed, the man who is to give you a brilliant position and honored name in the world. You, Laurence, will be able to press to your heart, him to whom you are about to confer your daughter's happiness, with the assurance that he will make her life happy and enviable. Yet you are both silent and thoughtful, as if something disagreeable had happened!"

"You are mistaken, Verboord. We are contented and happy."

"You ought to be wild with joy," continued Mr. Verboord. "Take me for example. There are bad news about coffee. Under other circumstances it would alarm and depress me. To-day it does not effect me. Your brilliant marriage, Felicité, is such a happy event, that it strengthens me against all care. I can understand that a young girl in such a position may conceal the joy which excites her. So be it, my child; but it is necessary to appear gay and pleasant, especially towards the father of your betrothed. You smile! now, that is right, you are sensible, and can be charming if you wish. I need only say to you, Laurence, that as the mother of the bride-elect, you are responsible for the dinner. I presume your orders have been already given."

"Do not trouble yourself about that," she replied. "Have full confidence in me; you will be satisfied."

11

The merchant entered his office, where he sat down before a table. He opened a paper and commenced to read the third page. He soon fell into thought. His face was grave and his lips compressed; occasionally he sighed deeply. Gradually his face brightened, and he murmured, with a smile

"Yes, everything seems to indicate a fall in coffee; but, why should I be alarmed? As Mr. Dorneval has promised me his credit, I need not be anxious about my notes. Besides, as soon as the money from Charleston arrives, I will be out of difficulties. Now that the future of my child is secured, I would be wrong to be depressed by the fear of a loss."

He resumed his reading; but, as before, he soon let the paper fall, and continued his train of thought.

"These are bad predictions in the London correspondence," he murmured. "If they should be realized I will lose a part of my fortune."

He anxiously shook his head.

"The fall is not yet very great," he continued, after a moment's silence. "Perhaps I would be wiser to sell my coffee. Certainly it would be a very disadvantageous affair; but I would be secure against a greater loss, and this anxiety would leave me. To sacrifice so much money! Perhaps it will rise to-morrow. A despatch from Amsterdam predicts it. But all the others anticipate another fall. What shall I do? I have no time to hesitate. If the market is firm this morning, I ought to take advantage of it, because at the Exchange there may be sudden changes. I must decide immediately."

He arose and rang the bell. A clerk appeared at the door of his office.

"Tell Mr. Banks to come here."

"Mr. Banks has not yet come to the office," replied the clerk.

"Yet he promised to be here at nine o'clock," murmured Mr. Verboord, with annoyance. "However, he will, doubtless, be here soon. Henry, go to the post-office immediately for my letters, you will oblige me by making haste. Tell them in the office that I wish to see Mr. Banks as soon as he comes."

"I will soon return, sir," said the clerk.

The merchant again resumed the paper, and for the third time commenced reading the accounts of the price of coffee in the different markets. He shook his head and glanced impatiently at the door from time to time.

At last the clerk returned, and handed his employer a package of letters and papers.

"What of Mr. Banks?"

"He has not yet come."

"Very well, Henry, tell him when he comes that I wish to speak to him immediately."

The clerk left the room.

In his impatience to learn the news contained in the papers, Mr. Verboord threw the letters upon the table, and was about to open an English journal, when his attention was attracted by the form and writing of one of the letters.

"Ah! from America! Charleston," he cried, in joyful surprise.

He quickly opened the letter.

But he had hardly read the first lines, when his hand commenced to tremble, and he turned pale, while a cry of pain escaped from his lips.

"Good heavens! What is this?" he sighed. "No, it cannot be possible! Such unparalleled news! The house of Ortado unable to fulfil its engagements!"

Mr. Verboord arose, and commenced to walk the floor of his office, with signs of the deepest agitation.

At last he threw himself in a chair, and said, as he looked at the letter :

" But why am I so needlessly alarmed ?   Oh, my nerves ! If I could only control myself!   The house of Ortado is firm and solid.   Particular circumstances oblige them to ask for a delay.   In a month they will be in a condition to fulfil all their engagements.   The sale of the cotton which was sent was very slow, contrary to every expectation ; but it was beginning to be better.   Some failures in the United States have somewhat embarrassed the firm of Ortado. What is there so terrible in that?   Mr. Dorneval's assistance will give me the means of waiting.   It certainly is not good news ; but I am wrong to be so alarmed.   I will probably not lose a florin by the house of Ortado."

The merchant reasoned in this manner till his alarm gave place to other thoughts.   He then took up an English paper and glanced at the commercial news.

His whole body was seized with a nervous trembling, and he became pale.

" The decline of coffee increases in London ! " he murmured, in a hoarse voice.   " Misfortune threatens me on every side !   It is enough to drive me mad!   How foolish I am ; I am dying of fright as if irreparable misfortunes had befallen me.   The new decline has only reached two per cent , but it will not stop there.   Ah, it is necessary to decide on something while there is yet time.   Banks ! Where can he be ? "

Filled with impatience, he left the inner office, and glanced around the outer one.

" He is not yet here ! " he murmured, with an expression of disappointment.

The merchant turned round to re-enter his own office, but paused at the door, and bent his steps towards the dining room, where were his wife and daughter.

In the middle of the room he paused, and struck his forehead with astonishment, murmuring, in a dissatisfied tone:

"Why have I come here! These anxieties are affecting my mind."

His wife and Felicité had observed how agitated his countenance was. They both advanced towards him; his daughter threw her arms around his neck, and cried:

"My poor papa, what has happened? Why are you so unhappy? Is it on my account; from love for your child? Oh, do be more calm; you will make yourself sick! I only pray that your anxiety for my future my not shorten your life; your health, dear papa, is worth more to me than all the treasures of this earth."

Mrs. Verboord also endeavored to comfort her husband with kind words, and to strengthen him against the unknown misfortune which seemed to have befallen him; for there was something extraordinary in the extreme dejection of her husband which frightened her.

Mr. Verboord was sorry to see he could not escape an explanation. He threw himself upon a chair, and endeavored to control his voice, and replied:

"You are both mistaken. I am tired of thinking and calculating. The life of a merchant is nothing but care and anxiety. Others have moments of quiet and rest; but we, while fortune smiles on us upon the one side, cannot feel sure but on the other side may be preparing a blow which will wound us cruelly. Is it strange, then, if sometimes after receiving unfavorable news I appear more anxious than usual?"

This explanation, instead of soothing his wife and

11*

daughter, increased their anxiety. The eyes of Felicité were filled with tears.

"Ah, you conceal from us the cause of your sorrow," sighed Mrs. Verboord. "Then, there is bad news? They must be very bad to cause you such alarm."

"Not so, Laurence," replied the merchant; "my face deceives you; it is in consequence of the agitation of my nerves. If you must really know what has happened I will tell you, although these matters are not of a nature to be confided to women. My Charleston correspondent, who ought to have sent me a remittance of money for a large amount, asks for a delay of a month. This would have caused me the greatest embarrassment if Mr. Dorneval had not promised me his assistance; for, during the coming week, I have large demands to meet. But I can wait a month, even longer. For a commercial house to ask a delay is a matter which would naturally cause anxiety; but, at present, I have nothing to fear."

"Thank God!" cried Felicité.

"Is that all?" asked Mrs. Verboord, doubtfully.

"Another matter also renders me sad, Laurence," replied her husband. "It is serious enough to cause me to feel troubled. Another decline has taken place in the price of coffee. I am threatened with a heavy loss."

The young girl sighed.

"Do not be troubled, my child," he said. "Under other circumstances the evil would certainly be great, but now I am in a condition to bear it without great trouble. Your happy marriage strengthens me against every adversity. Mr. Dorneval put his immense fortune and credit at my service. Therefore, Felicité, I beg of you be very agreeable at dinner; let a feeling of gratitude induce you to show the elder Mr. Dorneval that we appreciate his generosity at its true value."

The young girl promised to neglect nothing to please him.

Mr. Verboord gradually relapsed into thought. His wife took him by the hand.

" Come, Verboord, although you may be threatened with a loss, it is not sufficient reason to cause you to be unhappy and constantly anxious. It may not be great, and should it be there will be time enough for you to recover your position. To gain, to lose, to gain again, is not such the fortune of commerce? You are silent, my friend. Of what are you thinking?"

" Of what am I thinking?" he repeated, raising his head. " I am thinking if it would not be prudent to sell my coffee this morning. The decline seems to continue. It is a difficult question to decide, and I know not what to do. And Mr. Banks does not come! I do not know, Laurence, but it seems to me Raphael is beginning to lose his energy. He positively promised me to be here at nine o'clock. If anything prevented him from keeping his word, politeness alone should have induced him to send me a message. I ought and must speak to him."

In saying these words he rang the bell.

" Therese," he said to the servant who opened the door, " go to the office and tell Mr. Henry to go immediately to Mr. Banks' house, and tell him I am impatiently waiting for him."

" Very well, sir," replied the servant, handing a letter to his master. "Mr. Walput gave me that, requesting me to put it into your own hands."

Mr. Verboord looked at the address of the letter, and opened it, saying, with surprise:

" From Mr. Banks! What does this mean?"

These words produced a different effect upon the two ladies.

The mother rose up anxiously, while a smile passed over Felicité's face, which, however, she immediately repressed.

Suddenly Mr. Verboord stamped so violently upon the floor that the house shook; angry words and incoherent accusations against Raphael escaped his lips.

"It is unheard of. Benefit a young man, be kind to him, love him, interest yourself in his future as if he were your own son, and in the end to be repaid by cruel indifference."

"Oh! what does the letter contain?" cried Mrs. Verboord, in great alarm.

"What does it contain? Nice news, truly; listen, Laurence. You see, Banks, like a great many others, was only devoted in appearance. His letter not only proves he has forgotten his duty to me; but it is also rude by its brevity."

He read the following lines, trembling with anger:

Sir,—I have not the strength to fulfil my promise. Fate and duty control me. Do not accuse me of ingratitude; my soul will be eternally grateful to you. Forgive an unhappy man. May God bless you! I am going away. Adieu!

"Well! well! what do you think of such conduct? 'I am going away; adieu!' That is all. Oh, to be thus rewarded for kindness! But there may yet be time."

He recalled the servant.

"Is Mr. Walput still in the office?"

"I believe so, sir."

"Go and tell him I would like to have him come here, I wish to speak to him."

A moment later Francis Walput entered the room. He was probably doubtful of Mr. Verboord's object in sending for him, for his face was grave.

"Who gave you this letter, Mr. Walput?" asked Verboord, who could not conceal his anger and impatience.

"My friend, Raphael Banks," replied the traveling clerk.

"Where did he give it to you?"

"At his house last night."

"At his house!" cried the merchant. "Then you were with him last night?"

"Yes, sir."

"And he really wishes to leave?"

"He has left. This morning at daybreak I accompanied him to the English packet. He is already at sea."

Mr. Verboord bit his lips with rage.

"As you spent the night with your friend, Raphael Banks, you doubtless know the cause of his insane departure."

"I do know it, sir."

"Well, tell it to me, I beg you."

Francis Walput was silent. This silence exasperated Verboord.

"You must tell me what you know!" he cried. "I command you! You refuse! Do you not value my esteem, my patronage?"

"Be calm, sir," said the young man, with the same coolness. "The cause of Raphael's departure is a secret which no one knows, nor ever shall know, excepting him and myself. Spare me the pain of disobeying you. No power on earth can induce me to reveal what my friend has confided in me."

"Go, sir," cried the merchant, almost beside himself. "Your friend is ungrateful; to gratify his own foolish wishes, he forgets the benefits he has received!"

The traveling clerk turned towards the door, and said aloud, before he left the room:

"My friend is a generous man; and those who accuse

him so unjustly ought to be thankful that he had the courage to sacrifice his future and his happiness to duty."

Mr. Verboord would have inquired the meaning of these words, but the young man went out hastily, and did not seem to hear himself called.

Felicité, overcome by a feeling she could not repress, had bent her head on the table, and thus concealed the tears which fell from her eyes. Her mother, who, during this conversation, was trembling with fear, breathed more freely now that her husband had escaped the revelation.

The merchant beat the floor with his foot, and muttered reproaches against Raphael and his friend Walput. He was very angry.

"Do you understand any of this folly, Laurence?" he asked, turning towards his wife. "Secrets, strange secrets! The sacrifice of his happiness to his duty! He is grateful, yet he leaves me, in spite of the solemn promise he made me yesterday! Who can tell how much hypocrisy is concealed beneath it? If Raphael, learning the continued decline of coffee, and the delay in the receipts from America, has suspected the adversity awaiting me, he has betrayed me cruelly, in return for my kindness to him!"

A cry of horror escaped from Felicité, and Mrs. Verboord exclaimed:

"Oh, Verboord, do not be so unjust! Mr. Banks may be crazy, sick, or mistaken, but he will never be ungrateful or cowardly. Be assured, if he could have spared you any great trouble at the price of his life he would have given it without hesitation!"

Felicité rose up, threw her arms around her mother's neck, and concealed her tears on her bosom.

A sudden thought seemed to enter the merchant's mind. He raised his head, and said, calmly:

"Truly, this sudden departure gives me much pain; anger, doubtless, makes me unjust. Do not weep, Felicité. All these troubles, one after another, have stunned me; but now it is over. Sit down, my child, and be quiet."

He led his daughter to the sofa, and then returned to his wife, who turned pale beneath his look.

"Laurence," he said, gravely, "something is going on here which is concealed from me. You know what it is, and perhaps Felicité also. Tell me this terrible secret which I do not know."

Mrs. Verboord trembled, shrugged her shoulders, and remained silent.

"You, too," cried the merchant, in astonishment.

At this moment a clerk opened the door, and said:

"Mr. Dorneval is here, and wishes to speak to you."

"Mr. Dorneval!" repeated Mr. Verboord, impatiently. "Well, Henry, bring him here."

"He desires to see you alone, sir; I have shown him into the parlor."

Mr. Verboord joined Mr. Dorneval, wished him good morning, and held out his hand. Alfred's father gave his hand slowly and reluctantly. His smile was so constrained and his face so grave that Mr. Verboord was much surprised.

"I hear you wish to speak to me," said the latter. "Sit down, I beg you."

Dorneval looked at him suspiciously, and asked

"Have you not received news from Charleston?"

"Yes; bad news."

"Very bad news; I am sorry for you, Verboord."

"You need not be. Fortunately I can wait until the house of Ortado is again in a condition to continue its business regularly."

"What news have you received?"

" They wrote to me that in consequence of the failure of several firms in the United States, and the dullness of business, their house was somewhat embarrassed, and requested a delay of a month."

" I also received a similar request."

" It will amount to nothing; we need have no anxiety. Is not this your opinion also, Mr. Dorneval?"

" This news is false," replied Mr. Dorneval. " I received, by the same mail, a letter from one of my best friends living in Charleston. He tells me that the house of Ortado has entirely stopped payment."

" Good heavens!" cried Mr. Verboord, starting back in alarm.

" And the most favorable indications do not promise the creditors one-half of their money. It appears that the business of the firm has been involved for some time. My friend states that it has been very difficult to learn the truth. However, Verboord, take courage, and do not be too much alarmed. It is a great loss, but we are exposed to such every day. A favorable turn of fortune may give you back as much."

Mr. Verboord had put his elbows on the table and buried his head in his hands.

" Truly it is a hard blow for you," continued Mr. Dorneval. " You lose at least one hundred thousand francs, do you not?"

" One hundred thousand francs! Much more, you know very well!"

" If the house of Ortado pays fifty cents on the hundred, you will receive one-half your debt. You may, therefore, calculate upon fifty thousand francs at least; your fortune will be a little less, but you are not ruined by that, my friend: and really I do not see why you should lose courage."

Mr. Verboord shook his friend's hand warmly, much touched by his sympathetic words.

"Alas!" he sighed, "it is a terrible blow to me, but I thank God for having given me your friendship. Thank you for your comforting words. I feel they give me sufficient strength to struggle against my grief. Be assured of my everlasting gratitude."

Mr. Dorneval remained silent for some moments. He seemed to be embarrassed how to express something which was on his mind, and which was, perhaps, the sole object of his visit.

"Mr. Verboord," he said, at last, "I regret to have to tell you that it will be impossible for us to dine with you to-day. The marriage of which we thought is a matter, you understand, which must, of course, be put off."

"What! you refuse Felicité's hand for your son?" cried Mr. Verboord, in great consternation.

"Not at all," replied Dorneval, "but we will wait until the Charleston affair is positively decided. If your loss is not too great we can resume the arrangements for the marriage of our children. If, on the contrary, your fortune suffers an important diminution, we will say nothing more about the matter."

The merchant felt as if he had nearly lost his senses. Until this moment, the conviction that the future of his daughter was arranged, and she would have an honorable position in the world, had given him a little courage. This hope was now violently torn from his bleeding heart; for the words of Alfred's father indicated the positive breaking off of the marriage. Mr. Verboord gathered new strength from the excess of his grief and the bitterness of his disappointment, and with ill-concealed indignation, he exclaimed:

12

"But our agreement, sir? The contract we made together yesterday? Does the slightest misfortune which may threaten me suffice for you to withdraw from the pledge you gave. I did not think that a friend——"

"My dear Verboord," interrupted the other, "we are merchants. A verbal agreement which loses the basis upon which it was founded falls through of itself. You are actually unable to fulfil the conditions we had arranged."

'Do you think so? If it is necessary, I will pay in money the hundred thousand francs which is to be my daughter's dower."

"Really! have you then secret funds?"

"No; but, by selling my coffee, I can immediately realize the amount."

"That is true; but do you not need this money to pay the notes of which you spoke to me?"

Mr. Verboord gave a spring backwards, threw his hands in the air, while he uttered a cry of despair, and exclaimed:

"Do you refuse me your aid? Do you abandon me, without pity, to my sad loss?"

"It is not my fault, my poor friend," said Mr. Dorneval, shrugging his shoulders, "I would be most happy to be able to assist you; but I too am involved in the affairs of the firm of Ortado to a considerable amount, and it will be a loss to me, which will cause me much embarrassment."

"Good heavens!" sighed Mr. Verboord, shuddering from head to foot. "I will then be entirely ruined and disgraced! The traitors! The traitors!"

"If you sell your coffee——"

"But that will not be enough! I must dishonor my signature, and bring disgrace upon the heads of my wife and my poor child! I cannot bear it, I will die!"

Then summoning his last strength, he clasped his hands before his companion, and said in a beseeching voice :

"I conjure you, by all you hold dear, do not leave me without assistance at such a moment. I still possess some means ; I will give them all up. Oh, send me the sum which will be wanting after the sale of my coffee! Let me become poor, but let me honor my notes ; that my name, the name of my child, may remain free from all stain !"

"Let me see," murmured Dorneval, "perhaps I cou'd render you this service."

"For the love of heaven, help me, I feel as though I were dying!"

The door of the parlor opened suddenly, after a hasty knock. A clerk handed a paper to Mr. Verboord, saying:

"A telegram from London for you, sir."

Mr. Verboord. who, perhaps, had a secret hope that favorable news would give him more strength, took the folded paper, waited till the clerk had left the room, then broke the seal of the dispatch.

"Misfortune, misfortune! pity me!" he cried, as if his heart were broken. "Ortado has fled, a fraudulent bankrupt: all is lost!"

He fell upon a couch, white as a sheet, and trembling as if threatened with apoplexy.

Dorneval had picked up the dispatch, which had fallen to the ground and had read it.

He approached Verboord, took his hand, and said to him :

"I pity you with all my heart, Verboord. If you will come to my house after your feelings are calmer, I will help you to ascertain if there is not some means of assisting you. I must now leave you. This news calls me home. I will lose almost as much as you. Good-bye."

With these words he left the room.

Mr. Verboord was stretched upon the couch, and seemed to have lost consciousness.

He remained there for some time without moving, when he was seized with a sudden nervous attack. He rushed towards the dining-room, and opened the door violently.

His appearance and the terrible alteration of his face caused the two ladies to utter a cry of alarm. They ran towards him with open arms; but he bitterly repelled their caresses and exclaimed:

" Leave me; I am mad! Ruined, poor, deceived! No fortune, no honor, no marriage! All is over!"

He fell into the arms of his wife, who seated him in an arm-chair with lamentations.

While Felicité threw her arms around his neck, and shed tears upon his breast, he sighed in feeble tones:

" Raphael, Raphael! Abandoned, abandoned by him!— The traitors, oh! the traitors!—I am dying—"

He closed his eyes and fell back senseless in the chair. Mrs. Verboord rushed towards the door and cried with all her strength: "Theresa! Mary! Henry! Come quickly, and bring a doctor."

CHAPTER VII.

IT was about five o'clock in the morning. The sun had risen above the horizon, and flooded the heaths and the fields with the golden light of his first rays. The pearly dew of night sparkled upon the foliage; the flowers had not yet opened their chalices; while a slight mist hung over the meadows and the entrance of the woods.

But the morning lark already hovered in the waving grain; the sparrows, under the influence of the sweet month of May, sported and chirped amid the branches of the lindens; the cows lowed as though asking for their pasturage, and the industrious laborer walked along, singing and whistling, to the field which was awaiting his fertilizing labors. Notwithstanding these signs of a general awaking, complete silence still reigned in the hamlet behind Brasschaet; as the farms were at some distance from it, the noise of their active inhabitants could not disturb its repose.

The hunting lodge, which the merchant Verboord had intended to alter into a modern château, was not changed. It was still there, behind the iron grating with its white cornice, and its green shutters; but it looked neglected and deserted. Its walls had not been painted for years, and time, aided by rain and dust, had covered it in certain places with black or greyish stains."

12*

At this moment, some one opened the door of the house, and a young woman with a broom in her hand commenced sweeping the paved pathway which extended from the house to the iron grating.

This young girl appeared, at first sight, to belong to the better class of peasants. Her dress was very simple, and without the least display; she wore a small linen bonnet, white as snow, and an apron of blue calico, and a neck handkerchief, variegated with red flowers upon a green ground.

On a closer examination, however, it would have been observed that her dress was of a style which does not belong to the ordinary costume of the peasantry; something which indicated that the young girl must have procured her dress in the city; perhaps she had belonged to an elevated rank in society. Truly, the shape of her plain clothes, the extreme elegance of her slightest movement, something which could not be explained, showed at least that she had been well brought up.

Her features, though thin and browned by the sun, were remarkably fine and regular, and in her large blue eyes and the almost imperceptible smile which parted her lips could be traced the gentle and intelligent soul within.

After having swept the road, she entered a room on the ground floor and continued her work.

There was complete silence around her; she was all alone and no noise betrayed the presence of a living creature until the bleating of a goat was heard behind the house.

Then the young girl murmured in a low voice:

" Yes, yes, Micken, I have not forgotten you, my good little beast; but everything has its time. To-day you may feast as much as you like. To-morrow is a solemn day.

The twenty-first of May, St. Laurence! Ah! it is four years, four years since I saw him depart, he was there at the iron grating. He trembled, and his sparkling eyes spoke to me. Alas! I did not understand it! And now, now, he is dead, perhaps!"

She sighed. Troubled by this sad thought she ceased her work, and went to the wall where a crucifix hung, and knelt down with her hands joined.

The room had a strange appearance, and, like the dress of the young girl, showed traces of past riches. Near the hearth, where burned and sparkled a fire of birch-wood, all appeared simple. There were two or three common chairs, and a table of white wood; but on the other side of the chamber, before a mahogany desk covered with papers, was a large chair, with carved back and cushions of Utrecht velvet, worn by long use.

Many little objects, belonging to luxury and riches, and ornaments evidently made by feminine hands, proved that the inhabitants of the house made every effort to give to this apartment an air of cheerfulness and comfort.

The young girl arose from her knees and again took up the broom. Her prayer had doubtless comforted her, for the expression of her face was serene, and she smiled as she quickly swept out the room.

She carefully dusted the desk, arranged the scattered papers, poured some boiling water into the coffee-pot, put it upon the hot coals, placed some bowls on the table, and cut several slices off of a large loaf of rye bread, then fell into a reverie.

"What a strange dream it was," she said to herself, after a time, "which drew tears of joy from me this past night! He had returned; he stood before me with the same earnest look, with the same gentle sigh. His voice was soft and

melting. Nothing had happened ; my father was in good
health, and rich. I must drive away such foolish images.
It is very comforting, however, to hope that his love for me
did not render him altogether unhappy. Oh! God grant
he may soon have forgotten me. Can it be possible ? The
first impression of a virgin soul. Or, may it be ? Does he
still live ? "

Her voice trembled and nearly died away.

Still dreaming, she slowly went out by the back door,
took a sickle which hung from the wall, and went into the
garden.

There, a great change had been made. Of all the trees
and all the rare plants which shaded the winding paths,
there only remained a few shrubs, at the foot of the high
wall, which surrounded the garden. The ground was
divided into squares by straight paths, and converted into a
kitchen-garden. There were potatoes, peas, beans, salad,
and other vegetables, but no shrubbery, no flowers, except
ing, at some distance, a small bush, whose red flowers hung
in bunches towards the ground.

At the end of the garden the young girl stopped, her
back turned towards a green bank, upon which a worn spot
indicated that some one sat there frequently.

At her feet, near a square of salad, surrounded by a
border of box, was a row of simple flowers, of different
kinds, in the midst of which was the beautiful bush, whose
branches were so heavily laden with hanging flowers that it
resembled a shower of red corals.

It was upon this fuchsia, so carefully cultivated, that the
young girl gazed so earnestly. A strange light shone on
her face, her smile was full of enthusiasm, and although her
expression was calm and thoughtful, her whole soul seemed
to be in her eyes.

She was evidently under the influence of some powerful remembrance; for she soon bent towards the bush, gathered a flower, carried it tremblingly to her lips, put it in her bosom, and then raised her hands and eyes towards heaven. Perhaps she was asking the blessing of God upon an absent friend whose memory lived in these flowers. She breathed a sigh, and sadly bowed her head, as if it were difficult to leave this spot; but duty demanded it, she had to attend to household cares.

She turned into another path and knelt down in a small field of clover. She cut some of it with as much ease as if she had done it all her life, formed it into a bundle, and carried it into the little stable behind the house.

The goat, hearing her coming, began to bleat.

"Be quiet, my good Micken," said the young girl, throwing the food to the impatient animal; "there is your grass as tender as butter! You are always afraid Felicité will forget it! Is it likely? You who give my father the fresh milk which he likes so much! Eat as much as you want this morning, it is my mother's birthday. But I am late; I must milk you, pretty creature."

She left the stable and returned with a pail. Kneeling upon a bundle of fresh straw, she commenced to milk the goat, and said, as if talking to it:

"Hold still, Micken; I will not hurt you. Don't you know that? We are going to try once more if the good doctors cannot cure my father. To-morrow, when the stage for Holland passes, he is going to the city with mamma, to consult the best physician. It will cost a great deal, Micken, a very great deal; but what can mamma do better with her jewels. In our seclusion we see no one. And this afternoon, Micken, I am going to surprise mamma. She certainly does not expect a present; but, without her knowledge, I have worked at night, and yesterday, in the city, I bought a beautiful handkerchief with the money I had made. She will be so surprised she will shed tears of joy; and then, if the city doctor gives her hope, Oh, then, St. Laurence's day this year will be a bright day in our life! There, I have finished, Micken."

She arose and entered the house.

"Already down?" she exclaimed. "Good morning, dear mamma; have you slept well?"

Mrs. Verboord was seated near the window. Before her were two chairs, to which were attached something like a silk fringe. She was occupied in making knots in the thread, which hung down, and forming it into a pretty design.

Felicité placed the coffee on the table, and said:

"Let us breakfast, mamma, so that I, too, may work a little at the fringes before papa awakes."

"Bring the table nearer, Felicité," replied Mrs. Verboord. "I can take my coffee while I work."

"Come, come!" cried the young girl, discontentedly, "it will not take you five minutes; surely you may breathe while you breakfast, dear mamma."

"It is for your poor father, my child. The city doctor will charge a great deal. Mr. Drooms, the village doctor, was reasonable in his prices; but your father is angry with him, and will not hear his name mentioned."

"He is right, mamma. Mr. Drooms did nothing but bleed him, which only weakened him."

"That is true, Felicite; but we will find it very difficult to get the means to pay the city physician."

"Yet I do not wish you to work while you eat, mamma. I am young and strong. If necessary, I can work half the night. What will become of us if you also lose your health?"

Mrs. Verboord sat down at the table, and said, very sadly:

"I have not slept, Felicité. Your father had a bad night. He dreamed nearly all the time, and talked aloud. I heard him repeat Raphael's name six or seven times. It is a bad sign. When he dreams of Raphael he grinds his teeth, and struggles convulsively, while murmuring reproaches. I don't know, Felicité, but I am losing hope."

"Ah, mamma, you are sad because you have not slept," interrupted the young girl. "Is not papa always thus?"

"No, no; his condition has grown visibly worse for some months past."

"Come, come, do not despond, mamma. Are we not again going to try if medical care will not cure him? I am almost sure it will succeed this time! If it should be so, it seems to me life would be as bright and happy as though we had had no other misfortune."

Mrs. Verboord resumed her work; Felicité concealed the bowls and the black bread in a closet, placed a gilt china cup upon the table, and cut some slices of white bread. She took out some sugar, and put a silver spoon into the cup.

Then she sat down by her mother's side, and commenced to knot the fringes with rapid movements.

"How fortunate for us, my child, that my father was a lace-maker, and that I learned a work which is a resource to us in time of need! Will it keep us from want? I doubt it."

"How can you talk so?" murmured Felicité, reproachfully. "We earn a great deal of money by making these fringes, and it is said that the salaries of the workwomen are to be increased, mamma. Yesterday when I returned our work, the lady said she would give us as many fringes to make as we might wish."

"Yes, but can we make enough to pay the doctor? For we must continue him till he succeeds, if there is any hope of a cure, come what may. We ought to strive to economize above everything, Felicité. Do you not think we might give up the newspaper, *The Precurseur?* It costs us sixty francs; that is a large sum for us!"

"For the love of Heaven, mamma, do not speak of such a thing," cried Felicité. "Papa looks for the post every morning with impatience, and as soon as he has his paper he becomes calmer and more contented. Do not take this comfort from him! You are in a bad humor to-day, mamma."

"The future frightens me, my child. Our existence becomes every day more precarious; the clothes and furniture we kept are wearing out and all our jewels have disappeared."

"But we own this house and garden. Is it not a security against want, mamma?"

"Alas! that is the thought which troubles me!" sighed Mrs. Verboord. "If we should ever be compelled to sell this remnant of our past fortune, your father would have to sign the deed. It would certainly be a death-blow to him."

"But, dear mamma, we are not threatened with such a misfortune," said the young girl, in a voice which she tried to make gay and hopeful, though her heart was filled with anxiety. "We have still enough clothes. When I go to the city, and dress in my best, no one can suspect that we are embarrassed for want of clothes. In the garden we have all we need. Besides, I can still work more than I do now. Take courage, we will not suffer for anything, and papa will be cured, you may be sure!"

There was a moment's silence. Mrs. Verboord looked at her child with a strange expression. Her eyes filled with tears.

"My poor Felicité," she said, "it is still worse for you. We are old, and if the evening of our life is sad and unhappy, the grave is near to put an end to our sufferings. You, my child, have a long time to live on this earth. Your young years are passing in a gloomy solitude, with no other future before you. Other young girls, rich or poor, still enjoy some pleasures in life, liberty, friendship, love. They at least hope that some day God will bring them the one who is to be their protector; but you, Felicité, between two old sick people, are condemned to feed your weary heart with a sad remembrance. ' Oh, such thoughts are bitter to a mother's heart!"

She commenced to weep, while Felicité threw her arms about her neck and kissed her affectionately.

"Your love for me blinds you, my dear mother," she said. "I am not unhappy, just the reverse. If papa can be cured, and you do not grieve unnecessarily, I ask no more. The remembrance of which you speak is my only comfort. I know it is a childish feeling, but this fancy gives me courage and strength. Why, I cannot tell. Perhaps because it diverts my mind, and prevents me from feeling my loneliness. It is a caprice, mamma; you know very well I hope for nothing Raphael no longer lives, or he would have written to his friends and acquaintances in Antwerp. Since his departure no one has heard anything from him; but his love for me was the cause of his misfortune. I will cherish his memory to the grave. The heaviest trial to me is that papa becomes angry every time he hears Raphael's name, even when it falls from his own lips. So I can never talk of him to papa, and have to conceal that I think of him. Still, mamma, all this is nothing. Let us work quickly, the work is pleasant and easy; we make a good income by it; and, whether you like it or not,

13

to-night, after you go to bed, I will still make several yards.
By this means we will be easily able to pay for the doctor.
Have faith, mamma."

They remained silent for some time; their hands moved
quickly, and their work advanced rapidly.

Mrs. Verboord did not appear to expect much from the
doctor's attention; for while she worked she sighed heavily.

Felicité, to dispel the increasing depression of her mother,
exclaimed suddenly, in a gay tone :

" Ah, mamma, I forgot to tell you something. Yesterday,
returning from the city, I met, not far from the postoffice,
some one walking on the outer walls. Guess who it was !
Lucy Spelt, or rather Mrs. Walput, with a nurse and two
children—a boy and a girl. Such pretty children ! Little
angels ! How happy she ought to be !"

" Very happy, no doubt."

" Do you know, mamma, the name of the little boy ? It
is Raphael ! I did not dare to kiss him ; I feared Mrs.
Walput would notice my emotion."

" What did she ask you, and what did you reply to her ? "
asked Mrs. Verboord, anxiously.

" She complained, mamma, of the cool reception we gave
her when she came to see us three years ago. She said she
was inclined to make us another visit at Brasschaet, with
her husband and children."

" Surely, my child, you declined the visit ? Your father
dislikes Mr. Walput almost as much as Raphael himself.
He thinks Mr. Walput gave bad advice to his friend.
Besides, the presence of strangers terribly agitates your
father's nerves."

" I know it, mamma. Therefore, I replied in such a
manner as to make Mrs. Walput understand we did not
desire the visit. I told her papa was sick, and did not wish

to see any one. It was hard to refuse Mrs. Walput's friendship so coldly, for I am sure, mamma, she feels a sincere friendship for us. Thank God, she is happy. She, too, thinks constantly of poor Raphael, who was the means of her happy marriage with Francis Walput. It was, doubtless, for this reason she named her pretty little boy Raphael. I felt like kissing her hands for this remembrance; but I was afraid of betraying my feelings, and I left her hastily."

" Did she not speak of Raphael? Perhaps she knows where he is."

" No, mamma, she does not know; for she asked me if I had had any news. She, also, believes him dead; there were tears in her eyes. Mr. Walput has never ceased to use every means to obtain information of Raphael; but his efforts have been in vain. Ah, I hear papa coming down."

Félicité rose to get the jug of milk, then she went to meet her father, embraced him tenderly, led him to the table, and remained near him till she was quite sure he needed nothing. She then returned to her seat, took up her work, but still continued to watch her father.

Mr. Verboord had grown much older; his grey hairs had become as white as silver, his head was slightly bent towards one shoulder, and there was something painful, something wild in his vacant look. Otherwise, he showed no signs of sickness, excepting great emaciation. His linen was fine and very white, and his dress, at least, betrayed neither neglect nor poverty.

It was evident his wife and daughter endeavored, with affectionate care, to guard him from anything which could make him feel the loss of his fortune. For him they had light bread; he had a silver spoon and fork; his clothes were always neat and elegant, and he was surrounded by furniture which had adorned his office as a merchant.

He had for a long time murmured at the strange existence of his wife and daughter, their simple dress, and the
change of the English flower-beds into a kitchen garden.
But they had made him believe that they had all at once
conceived a passion for country life, and they found much
pleasure in its employments.   Although Mr. Verboord
believed himself richer than he really was, he knew that
his fortune was considerably diminished.   He admired the
industry of the two women, although he could not see the
necessity, and he had ceased to oppose them in their strange
taste.

When Felicité had embraced him, he had pressed the
young girl against his heart with a smile, and said a few
kind words to her; then his face became serious.   He sat
down near the table, and commenced to eat his breakfast in
silence, while the two ladies tried to read in his face how
much the wakefulness of the past night had excited his
nerves.

Suddenly he raised his eyes and looked at them for a
moment in silence.

"Ah! Laurence," he asked, "when will this work be
finished?   Have these fringes no end?"

"These are not the same," replied Mrs. Verboord.
"They will be finished in a few weeks.   They do not progress rapidly, it is true; but how would we spend our time
here, if we did not amuse ourselves with work?"

"For whom is this new fringe?"

Mrs. Verboord hesitated for an answer.

"For the daughter of the elder Lavans, who lives behind
the church, in the meadows."

"They make fringes for all the village.   What a strange
taste!" said Mr. Verboord, to himself.   "There is a story
of a certain Penelope; she was a queen, and she worked on

a fringe which had no end. If there were much money to be made by it, I could understand it. Make money?. Why not? Is not all uncertain in this world. A single reverse of fortune may rob us of all our money; but one smile from her may render us ten times richer. The price of coffee is rising. Of course, of course, it is wavering now; but yesterday's news were favorable. Listen, Verboord, take advantage of the opportunity! There are great speculations to be made."

As he said these words, he walked towards the desk.

He took up a number of the "*Precurseur*," and read the commercial news on the third page. What he saw did not seem to please him. He opened quickly a package of old newspapers, and began to look for something he could not find; for he became gradually very angry and commenced to complain in harsh tones. His nerves appeared much excited, he trembled visibly, and his brow was wet with perspiration from his impatience.

The two ladies remained quiet and continued to work, looking at him sadly from time to time.

"Ah, ah! now I have it," suddenly exclaimed the old man, with enthusiasm. "This is it! this is it! The coalition of the commercial houses of London has greatly depreciated the price of coffee! I will make a hundred thousand francs. I will put all my fortune in coffee; yes, yes, it will enable me to make one or two millions—a great many millions!"

With a vacant smile, he gazed at the paper which gave him such favorable news.

The ladies did not dare to correct his error, for Felicité said in a suppressed tone:

"Poor papa! He is not well to-day, his nerves are

13*

much excited. Fortunately, he will go with you to the city; the doctor will give him something to quiet him."

"Alas! it is always the same thing," said Mrs. Verboord. "When he is so excited, he always meets with something to excite him more. The paper he has in his hand is the "*Precurseur*" of four years ago. The news which makes him so happy are really there, and he believes them perfectly now. We must take this paper away, my child."

"Oh, no, mamma," begged the young girl, in alarm. "Papa would look for it without ceasing; he would not have a moment's rest."

"That is true," sighed Mrs. Verboord, "it might be worse. By the grace of God——"

She was interrupted by a piercing cry from her husband. His hair stood on end, and his face was livid; he said in an altered voice which passed from anger to fury:

"What! is it possible! Such a misfortune! The house of Ortado has failed! My fortune is lost! The letters of exchange, the letters of exchange! The name of my poor child dishonored forever! No, no, I will sell my coffee; I will make money. I will escape the shame. I must go to work at once. Banks! Banks! where is he? I have been kind to him, I have loved him; now, in the hour of my adversity he has abandoned and betrayed me. God will punish his ingratitude. Oh, what traitors—dishonor, shame! Help me, help me, I am powerless. Take my life's blood; but, in mercy, do not dishonor the name of my wife and daughter!"

His head fell heavily upon the desk, and he continued to moan.

The ladies had evidently witnessed such scenes before; for although their eyes were moist, they did not weep but continued their work in silence.

The old man ceased to sigh, and remained motionless for some time. This apathy frightened Felicité. She arose, saying

"Mamma, I am going into the garden with papa. The fresh air will revive him, and I will try to divert his mind from these sad thoughts."

She approached the desk, took her father by the arm and said:

"Come, dear papa, let us walk out in the garden. It is a delightful spring day."

Mr. Verboord arose and followed his daughter in silence. His face was calm, and he seemed to have forgotten what had excited him so much.

"Felicité," he said, as they entered the garden, "my nerves are weak; I am not well to-day."

"Mamma is going with you to see the doctor, he will cure you, papa," replied Felicité.

"Well, let us go immediately. Why should we wait?"

"But, papa, you know you will not find him home till to-morrow. He is going to Brussels to-day. He told me yesterday, that he had infallible remedies for nervous complaints. Come, papa, let us continue our walk. The sun is so warm, the sky is so blue! Walk by my side, the path is broad enough, and I love to walk arm-in-arm with my dearly loved father. The heath sends us its fragrant perfume; the east wind plays in the foliage; do you not feel the refreshing breeze about your head? Does it not do your brain good?"

"Yes, yes, of course, my good Felicité," replied Mr. Verboord; "but I do not wish any more peas."

"Why not!"

"Because this ground has been watered with the sweat of my daughter's brow," he sighed. "Do not deny it,

Felicité, I know it is so. I have seen you working like a man; the perspiration dropping from your forehead. Since then, I have hated peas."

"But you are mistaken, papa," replied the young girl. "Your love for me makes you blind. You know very well the old gardener Etien comes to do all the work here."

"It is a long time since I have seen him."

"Let me tell you. I went to the gate to tell him to plant our peas, when an idea came into my mind. My father, I said to myself, dearly loves peas. They will taste so much better to him when he knows that Felicité planted them. The thought pleased me. Five minutes later I had the spade in my hand. I did not conceal my work; for I wished you to see me. The color in my cheeks was the excitement of pleasure. Oh! I was impatient to see them on the table. They were for my father: I felt as if I should weep for joy, the first time you would say to me : 'how tender these peas are, which my Felicité planted for me!'"

The old man raised his hand to his brow, and said, as he continued his walk:

"The brain! Yes, yes, the brain. It is said to be the seat of the human soul. But the poor soul is much too confined there. This is the reason she so often forcibly leaves her dwelling; then the eyes grow dim, and the thoughts wander. It is frightful, frightful! There where the light of intellect ought to shine, eternal darkness reigns! Confused remembrances, disconnected ideas, foolish dreams, fancies, apparitions. This is what is called the soul!"

He endeavored to hasten his steps, as if to escape his painful reflections; but Felicité stopped him, and cried, with childish joy:

"Ah! dear papa. The happy time has come! See the young peas are already in flower. You love them so much!

The first are for you. They will be ready to eat in a few days. Then new potatoes will soon follow. New potatoes, green peas, fresh butter—what a feast it will be. How kind it is in our good Lord, papa, to make the first fruits of the earth, which are given to rich and poor, so delicious."

These artless remarks and his child's gentle voice touched the old man, and restored quiet and reason for a time to his mind.

He stopped, took his daughter's hands, looked into her eyes, and said very gravely:

"How pure your heart is, how sincere your love! You watch over your father's troubled spirit like a guardian angel. You sacrifice for him not only your inclinations, but your youth, your future, your life. Yes, I know it. It is not always dark within—Alas! I am powerless, fortune has deserted me; but that is nothing, Felicité. There is One in heaven who pays the debts of fathers to children. If He punishes the ungrateful without pity, He also rewards those who do more than their duty. Trust in Him, Felicité—Yes, yes, my noble and generous child, believe your father's words: some day, you will be happy; for God is just and forgets nothing!"

The young girl, deeply moved, threw her arms around her father's neck, and embraced him with delight; but she saw that his eyes began to shine with increased brilliancy. She recognized the symptoms, restrained herself, remained outwardly calm, took her father's arm and continued her walk.

She knew that deep emotion gave her father a temporary sanity, but an increased excitement was the usual consequence. A quiet and cheerful conversation on indifferent subjects had a better effect than anything else.

She commenced to speak of the vegetables they saw along

their path.   The most trifling thing answered as a subject
for conversation; a butterfly on a cabbage leaf, the bees
amid the flowers, the lark hovering over the neighboring
field, the flower lost among the weeds, the little ant in the
path, air, space, the sun, the goodness of God proclaimed
throughout Nature.

Mr. Verboord listened at first with pleasure to Felicité's
gay prattle; but gradually his thoughts wandered, he fell
into a reverie, and every now and then made a gesture
which had no relation to his daughter's words.

The latter observed his absence of mind, and to divert his
thoughts changed her conversation from one subject to
another.

When they had walked to the end of the garden for the
fourth time, and were passing in front of the green bank,
the old man said:

"Let us sit down here, my child, and remain quiet for a
few moments; I am very tired."

They both sat down   Felicité respected her father's wish,
and they remained silent for some time.

"Would you like to walk a little more?" asked the
young girl.

"Oh, I am very sick," sighed the old man.   "There is
something in my head which is always turning round, and it
bewilders me."

"It is a symptom of your disease, papa," she replied,
kissing his hand; "but you will soon be relieved."

"Do you really believe, Felicité, that the physician will
be able to cure me?"

"Certainly I do.   Nervous affections, he said, usually
require much care before they are relieved; but this doctor
has a peculiar mode of treatment, and has already cured
more than a score of persons who were worse than you are."

"If he can only cure me, Felicité!"

"Oh, yes, dear papa, let us trust in the goodness of God. We will have a happy life. All will be sunshine. I will sing from morning till night, and will be as happy as the angels in heaven!"

"How I will reward your love!" cried Mr. Verboord, with joy. "I will resume business, I will make money and become rich. The first thing I shall do will be to make a large and beautiful pleasure garden for my Felicité, a garden of several acres. Do not fear; as you love so dearly to cultivate your vegetables, I will not touch the kitchen garden, but behind it, beside the brook, I will lay out a grand park for you, Felicité, for you alone, because you have watched over your sick father. The brook shall pass through the garden and bring fresh water to the ponds. A broad lawn shall extend to the farthest point of the view; there, upon a hill, shall be an open temple, with a group of statuary upon a pedestal, like an altar. But what shall this group represent? It is difficult to decide. Ah! I know. An old, sick man, leaning upon the shoulder of his young and beautiful daughter, who will carry a torch in her hand, the flame of love, by whose light she will remove the briars and thistles from his path. This elegant building will be called 'the temple of filial love.' When our brain grows weak and we forget the past, we will come here to be reminded of it."

The old man trembled with emotion; tears filled his eyes, and he remained absorbed in the contemplation of the paradise his wandering mind had created.

Felicité did not dare to open her mouth, for fear of increasing her father's agitation.

"Well, my child," he said at last, "what do you think of that? It is beautiful, is it not?"

"Very beautiful, papa," she replied; "but now I only

wish for one thing : to have the doctor cure you. I am indifferent to everything else till that is accomplished."

Mr. Verboord no longer listened, but talked to himself, and rubbed his forehead, like some one endeavoring to remember something.

"Yes, that is it," he cried, joyfully. "I knew very well I had forgotten something. A pleasure garden without a dwelling! How absurd! There will be a chateau with a carved front, large marble steps before the door, and a portico, with high columns on both sides. A princely palace! That is pride, is it not? Yes, but when one is rich, worth millions. Ah! what is there on earth too beautiful for my Felicité! Time is short. We must take the chance that offers ; for we are rich to-day and poor to-morrow. I must decide at once. Banks does not come. I ought to consult him about the plan. He promised me to be here at nine o'clock. Where can he be? Do you know, Felicité?"

Suddenly he was seized with a violent attack, his features contracted, and he cried, furiously :

"Banks, Banks! He has abandoned and betrayed me, because misfortune has befallen me. My love for him, my kindnesses, my misfortune, he has forgotten all, all! Thou, O God, will demand an account of his ingratitude."

Felicité tried to calm him. She endeavored to induce him to return to the house, and told him her mother had already called him twice ; but the old man did not hear her, and suddenly cried, in tones of despair :

"Poor, ruined, dishonored! Raphael, Raphael, what have you done? There they are, there they are, the phantoms which pursue me, the death which threatens me! Let me fly—The notes! the notes!"

Felicité sadly followed her father, but his imaginary fear caused him to run so rapidly that the poor girl could not overtake him till he was entering the house.

CHAPTER VIII.

IT had been a very warm day. The sun, bathed in purple and gold, sank into the west, and disappeared behind the Flemish hills. His oblique rays still fell upon the waters of the Scheld, and gave the river the appearance of melted gold. The houses along the quays were of an orange color, while their panes of glass shone like rubies, and the whole atmosphere had a crimson tint.

Thousands of citizens of all classes and ages were walking along the wharf enjoying the evening breeze. There was nothing in particular to attract their attention; work was finished, and with the exception of two or three large vessels at anchor in the middle of the river, the Scheld was entirely free and quiet.

Suddenly there was a movement among the people. Many stopped and gazed with interest upon a column of black smoke which was visible behind the "Tête de Flandres." The London steamer was approaching the city. Of course such a sight was seen in Antwerp several times a day; but, in the quiet of the sunset hour, when all bustle had ceased, the arrival of the large London steamer was a striking spectacle. It plowed the waves like a triumphant colossus; a long line of smoke marked its way; it tossed noisily, and rushed along upon a bed of foaming billows. Her deck was crowded with people. Some of her pas-

14

sengers who had come from America or the East Indies, and saw their native city again after a long absence, waved their hats and threw up their hands.

On this occasion the steamer had many passengers on board, and there was a crowd of ladies and gentlemen on her deck, who each endeavored to have their baggage examined before the other by the custom-house officers.

There was one traveler, with black hair, who showed more impatience than the others, and succeeded in placing his trunks in advance of his neighbors. He quieted some by his politeness, others he awed by his determined expression and decided manner.

He had evidently been accustomed to live among a savage people, for, in the midst of the cries of his companions, he remained indifferent, and looked upon the crowd with a quiet smile. This passenger was still young. His face was burned by a long sojourn in a warm climate, and it was apparent at the first glance that he was familiar with the ocean.

His dress was rich, and he wore it gracefully; this elegant appearance, combined with his noble features, the dignity of his manners and speech, caused him to be taken for an important personage. So his baggage was first examined, and immediate permission was granted to him to leave the steamer.

He entered a carriage, and called to the driver:

"Place Verte, Hotel St. Antoine."

At the office of the hotel he was informed that they only had some very small rooms on the upper floor vacant, and an elegant apartment on the first floor, front. The price of the latter was very high; but the stranger, without any other remark, replied, with indifference:

"Very well, madam; show me to the room on the first floor."

" Will you have supper, sir ? "

" No," he replied, "not to-day; I have already supped on the steamer. Let my baggage be sent up."

When he had taken possession of his room he changed his dress to go out.

He went down stairs and asked for a directory. When he had found what he wanted, he murmured to himself:

" ' Walput-Spelt, merchant, Emperor St.' Ah, I understand."

He left the hotel, walked slowly and looked around him with a smiling face, as if each house awakened some remembrance.

When he had reached the " Place Verte " he walked slower, his heart beat quickly, and he uttered an exclamation of admiration.

It was night, and the gas lights were already lighted, but in the west the sky was still bright, and in this faint light the tower of Notre Dame stood out majestically like a dark pyramid.

The stranger was, doubtless, a native of Antwerp; otherwise his heart would not have beaten so rapidly at the sight of this great architectural work. To a native of Antwerp this tower is a part of his childhood's faith. Since his infancy he has always seen, from every corner of the city, and even from the country beyond, this giant of stone, which is a light-house to the city. Thus the tower mingles in all his recollections, and when he sees it again, after a long absence, his eyes fill with tears, and his whole life passes before him in a moment.

The stranger allowed his emotion to subside, and then continued his walk; but he suddenly paused, his looks fixed upon a large house. Ten minutes passed without his making the slightest movement. He kept his eyes upon the house, but it would have been impossible to imagine what attracted his attention, for there was no light visible nor any movement apparent within. At last the stranger sat down upon a bench which was behind him under the lindens, and murmured:

" It is there she lives! rich, contented, happy, adored by her husband, petted by every one. She does not imagine there is any one on earth who, for each one of her joys has suffered a life-long grief! Incurable heart wound! Nothing relieves it. I thought I had become strong enough not to recall this love excepting as a dream of my youth, and my soul is moved, and I tremble here with fear and sadness at the remembrance of my crushed hopes! O my God, I created for myself a paradise on earth. Thou hast punished me for so much pride, and Thou hast condemned me to a sad and lonely life, without hope and without end. I have begged Thee for riches, when money could have given me happiness. Now, I am rich—but it is too late; all the gold in the world could not now fill up the deep gulf which lies between her and myself for eternity."

He then observed there was a light in a room on the first floor. The shadow of a woman, carrying a child in her arms, passed before the curtain. The shadow soon disappeared.

A few moments after the stranger sighed:

" Yes, she lives before my eyes. She is seated there, with two children on her knees. What affection in her beautiful eyes! How her lovely face shines with maternal pride! Her husband, Alfred Dorneval, is near her. How happy she is, alas! alas!—"

He bowed his head, and became absorbed in his gloomy thoughts. At last he murmured:

" What means this tear upon my cheek? I am still

dreaming, as if fate had not irrevocably destroyed my dreams. She might have been the mother of my children What folly! this place fascinates me. It is as if four years of grief and suffering had had no effect upon me. The strong man who has wrestled with fortune like a desperate prize-fighter, to sigh here over the remembrance of a lost hope! How lasting is this first feeling of love!"

He arose and walked in front of the house. He was obliged, however, to stand aside, for a carriage drove up; but when he saw that it stopped before the house he was watching, he turned round and approached nearer to the door. He was overcome with an emotion he could not control, when he saw a gentleman descend from the carriage and offer his hand to a young woman.

The gentleman was Alfred Dorneval. His face was turned towards the stranger, who knew him well; but the lady wore a lace veil, and her features were not visible.

Yet the stranger thought he recognized her, for a name escaped him:

"Felicité!" he murmured.

The gentleman and lady entered the house, and the carriage drove away.

A servant came out to close the window shutters. The stranger approached her, and asked:

"Was not that Mr. Alfred Dorneval who just entered?"

"Yes," she replied.

"And the lady?"

"My mistress, Mr. Alfred's wife," said the servant.

"Thank you."

The stranger sighed as he walked forward into the darkness. A few minutes later, he arrived at Emperor Street, and stopped hesitatingly before a handsome house, as if doubtful what to do.

14*

"Shall I go to see Walput?" he murmured. "It may not be convenient, it is too late. To-morrow morning—if I only announce my arrival. Yes, yes, Walput lives here near his father-in-law. I must clasp my good friend in my arms to-day——"

He passed four or five houses and rang the bell of one.

"Does Mr. Walput live here?" he inquired of the servant who opened the door.

"Yes, sir. but he is not at home."

"Is Mrs. Walput in?"

"No, she is also out."

"I am sorry. I would be so glad if they were at home! Will they be long out?"

"They have gone to see Mrs. Walput's mother. They will return in a quarter of an hour. Will you not wait for them? Come in, sir."

A child's voice cried from an adjoining room:

"Catherine, Catherine! Sister Victoria wants to look at the pictures all by herself!"

"Ah! Mr. Walput has children?" exclaimed the stranger with delight.

"Two little angels," replied the servant. "You shall see them, sir."

She led him into a room where a little boy and a little girl of three years, evidently twins, were standing near a table looking at the pictures in a large book. The little boy had brown curly hair, rosy cheeks, and large bright eyes, the little girl was fair and pale, but her face was beautiful.

"How happy he ought to be," said the stranger "It is his likeness; he lives again in his son. And this little rose-bud, is Lucy!"

"Children," said the nurse, "come with me into another

room, this gentleman is going to wait for your father to return."

"I beg you will not take away the little angels," he said. "They need not be afraid of me."

"You love children, I suppose, sir," said the servant, with a smile.

"Oh! extremely; especially these."

"If you wish it, sir, I will stay here to take care of them."

"I will be very glad."

At the appearance of the gentleman with the black beard, and brown skin, the two children were a little frightened, and they looked at him with surprised and questioning glances; but the smile which lighted his face was so full of love and kindness, that the little boy also commenced to smile as if he had met an old acquaintance.

The servant turned towards the child, and said:

"Give your hand to the gentleman, Raphael."

"Raphael!" exclaimed the stranger, raising his hands, "is he named Raphael!"

But he restrained his emotion, took the child's hand, who approached him timidly, and covered him with kisses.

He sat down, took the boy upon his knees, and embraced him again and again as tenderly as if he had been his own child, still repeating:

"Raphael! my little pet, so you are called Raphael! Bless you for the happiness you give me!"

Surprised by the impression the child's name had made upon the visitor, the servant said to him:

"Do you know, sir, why he is called Raphael? My mistress has often told me. His father had a friend who left four years ago for America, and, without doubt, died there, for nothing has ever been heard of him. It seems that this friend was dearly loved by my employers. In memory of him, they named their son Raphael."

The stranger held the child close to his breast, and embraced him with emotion. Tears filled his eyes, and it was some moments before he could reply:

"I am that friend they mourn. I am Raphael Banks."

"And my employers believed you dead!" cried the woman. "Oh, how happy they will be."

Raphael paid no attention to her remarks, but promised a thousand presents to the child. There was nothing too beautiful for little Raphael; he should have a wooden horse, a little carriage drawn by two living lambs, books full of pictures, and sugar plums in abundance. The little girl, who heard him talk of these wonderful things, approached him timidly, and was soon upon the stranger's other knee, sharing in his caresses and promises. Poor Banks! He had no children of his own, fate had declared he should not know the happy name of father. The hope of his youth was lost forever; the only woman he had ever loved was married, and the law of duty and honor prevented him from seeking even to see her. His life was blighted; he would never love again and would live without children, though he loved them so much.

Such were the thoughts which, at this moment, passed through his mind.

While he forgot all the rest of the world in holding the two children on his knees, a key turned in the lock of the door.

"There are Mr. and Mrs. Walput," said the servant.

The stranger put the children on the floor, and walked towards the door; but his friends were already on the threshold.

Walput looked for a moment at the visitor who smiled so

strangely. Suddenly he opened his arms and rushed forward· "Good heavens! Can I believe my eyes!" he exclaimed. "Raphael! Raphael!"

"Francis, my dear Francis!" cried Banks as he threw himself joyfully into the arms of his friend.

Lucy also embraced him. Tears fell from the eyes of all. After a moment, Walput exclaimed:

"It seems to me impossible. It is true, however. My dear Banks, we have so often mourned for you as dead— and you still live! You have returned to your own country in good health!"

"I have remembered you every day in my prayers," said Mrs. Walput. "God be praised for granting them."

"Have you prayed for me?" stammered Raphael, deeply moved "Ah! how have I deserved such constant and devoted friendship?"

"But, my dear Mr. Banks, do you not know how much more we owe you," replied Mrs. Walput. "You were the means of my marrying the chosen of my heart. Since then, fortune has not ceased to smile on us; our existence is truly a paradise. See these children, our hope and our pride! Without your aid we would have been wretched! My son is named Raphael. So your remembrance continues to live in what is the dearest thing to us in the world."

"Spare me, dear friends," murmured Banks, with tears in his eyes. "I thought my rude life had blunted my feelings; but I was mistaken; your friendship touches me to the bottom of my soul."

"But, Raphael," said Walput, "your face is very much burned! You must have lived in a hot climate. Where do you come from? Has fortune favored you? Come, gratify our curiosity. Tell us some of your adventures."

"It is a long history," said Banks, smiling. "I am a little fatigued."

" Give us at least a brief account," begged Lucy. " We want to know what has happened to you. You cannot refuse us this gratification."

" Let it be so, as you desire it," replied Raphael. " I will try to give you a sketch of my adventures. On some other occasion, we will have time to talk more fully; then I will tell you some wonderful things. Listen now, my friends."

" Excuse me a moment," interrupted Mrs. Walput. " My children ought to kiss Mr. Banks and go to bed."

Their friend pressed them several times to his heart; and Lucy felt very proud as she looked at Banks and heard him praise the beauty and amiability of her children.

" Ah, friend Raphael," cried Mr. Walput, " we are forgetting the laws of hospitality. Have you supped? "

" Yes, an hour ago."

" Will you not take something ? "

" Nothing, thank you."

" Then we will drink a bottle of - wine to your happy return; I have some excellent *Hockheimer*."

The wine was poured out, Mr. and Mrs. Walput brought their chairs nearer, and Raphael commenced :

" You know, Francis, the state of mind in which I was when you accompanied me to the steamer. I remained some days in London, seated in my chamber, my head in my hands, until the time of my departure for New York in the Atlantic steamer. I was hardly at sea, before I became seriously ill. It was a kind of delirium, which sometimes became so violent that it was necessary to tie me in my bed. All I had hoped, all I had feared, all the events of my life rushed through my brain in a giddy whirl. I had been bled freely, and I refused all nourishment. In my insanity, I wished to die of hunger. My disease was so severe that each day it was predicted would be my last. There was an old Hollander on the steamer, who, under an apparent coldness, concealed a kind heart. He, alone, pitied me, and was day and night at my side, struggling with the disease which was consuming me. The fever left me at last; but I was so weak that when we arrived in New York, I had to be carried from the vessel. The Hollander, who had watched over my baggage and my money as if it had been his own, procured me lodgings in a private family, and then sailed for Mexico, where he was going to try his fortune, which had been unfavorable to him in his own country. I was still very sick, especially my head. From morning till night, and even in the night, I thought of nothing but the wound which was bleeding in my heart. I hoped to die, life was to me a miserable burden. However, after a month or two, my strength was entirely restored, and at the end of the third month, I was stronger than I had ever been. I could not remain idle. I felt an overpowering need of active work. I wished to escape from the despair which oppressed me, like a mantle of lead. Of course, it was the effect of my mania; for I resolved to risk the nine thousand francs I still possessed in a single venture. The idea of becoming poor and being compelled to struggle against want was pleasant to me. I did not like New York. The remembrance of the good Hollander led me to the South. I bought gilt jewelry in New York to the amount of eight thousand francs; ear-rings, rings, chains, small crosses, and other jewelry for ladies. With all this I started for Mexico in the hope of finding there my saviour, the Hollander. In Vera Cruz I was attacked with yellow fever, and death again held his arms very near me. I recovered at last, and started, with some traveling companions, for the interior of the country, to take the mountain road to Mexico, the capital. On our way we were attacked by bandits. One of our party was killed, and I received a ball in my arm. It was not serious, however, and in a few weeks the wound was cured. We put the robbers to flight after an exciting fight. At some other time I will give you the details of it. When I arrived in Mexico I could not find my Hollander. I made some splendid sales of my gilt jewelry. I sold them for silver, or exchanged them in the villages or farms in the interior for cochineal, indigo, vanilla, and other precious articles. Thus I obtained for my jewelry five or six times the price of my purchase. At the end of a few months I found myself in the possession of more than fifty thousand francs. It was marvellous! I made all sorts of speculations; the greater the risk the more eagerly I entered into them. I tried to defy fate; but it was like enchantment, whatever I undertook yielded me large profits. I was certain of acquiring a large fortune in a short time in Mexico; but learning from some travelers that the Hollander was engaged in business in San Francisco, California, I sailed from Acapulco, and soon arrived in San Francisco, where I found the Hollander in good health. It was the first feeling of pleasure I had experienced since I had left Antwerp, for I was equally indifferent to joy or sorrow. The Hollander was an old merchant who had failed in Europe. He had tried his fortune again, and had increased his capital to forty thousand francs. He was a very bold and venturesome man; but his apparent rashness was founded upon great experience, and an exact calculation of the chances. We associated ourselves together under the name of Peters & Co. It was, doubtless, because my name did not appear in the firm that your efforts to learn something of me were unsuccessful. As for myself, I wished to have no association with Europe, and I did not write to you. Forgive me; it was a consequence of my despair, an insane resolution. Our principal business consisted in sending to the mines all kinds of provisions, tools, and clothes, and selling them to the gold-diggers or store-keepers. As I could not overcome my continued depression, I became the traveling partner of the house. I did not give myself a single day's rest. One day I was in the mines, at the foot of snowy mountains; the next day I was in San Francisco, then in Sonora, then in Texas, then again in the Sandwich Islands. I traveled, I bought, I sold, and I gave great activity to our house. We made an immense amount of money. In the meantime the Hollander had entered into a speculation which was to yield us a fortune at once. There lived in San Francisco a Swiss, who, at the time of the discovery of the gold mines, owned a large tract of land at the other end of the village. This Swiss, who was a friend of my partner, wished to return to Europe, and offered to sell his land, for cash in hand, for twenty-seven thousand piastres, equal in our money to two hundred thousand francs. The bargain was concluded. The Hollander immediately divided the property into lots, and sold it at public auction for building lots. The product was nearly a million. What shall I tell you? We met with some misfortunes which prevented us from increasing our fortune as we had expected; yet at the end of three years we each had a capital of six hundred thousand francs!"

"You own six hundred thousand francs!" exclaimed his astonished listeners.

"At this time I own a great deal more. Fortune favored me in a short time so wonderfully that I am worth more than eight hundred thousand francs. But listen one moment longer; I ought to tell you why I returned to Antwerp,

15

although I had decided never to return to my native country. Time had nearly cured the wound in my heart, at least I thought so. I still remembered of the bitter disappointment which had caused me to leave Europe, but there was no longer anything painful in the recollection ; on the contrary, my only joy consisted in recalling the hopes of my youth, and in living over in imagination that world of dreams and sweet emotions. Then, when I found myself the owner of a handsome fortune, I thought of my old employer, Verboord. My mother said to me on her deathbed: ' My son, never forget the generosity of these good people; pay them my debt, if it is possible, and be grateful to them all your life.' These words, which my mother said to me as she blessed me, always sounded in my ears. But I know not what to do. The Verboords are rich. What can I do for them ? "

" The Verboords ! " interrupted Walput ; " they are poor ! "

" Poor ! " repeated Banks. " What do you mean ? "

" It is easily explained. The house of Ortado, in Charleston, failed, and Mr. Verboord was involved by them. Besides, coffee fell considerably, and the price remained for a long time at a low figure. Verboord was entirely ruined, and had to sell all he had to satisfy his creditors. How much you are affected by this news, Raphael! The misfortune of Verboord did not awaken much of my sympathy, I confess. These people have injured you too deeply, and I look upon their misfortune as a punishment of Heaven. Be calm; do not be so much overcome by their troubles ; really they do not deserve it."

Raphael had not heard his friend's last words.

" Then it truly was my mother's voice which made me come to Europe," he murmured. " God permitted me to amass riches only to pay a debt of gratitude."

When he raised his head he was pale ; but a bright smile parted his lips.

" You say Mr. Verboord is poor ? " he asked. " Where is he now ? Can I see him to-night ? "

" He is not very poor," replied Walput. " When all his creditors were paid, something was still left for himself ; for he kept his little country-house at Brasschaet, and lives there without doing anything. No one knows on what he lives. It appears he is sick, and suffers from a severe nervous affection."

" A nervous affection ! " sighed Banks. " His nerves were always very sensitive."

" The Verboords are proud."

" Ah ! it is in my power to cure him ! " cried Raphael. " To-morrow he will forget his misfortune ; I will restore to him what fate has robbed him of ; my mother will rejoice in heaven."

" What ! you will sacrifice your fortune to one who has made your life so bitter ? "

" But this was my only object in coming to Europe. I wished to form a business connection with Verboord. He would have sent us large consignments of all sorts of merchandise ; we would have sold them in California or Mexico on his account. My intention was, in a short time, to double Mr. Verboord's fortune ; for I am altogether indifferent to money, and what better use could I make of it than to grant the last prayer of my dying mother. Now that a great misfortune has befallen him, I must necessarily alter my first arrangement. This is what I will do. I will propose to my old patron to become my partner, under the name of Verboord & Co., in Antwerp. I will establish another branch in San Francisco. With eight hundred thousand francs, experience, large connections, and indefatigable

activity, we ought to succeed. In this manner I will return
to my benefactor not only his fortune, but also his position
in the commerce of Antwerp. It is the panacea which will
cure him of his nervous complaint. Oh! now I know the
value of money."

Walput shook his head discontentedly and with astonishment. There was a moment's silence.

" But there is one thing I cannot understand," suddenly
exclaimed Raphael. " How is it that Mr. Dorneval allowed
my poor patron to become so embarrassed without coming
to his aid? And Felicité!"

" True, you do not know," replied Mr. Walput, with a
strange smile. " This at least was a just punishment. Mr.
Verboord and his wife allowed you to cherish a false hope.
Felicité seemed to reciprocate your affection, till she was
dazzled by a large fortune. Then they sacrificed you to
money without pity, they made you unhappy, and nearly
ready to die of despair. Well! they were all deceived.
The Dornevals broke the marriage contract."

" Is it possible!" cried Raphael, turning pale. " Then
she is not Mr. Alfred's wife. It was not she I saw? She
is not married?"

"No, she is not married."

" What news! I am overcome; everything swims before
my eyes."

" Raphael, my friend, how much this information seems
to trouble you! You tremble. Do you not feel well?"

" She is not married, not married!" murmured Raphael.
"My despair, my sufferings, my hatred for life, all was a
delusion! If I had only known it! Felicité not married!"

Walput and his wife went up to him and took his hands.
They feared their friend was ill, and tried to quiet him by
kind words.

He remained for some moments insensible to their attentions. Only when Walput reminded him again that Felicité had treated him cruelly, and had never loved him, did he sigh, and say, with a sad smile:

"Ah! my good friends, have pity upon me. The wound of my heart is not yet cured, it will never be cured. I know Felicité never loved me. 1 respect myself too much to accept happiness which money alone procured me. My emotion is caused by the revival of past hopes; but the dream has vanished."

"Will you go to Brasschaet to-morrow?" asked Lucy, with hesitation. "How surprised Felicité will be to see you! Will you be able to conceal your feelings, Raphael?"·

"I understand you," replied Banks. "Do not be afraid. I am a man, and duty alone would give me strength to control myself. I shall probably see Felicité; but I would not be generous if, in her present position, I manifested anything but respect. Was it not my intention to offer her father money under a disguise. In any case, by returning her father the benefits I have received in the past, I will ameliorate her condition. The reflection that God has permitted me to benefit one whom I have loved with my whole soul is sufficient reward."

"May I give you some advice, my friend?" asked Walput. "Your generosity blinds you. It is probable that your only recompense will be a bitter disappointment. The Verboords are a proud set, I would even say wicked."

"I beg you, Francis, do not unjustly accuse those who have been my benefactors," sighed Raphael, sadly. "How difficult it is to eradicate a feeling of hatred from the heart of man. The evening before I left, and even during that night, I gave you a thousand reasons for altering your opinion of the Verboords, but in vain. You are wrong,

15*

however ; I alone was deceived. Felicité did not love me ; she did not know my feeling was anything more than friendship. Neither Mr. Verboord nor his wife knew of my ambitious hopes."

" Do you believe that ? " asked Walput, with a sneer. " Why, then, did they hate you ? You never did them any harm ? "

" Hate me ; impossible, Francis ! "

" I have never been able to forgive the Verboords their conduct to you. However, through Lucy's persuasions, I resolved to serve them, if necessary to assist them pecuniarily. With this intention we went to see them at Brasschaet. They received us very coolly, and made us feel that the greatest favor we could do them would be not to return again. Verboord left the room soon after our arrival without saying a word, and we did not see him again, even to take leave of him."

" I do not understand it," murmured Raphael. " They were always so polite to every one."

" Ask my wife," said Walput ; " she has always taken the Verboords' part ; but since she talked with Felicité day before yesterday she has changed her opinion."

" Did you see Felicité day before yesterday ? " cried Raphael.

" Yes," replied Mrs. Walput. " I am sorry, but I must admit her conduct made a bad impression on me. I expressed a wish to take my children to visit her at Brasschaet, and she gave me to understand very plainly that she would rather not have me come. Another thing made me still more angry. I thought that Felicité, when I saw her for the first time in three years, would have asked for some news of Raphael Banks, or have perhaps given me some. She left me without even mentioning your name. I called

her back and told her of our ineffectual efforts to learn anything of you. The tears came into my eyes, as I thought
you might, perhaps, be dead. Felicité listened indifferently, changed the conversation, and left me with a cold
adieu."

"What can it mean?" murmured Raphael. "Do they
fear the observation of the world? Perhaps they are concealing some sad trouble."

"No," replied Walput, "they are not poor, as they still
possess their country-house and the ground attached to it.
I will tell you what it means. They have done wrong, and
know it very well. As is usual, they hate their victim, and
hate us also, because we are his devoted friends."

"For the love of heaven, my friend, do not talk so!
Hate me! For what reason?"

"I have told you; they wish to quiet their conscience.
Verboord called you ungrateful in my presence, and accused
you of having abandoned him because you foresaw the misfortune which befell him."

Raphael sighed, and bent his head upon his breast.

"It may surprise you," continued Walput, "that I tell
you such unpleasant things at this time. But I am your
friend and will do my duty, however disagreeable it may
be. You are going to Brasschaet to-morrow. I dread two
things. In the first place, it is very possible the Verboords
will treat you with extreme coldness, and proudly refuse
your assistance. It is against such a reception I would
warn you. The thought of your being insulted by the
Verboords troubles me. On the other hand, it is possible
that your riches may tempt them to try to conceal their bitter feelings. In this case you would be the victim of their
treachery."

"No, no!" cried Raphael, in an excited voice, "it is

not possible. You are under a strange delusion. That Felicité should not have loved me, that her father should have blamed my departure under the pressure of his misfortunes, I can understand. But that they should hate me, should deceive me! They are as incapable of cherishing a feeling of hatred as of committing a bad deed. Can these angels of kindness have suddenly lost all their virtues? There is some mystery behind it, I tell you. To-morrow, I will find it out; to-morrow, my friend, you will regret a mistake which arises from your affection for me."

"I hope so, Raphael. If I am really deceived, and your heart has guessed it, I will give you credit. But, in the uncertainty, be prudent. Spare yourself the pain and shame of an open refusal. You have been the victim of their egotism, do not be the victim of their pride."

Walput's continued accusations against the Verboords pained Raphael. He arose to go, and said:

"My dear friend, what I have learned from you has disturbed all my ideas. I am tired, and long for rest and quiet. It is past eleven o'clock. I must leave you. To-morrow, on my return from Brasschaet, I will come here."

"At what hotel are you staying?" asked Mrs. Walput.

"At St. Antoine."

"It must only be till to-morrow, then. You will bring your baggage here, and stay with us, Raphael."

"I will be happy to accept your kind offer," replied Banks. "I must now say good night, blessing you from the bottom of my heart for your sincere friendship and kind remembrance."

Mr. and Mrs. Walput pressed his hand with every expression of friendship, accompanying him to the door.

Raphael walked rapidly like one who hastens to a desired end.

He was almost running as he passed the Jesuit Church, then he walked slower and slower, and pressed his hand to his brow.

He was evidently wrestling with his own thoughts, for he stopped suddenly at a dark corner, and murmured:

"Not married! Felicite is not married! Alas! if she had ever loved me, all I dared to dream of in my pride might now be realized. My future would suddenly become bright. No,-no, let me not cherish so vain a hope, or my heart may be again cruelly lacerated. She hates me! It is impossible! But she never loved me! I do not wish to buy happiness with money. She is not married, she is free! Oh! if she had only loved me!" As he uttered this sad complaint, he crossed the market place; and a few minutes later, entered his hotel.

CHAPTER IX.

IT was scarcely nine o'clock the next morning when Raphael reached Brasschaet. He left the carriage and directed the driver to wait for him at the Swan Tavern. There was an expression of sadness upon his face, and he appeared to be indulging in unpleasant reflections.

It was, however, a glorious day in May. The birds sang joyously in the trees, the leaves waved gayly in the sunshine, and the air was filled with the fragrant perfume from the heaths. The season, the hour, smiling nature, all were the same as four years before, when the young man, full of dreams and hopes, followed the road to participate in the fête of Mrs. Verboord.

Indifferent to the beauties which had charmed him at that time, Raphael walked dreamily along.

Was it not on the day of that fête when he first heard Felicité pronounce the name of Alfred Dorneval? Had not his heart, at that time, received the wound which would continue to bleed until the end of his life?

Alas! Night with its sad reflections had thoroughly depressed him. His friends had told the truth. The Verboords were, doubtless, angry with him. What reception would they give him, he wondered. Would they forget the past and forgive one who for years they had accused of ingratitude, and accept assistance from his hands?

Poverty and misfortune render the noblest hearts proud and suspicious. If the Verboords declined his proposition and all assistance from him, he would not then be able to fulfil the last wishes of his mother. What then would be accomplished by his voyage to Europe, and of what use would his fortune be? Two dreams had filled his whole life. The first had been rudely broken, when the news of Felicité's marriage had proven to him the state of his affections; the second had arisen from a feeling of gratitude. If this last object should also disappear from before his eyes, there would be no longer any hope to brighten his sad future. He would then remain a few days with his friend Walput, give him a proof of his regard, depart for America, never to return to his native land.

As these thoughts passed through his brain, Raphael arrived at the open gate of the hunting lodge. He entered the garden and looked around him. The grey stains upon the walls, the pot-herbs in the beds which were formerly filled with flowers, the appearance of poverty which was everywhere apparent, pained him deeply.

His heart commenced to beat rapidly when he approached the door of the house. In a moment, he would enter the dwelling of his master, a moment later he would see Felicité.

He hesitated, full of apprehension; it seemed to him he could already hear reproaches and accusations. He summoned all his courage, strengthened by the conviction he was about to pay a debt of gratitude, and walked with a firm step toward the house. He rapped, he called; but all remained silent save the plaintive bleating of a goat. He took a step or two forward and found himself upon the threshold of the room where the Verboords usually sat. There was no one in the room, and perfect silence reigned within the dwelling.

Attracted by certain articles which recalled past days, he advanced into the middle of the chamber. He saw the mahogany desk which had been in his master's office, papers and books, as of old, the velvet chair, and many little things which ornamented the walls of the room.

It was evident the Verboords were not so very poor, or they would not have reserved this handsome furniture. The papers and books seemed to indicate that Mr. Verboord was still engaged in commerce. And in this small business he, perhaps, found sufficient resources for the wants of his household without being indebted to any one.

This thought pleased Raphael, and a smile passed across his face ; but his expression soon became sad, for he felt that this prosperous situation of the Verboords gave him less reason to hope they would accept of his assistance.

He turned his eyes and looked around upon the other side of the room. There he saw common chairs, a table of white wood, on the hearth a fire of willow wood, and kitchen utensils No more velvet lounges ; there were only three chairs and a table. It was, therefore, off of these bare boards the Verboords dined, and on one of these straw chairs Felicité sat.

Raphael sighed—after waiting a few moments, he rapped several times on the door and made a noise, hoping some one in the other part of the house would hear him, but the same silence continued.

The back door which led into the garden was open. It was evident the Verboords were not at home, and the servant who was in the garden had forgotten to close the door .

Raphael crossed the room and looked out into the garden. He discovered at a distance a young peasant woman, who was kneeling in a path with a sickle in her hand, cutting the weeds out of a bed of lettuce.

This peasant had her back turned towards him, and was not aware of his presence until he said to her :

" Well ! my girl ! is not Mr. Verboord at home ? "

She sprang up and looked at the stranger with an expression of annoyance.   Her eyes seemed to reproach him with having surprised her ; but, suddenly the sickle fell from her hands, and she uttered a piercing cry:

" Raphael ! " she exclaimed.

" Felicité ! " murmured Banks.

They both raised their arms as if to embrace each other ; but a mutual feeling restrained them and enabled them to overcome their emotion.

They looked at one another for a moment in silence, and each endeavored to read the mind of the other.

This hasty examination seemed to depress them, for they both sighed deeply, as if they had met with a bitter disappointment.

Felicité suddenly remembered she wore her every day clothes.   A deep blush suffused her cheeks; she looked with a mortified expression on her coarse apron and let it fall to the ground.

" Miss Verboord," said Raphael, stammering from emotion, " forgive me, I pray you, for having surprised you. I knocked at the door, but no one answered.   I have come from America to see your father, my old employer, and to talk with him.   He is probably not at home.   Be kind enough to tell me when he will be able to receive me; I will come again."

Felicité trembled, her brain was bewildered.   How deeply Raphael's kind and gentle tone affected her!   It was still the same voice, frank and pure, to which, with childish joy, she had formerly listened as to enchanted music; but he called her Miss Verboord and there was

16

something so reserved and respectful in his accent, that she was completely overcome; time had then broken those early ties, and perhaps, the remembrance of that love no longer existed in Raphael's heart.

"My sudden appearance troubles you," said Raphael. "Excuse me, I will return later."

"No, Raph—; no, sir," stammered the young girl, looking up. "I am alone. My father is in the city with my mother; they will not return till after dinner. Will you not rest a little, sir? Why leave so suddenly? It is four years since you left your country to go to America. Ah! how the fortune of man changes!"

As she uttered these words she walked towards the house. Raphael followed her with beating heart and so absorbed in thought, that he did not attempt to break the silence. Felicité was still beautiful. More so, perhaps, than formerly. Her simple dress was very becoming to her, while her sunburnt cheeks, and the decision of character expressed in her face, marked the fully developed woman in the place of the pretty child. He had surprised her with the sweat of labor upon her brow; embarrassed and blushing, she had taken off her coarse linen apron, mortified that he should witness their poverty. It deeply pained the young man, though pity increased the strength of his love, and he said to himself as he raised his eyes to heaven:

"Oh, that she had only loved me!"

His conscience whispered that the poverty of Mr. Verboord should cause him to show the greatest respect, and it would be ungenerous to let Felicité see what was passing in his heart.

When they had entered the house, Felicité tried to speak; her eyes were fixed on Raphael. She shuddered and turned pale, while tears ran down her cheeks. She threw herself into a chair with a cry of despair, and covered her face with her hands. While she, in her isolation, had thought of no one but him—whilst her love for him had only increased and changed into a mysterious faith—he had forgotten her. He met her after four long years of absence with such cold looks and polite words as he would give to any other woman.

It required a great effort for Raphael to conceal his pity; he attributed the grief of the young girl to her being ashamed of their poverty.

With moist eyes and beating heart, he attempted to comfort her; but every word was one of respect. He did not even make any direct allusion to Mr. Verboord's situation.

Felicité, who had at last overcome her emotion, dried her tears, and said with a smile:

"Do not notice me, sir; it is over. Thank you for the trouble that you take to— You come from America; have you been successful? Have you not suffered a great deal, so far from your country and your friends? A terrible misfortune has befallen us. You know it, perhaps? Ah, since then our life has been very bitter and unhappy!"

Raphael felt that he would not accomplish his object by vague words; he summoned all his courage to overcome his agitation; the depression of the young girl gave him the necessary strength, and he replied in a firm and decided tone ·

"Yes, Miss Verboord, I learned yesterday evening of the misfortune which had befallen my benefactor; the news filled me with grief, but with this grief was mingled a feeling of joy and gratitude to God, who has given me the power to restore to my good master all he has lost."

"Impossible, impossible," sighed Felicité, shaking her head.

"Believe me," replied Raphael, "the desire to see my

old employer again, and to be of use to him, alone induced me to return to Europe. I do not forget all that you and he and Mrs. Verboord did to comfort my mother on her death-bed; I have neither wife, nor children, nor family—"

Felicité took a deep breath.

"My mother—you were at her bedside—often repeated the same prayer, and left as my inheritance eternal gratitude to your father. I have therefore a sacred debt to pay, and I implore heaven to permit me to pay it. Means are not wanting, for I am worth more than a half million—"

"You are rich! Oh, God! he is rich!" murmured Felicité, in despairing tones and again turning pale.

This exclamation surprised Raphael; he did not quite understand its meaning, but Felicité soon looked proudly up.

"Your father, Miss Verboord, may well feel very unhappy, not alone on account of the loss of his fortune, but also because he is compelled to lead an inactive life, after always being accustomed to one of labor. Ah! well! I have come to return to him all he regrets—at least to offer it to him as a proof of my gratitude. I intend to propose to him to become my partner; we will open a store in Antwerp, of which he will be the head, for I will return to America to open another store in San Francisco, under the same name. I possess the means of giving to each house a large business, and there will be no necessity for your father to receive anything from me, as his share of the profits will be large enough to enable him to live handsomely. Oh! I pray I may not meet with a refusal. Your good parents, my benefactors, will resume their position in the world, and you," he added, with hesitation, "you will doubtless meet with a husband worthy of you, and who will render you happy."

Tears glistened in Felicité's eyes—at first tears of admiration at the young man's generosity, then tears of grief because his last words wounded her heart.

"May I hope Mr. Verboord will accept my proposition?" asked Raphael.

"May God bless you for such generosity," she sighed. "Alas! my father will refuse."

"Refuse?"

"Positively."

"Perhaps I am mistaken, Miss Verboord. Your father may have saved a large part of his fortune, and so not need assistance."

"Ah! we are poor; we earn our daily bread by the labor of our hands!"

"Poor! and he would refuse! Then my friend Walput told me the truth. My benefactor hates me! Oh, God! Thou knowest I have not deserved it, and if I yielded to a delusion, I have bitterly expiated the error of my youth."

"It is true that my father is angry with you, sir," said Felicité. "He thinks you left him because you foresaw that misfortune was about to befall him."

"But I left before it was possible to foresee it. Has no one justified me to him? Can any one believe me capable of such injustice? Was there no one who had faith in the honesty and purity of my soul?"

As he uttered these words he looked reproachfully at Felicité, his voice trembled, and he appeared to accuse her of injustice towards him.

The young girl trembled beneath his look; she tried to speak, but she only muttered some unintelligible words. Perhaps the avowal she was about to make frightened her.

She suddenly burst into tears, and, raising her hands to the young man, exclaimed:

"Raphael, Raphael, forgive my poor father's injustice: he is insane!"

16*

"Insane!" repeated Raphael, turning pale. "My good master insane!"

This sad news completely overcame him; he put his hand to his face to hide the tears which fell from his eyes. Now he understood all. The hatred of his employer to him was a sick man's fancy; Felicité did not participate in this hatred, since she called it an injustice. The retirement in which Mrs. Verboord and her daughter lived, their dread of the visits of strangers, their refusal to explain to the Walputs: all this had its origin in a feeling of love for an unhappy husband, an unfortunate father; doubtless they still hoped he would be cured, and did not wish to have him blush at the loss of his mind. But insanity is often an incurable disease. So that Raphael, who had crossed the ocean to benefit Verboord, might still be unable to do it. This thought plunged him into despair.

Felicité arose and approached him. She saw that tears filled his eyes. An irresistible impulse possessed her; she took his hand and said:

"Raphael, you are weeping with pity for my poor father. Besides my mother and myself, you are the first person who has shed a tear over his misfortune. O my friend, may God bless you for your sympathy!"

The touch of her hand thrilled the young man; the word "friend," pronounced by her sweet voice, moved his whole soul; he arose and looked at the young girl with a surprised and questioning glance; but Felicité, ashamed of this moment of forgetfulness, resumed her first expression.

"Insane! Mr. Verboord insane!" he repeated with distress. "Oh, let me be calm! He is excited against me; Francis Walput said he hated me. Did my departure increase the trouble? Must I accuse myself of being the cause of such a misfortune? Impossible! It would be too cruel!"

" No, sir," she replied. " My father's sickness has other causes than you can imagine. When my father learned, on the same day, of the failure of the house of Ortado and the extraordinary decline in coffee, he knew that his entire fortune was lost. Dreading the future for my mother and myself, he sank beneath the blow. He became extreme'y feeble, and remained for months upon a bed of grief. He sold everything to satisfy his creditors. We came here to live. My father seemed cured; his body at least was no longer sick; but we soon observed his brain was troubled. The evil increased daily. He would speak of business, of great undertakings; he wished to make money; he wrote, he calculated, and watched the state of coffee."

"Ah! is that so?" cried Banks, with delight.

" It was necessary to let him do so," continued Felicité, "for at the slightest contradiction he became unhappy and excited. Every time he met with anything disagreeable he was so much agitated that we had to lead him to his room and put him to bed to quiet him. The face of a person we had known before our misfortune was sufficient to disturb and excite his brain for several days. It is this condition of things which has compelled us to live in such close retirement."

" Now I understand what Mrs. Walput told me," murmured Raphael.

" Yes, I suppose she accuses me of rudeness. Alas! I think of her constantly; I know she still remembers our past friendship, and I feel grateful to her for it. I have only seen her twice, and each time I wept the whole day because I was obliged to repel her kindness with coldness."

" But the insanity of your father has its lucid intervals. If he remembers my sudden departure, the trouble cannot last forever. He will recover, be assured."

Tears ran down Felicité's cheeks, as she despondingly answered:

"No, no, my poor father is fated to lead this wretched existence till death relieves him."

"What!" cried Raphael Banks, "he cannot recover. My gratitude, my wealth, the science of the best physicians will avail nothing! No, no, a new aim in life is presented to me. A cruel enemy has arisen before me. I will fight with it till I conquer."

The young girl sadly shook her head.

"I am rich, I have strength," he continued; "your father was my benefactor, and I will devote my entire fortune, my life, my strength to this end. I will not return to America till he recovers his strength. You see, Felicité—you see, Miss Verboord—the chief cause of his disease is his depression from not being engaged in business. I will give him occupation. Ah! if I can only succeed, the light will suddenly return to his mind."

"Yes, my friend, if he would accept your noble offer," she sighed, "but he will refuse."

"No, no, to soften his heart I will implore his pardon, and if necessary I will entreat him on my knees to let me pay my mother's debt. No, he will not be insensible to my tears; he will have pity upon me; the voice of one whom he loved as a son will move him. Yes, God will bless me; your father will be cured. You weep. Is your heart closed against all hope?"

"No, sir," she replied with enthusiasm; "on the contrary, your words have awakened hope in my breast. It is perhaps only a delusion; but, whatever it may be, your noble conduct fills me with gratitude and admiration. There was a sad day in your life, with which you might have reproached my father. You have crossed the ocean to return what you choose to call his benefits. Your noble soul has forgotten the pain and suffering, and only remembered his friendship and kindness. Oh, may God bless you for my father's sake!"

"Do you then know what I suffered so deeply?" said Banks, endeavoring to restrain his feelings. "Excuse my emotion; but tell me how you learned this?"

"Certainly," she replied, "the feelings of our youth grow weaker as time passes, and end by leaving us entirely; but, at first, the chalice of despair is very bitter to drink!"

"Have you then had news of me during my absence?"

"None whatever."

"But how do you know what I have suffered?"

Felicité bent her head, but did not reply.

Raphael seemed much agitated, his eyes sparkled, and a smile full of hope lighted his face; with trembling tones he repeated his question.

A deep blush suffused the cheeks of the young girl, while she murmured:

"I judged by my own heart; I was very unhappy, crushed by my grief."

"Alas! yes, the Dornevals treated you cruelly!" sighed the young man.

"The Dornevals!" repeated Felicité, contemptuously.

"I mean in breaking off your marriage."

"My marriage? I blessed God that He at least spared me an alliance of which the thought alone filled me with horror and fear. Of course I would have submitted to my father's will and wishes, but—"

She seemed to shudder at the thought.

"But—but—" replied Raphael with feverish impatience.

His emotion recalled her to a consciousness of her situation. The tone of her voice changed, and with surprising calmness she answered:

"I tell you this, sir, to prove to you that I was not insensible to your grief. You are so generous that I do not wish you to think me ungrateful. Four years have passed since then. Time has healed the wound; and if I speak to you freely, it is because those things are now only a dream of your youth."

Raphael could no longer restrain himself:

"Oh," he stammered, "if my words should pain you, I beg you will forgive me, I hardly know what I do, I feel stunned, as though some strange dream possessed me. The feeling which gave me so much sorrow and grief, which has made my life a long and inconsolable regret, has continued to live against my will; it has given me no rest, it has filled my heart. The angel of my youth has never left me; her sweet image has been ever before my eyes during these four sad years. Yesterday, to-day, and forever. I will carry the feeling with me to the grave, and though I may die of despair, your dear name, Felicité, will be the last word upon my lips in the hour of death."

The young girl was seated, with head bowed and eyes fixed upon the ground, while tears rolled down her cheeks.

Alarmed at his own vehemence, the young man looked at her for a moment, and said:

"I have offended you? Be generous, and forgive me."

"Raphael, Raphael, I have nothing to forgive," she sighed, in a scarcely audible voice, and without lifting her eyes.

"Then the avowal of my weakness has not wounded you. You smile amid your tears. Oh, Felicité, have pity upon me! My brain is turning. Do not remain indifferent to my sufferings. Have you forgotten those enchanting hours, and their innocent joys? Do you still think kindly of me? Speak to me, speak to me. God has sent me deep sorrows; but if he has only permitted my remembrance to live in your heart, however faint it may be, I will fall upon my knees and bless His holy name with joy. Ah, in mercy, Felicite, give me a word, a single word!"

The young girl arose and looked strangely at Raphael. A light beamed in her eyes, the smile had disappeared from her lips, and her expression was grave.

"Raphael," she said, "it may not be right for me to give you the reply you desire, but your heart is noble; you have come here to benefit my poor father; you will seek to have him cured, will you not? Perhaps my answer may make you happy. Well, listen. I have lived here in a sad retirement, with an insane father and a heart-broken mother. Everything was dark and gloomy around me, yet my soul still felt joyful, and I have had a source of consolation and strength. I have made for myself an altar of remembrance, and before this altar I have come constantly to pray for one whom I mourned as dead, or to dream of the happy days of my youth."

"Ah, Felicité, can it be possible! But one word more, hope and doubt bewilder my senses."

She took a little faded flower from her bosom, and said:

"You do not know this flower? Every morning, I gathered one from the altar of remembrance, and it has thus faded on my heart, speaking to my spirit of the one who gave it. Follow me, Raphael, I will show you the bank on which I have so often knelt."

She went out by the back door, and turned towards the lower part of the garden.

Raphael looked in astonishment at the small flower-bed, surrounded by box, in whose centre grew a beautiful fuchsia.

"Here I came to pray," she murmured, "for him who on a festal day gave this flower to my mother."

"Oh, Heaven, St. Laurenco!" cried Raphael. "Your prayer was for me, Felicité, dear and good Felicité," and he opened his arms to press the young girl to his heart; but she stepped back in the path, and joined her hands in supplication. He understood her, and restraining his emotion, sank back upon the bank, unable to speak another word. Felicité sat down beside him, and said, gently:

"Raphael, my friend, be calm. I trust to your generosity and strength of mind. Remember, my parents have not yet seen you. I am alone, and I do not know how my father will receive you."

The happy young man fixed his eyes upon those of the girl; a smile lighted his face, he doubted his happiness still, in his excitement he seemed about to throw his arms around his companion.

The young girl again arose, and said reproachfully:

"When you thought I had forgotten you, Raphael, you treated me with respect."

"Oh, grant me strength to restrain my feelings," he sighed. "Give me a word, a sign! Tell me, Felicité, that you have loved me, still love me?"

She pointed to the flowers, and remained silent.

"Truly," he cried, "no word would be equal to this proof of your pure, and lasting love. Thank you, thank you."

"Raphael, grant me a favor?"

"Anything, even my life."

"Now that you know the secret of my heart, we ought not to remain alone together."

"What, leave you already?" sighed the young man. "Your parents will not return till afternoon; no one can either see us or hear us."

"My conscience, the respect you owe me," she said, gently, but firmly "I cannot talk to you any longer till my father or mother know what I have dared to tell you."

"You are right, you are an angel," he murmured, as he arose. "I will obey you, Felicité, I will go."

Together they turned back towards the house. "O, Felicité!" cried Raphael, "may the God of mercy favor me with your father!"

"I will try to prepare him to see you," she replied. "Give me the necessary time. Do not return till three or four o'clock. Let us hope, Raphael."

"If I can only succeed! I will never abandon your father; we will live with him and your mother. It will be an earthly paradise!"

When they had re-entered the room, and Felicité was already murmuring adieu, the young man hesitated, and looked at her in silence with beating heart. How beautiful she was! How noble was the soul which shone forth in her lovely face. She was truly the good angel of his dreams and his griefs. Time and trouble had left no traces upon this pure flower. If God had kept her for him, and he might one day lead her to the altar as his idolized wife!

"Take courage, Raphael," she said. "The heart must submit to duty."

"I am going!" he sighed. "Good-bye, good-bye, Felicité, till this afternoon."

He left the room without turning round, as though he feared that the slightest glance behind would take away the power to go away.

The young girl looked after him, till he had disappeared among the trees on the road; then she uttered a cry of joy, took a few steps backwards into the room, and overcome by an irresistible emotion, she sank into a chair near the table, and remained motionless, with her eyes fixed on space.

CHAPTER X.

FELICITÉ became extremely impatient as she looked out for the fifth time on the road from Brasschaet and saw no one.

She had spread a cloth on the table and placed the plates for dinner. Upon the coals, on the hearth, were two or three copper pans whose smoking contents proved the gentle girl had not forgotten her duties in her new joy.

When she went out the sixth time, she uttered an exclamation of delight as she met her parents.

After embracing her father with more than usual affection, she led him into the house, saying:

"Dear papa, you smile, you must feel better. I am delighted to see you so cheerful. I have prayed earnestly to God to give the physician power to cure you. How glad I am if you are really better."

"Thank you, my dear Felicité," said Verboord. "My new physician is, undoubtedly, a scientific man, as well as one of kind feelings; he gave me something to quiet my nerves, and I have felt better ever since. Who knows? Perhaps he may cure me!"

"Yes, yes, papa; you must be hopeful."

"What is the matter, Felicité?" asked her mother. "You seem excited."

"Yes, mamma, excited from joy. But be quiet now. After a while I will tell you all."

They sat down, and Felicité put the dinner on the table, and Mr. Verboord ate the peas his daughter had prepared, with much pleasure. He was in a charming mood, apparently without a shadow upon his mind, and Felicite, who watched all his movements, was delighted. When dinner was over, Felicité placed the velvet chair before the desk, on which she laid an open newspaper.

"Come, dear papa! your trip must have fatigued you; the postman came while you were absent. You have not yet read the "*Precurseur*." Sit down and rest a little. In the meanwhile, I will go up stairs to finish some work I have commenced, afterwards you must tell me about your journey and what the doctor said."

When her father was seated and had the paper in his hand, she left the room and went up stairs. Her mother followed her immediately.

Felicité took both her hands, and exclaimed, with emotion:

"Mamma, mamma, while you were away Raphael arrived."

"Who? Raphael Banks?"

"Yes, mamma, Raphael Banks, whom we mourned as dead."

Mrs. Verboord looked incredulously at her daughter, as if doubting the truth of what she heard.

"Raphael is rich, mamma; he is worth more than half a million."

"Thank God for having preserved so good a man."

"But do you know why he has returned from America? You will admire him more than ever when you hear what he said. Ah, my father had good reason to love him as a son. Raphael has the noblest and purest heart that has ever beat in the breast of man."

She then repeated to her mother all Raphael had said, which recital frequently brought tears to Mrs. Verboord's eyes.

"Noble Raphael," she exclaimed, "I never doubted your integrity of character."

"Well, mamma, he is to return in an hour. I have promised him to prepare my father for his visit. It is a difficult matter, and I am frightened at the thought. Fortunately, my father is in a good humor. I will caress him, entreat him, beseech him. The God of mercy will give strength to my words. Alas! if my father, in a fit of derangement, should repel Raphael!"

Mrs. Verboord sadly shook her head.

"You despair of success, mamma?" sighed Felicité.

"I have very little hope, my child. You know the name of Banks is sufficient to bring on an attack. What will it be if he sees him in person? Perhaps it may increase his disease!"

"But Raphael cannot return to America till he sees my father, and tells him of the resolutions he formed in his gratitude. No, no, it would be too cruel! The conversation may perhaps be trying to my father. Yet who knows? It may have a good effect on him. If necessary, Raphael will go down on his knees to him. If my father, touched by his prayers, forgives him, one of the causes of his sickness will be removed; and the idea of again being at the head of a large commercial house may perhaps cure him entirely. Banks thinks so. Activity of mind and constant occupation, with the handling of money, are the only remedies which can restore my father to his senses."

"Banks is right," replied Mrs. Verboord; "but how will you keep your father calm?"

"I will try, mamma. There is something which encourages me and gives me hope."

"Well! so be it, Felicité; he is in a good humor, and you have much influence with him. If he does not repel Banks, what happy results may ensue from the interview! His cure, his happiness in his old days! Go, Felicité, tell him of Raphael's return, but gradually, and with prudence. Be gentle and affectionate; do not contradict him, and always give him a reason for what you tell him. Ah! perhaps you may overcome his anger!"

"Dear mamma, there is another thing I have not yet told you."

Mrs. Verboord was astonished at her daughter's embarrassment, and looked at her interrogatively.

"Oh, mamma," she exclaimed, · "I am so happy; my joy seems like a wild dream—but I am unable to express the feelings which carry me away Raphael still loves me with his whole soul!"

There was a moment's silence; Mrs. Verboord thought over this unexpected revelation, and sighed as she shook her head and murmured:

"He loves you still?"

"Yes, he told me so,· with tears in his eyes; and I, dear mamma, overcome by his generosity and despair, led him to my flowers, and there—forgive me, mamma—my lips for the first time in my life uttered a confession of love. I wished to reward him for the affection he felt for my unhappy father, and I said to him: 'I have loved you from my childhood, and will love you still.'"

"My child, my child," said Mrs. Verboord, severely, "what an indiscretion! All alone with him? Did he stay here long?"

"No, no, dear mamma, do not be angry with him. If

17*

you had seen Raphael's respectful manner, as he earnestly begged for one word of comfort, you would have pitied him yourself. Although my confession filled him with delight, he did not even venture to take my hands; and when I said to him that after what I had told him I ought not to remain alone with him, he obeyed like a child, and left the house without a word. Oh, dear mamma, Raphael is still the same; he has as pure a heart and noble a soul as an angel!"

"Félicité," said Mrs. Verboord, looking annoyed, "you have been imprudent. What can such an affection avail?"

The young girl threw her arms around her mother's neck, kissed her, and exclaimed:

"If God is merciful to us, Raphael will cure my father, and never leave us. Come now, time is passing."

Félicité ran down stairs and met her father with a smile, to which he responded in like manner.

She sat down beside him, put her arm on his shoulder, and looked so lovingly at him that the old man was touched.

"My dear Félicité," he said, "you seem very happy to see me a little better. Really, it is astonishing how the doctor's remedy has quieted my nerves! Ah, if I could only be cured! I would resume business, I would enter into large speculations, I would make a great deal of money, and I would reward your devoted affection."

The young girl shuddered at the thought that a single unpleasant word would be sufficient to disturb her father's mind. He was talking of business matters and making money. It was a very bad sign.

She was silent for some moments, to give her father time to forget what he had just said. She hesitated, but to draw back was no longer possible. Raphael would soon return, and the consequences of his appearance would be more serious if her father were not prepared for him. She commenced caressing the old man, and, when he pressed her to his heart in return, she murmured in entreating tones:

"Dear papa, I wish to ask you something. I know you are goodness itself, and if you promise me the favor I implore, I will bless you for making me happy by such a proof of your love; but I dare not—"

"Speak, my child," he replied; "ask anything you like; if not absolutely impossible, your wish shall be granted."

"Oh, may I hope it?"

"Do not doubt it; to give my Felicité pleasure, I would give my life's blood."

"But, dear papa, if my request should be unpleasant to you, would you forgive me? would you remain calm and try to control your nerves?"

"Fear nothing. I feel very strong. To-day is a bright day for me."

Felicité glanced joyfully at her mother, who pretended to work, while listening with beating heart to the conversation. She gave a sign of encouragement to her daughter, who continued:

"Then you will grant my prayer, if it is not altogether impossible?"

"Rest assured of it, my child. You arouse my curiosity. Speak! What astonishing thing do you wish?"

"Papa, suppose I should tell you an old acquaintance wishes to see you, and should ask you to welcome him here?"

The old man bit his lips, and his brow contracted.

"Ah, papa," sighed Felicité, quite discouraged, "I have hardly said a word, and you are already provoked! I know visitors are not agreeable to you; but, if you would grant me the favor I ask, you would find strength in your generous heart to overcome your repugnance for once."

"Certainly, Felicité, I would find the strength in my desire to gratify you."

"If you say so, papa, I will submit, and never speak to you again of such a thing."

"I will receive the visitor politely, kindly, if it will give you pleasure; but do not ask too much of me. Do not let him stay too long."

"Suppose it should be a person whom you used to dislike?"

The old man's expression became sad; but his daughter's beseeching look overcame him.

"Walput!" he exclaimed. "So be it; I will conceal my dislike. Of course, Felicité, it will be difficult for me to appear friendly to that man; but I feel stronger than formerly, and since you are so desirous of securing a kind welcome for him, I will show you that nothing is too much to please you."

"It is not Mr. Walput who is coming," stammered the young girl, timidly.

"If it is not Walput, who else can it be? Mr. Dorneval? He certainly has not behaved very generously to us; but he acted like a merchant, and he owed me nothing. Let him come!"

Felicité did not reply, but looked down on the ground; a cold perspiration moistened her forehead, and her heart was filled with anxiety. The important moment had arrived; she would now have to utter Raphael's name, and she feared her father would have a violent attack as soon as he heard it. He would then no longer be in his senses, and all hope would be lost.

After struggling a moment against her despair, she summoned her strength, concealed her depression, caressed her father very tenderly, and replied:

"Listen, papa—be good to me—listen quietly. There
is a person who once committed a wrong act, and who apparently forgot your great kindness. You do not know the
reason of his conduct; you very properly accused him of
ingratitude. Notwithstanding, he was grateful, and he has
come across the ocean, thousands of miles, to ask you to
forgive him. Oh, papa, do not be angry! I will be quiet,
I will be silent!"

At these last words, the old man commenced to tremble,
his eyes flashed, and his teeth were clenched, as he muttered:

"Impossible! God has punished him; he has long been
dead."

"Oh, do not be so hard, papa!" she said, with clasped
hands. "He will ask your mercy on his knees. Have
pity on his grief, hear his humble prayer, grant him his
pardon!"

"Then it is of him you speak?" he cried.

"It is of him."

"Of Raphael Banks?"

"Of Raphael," she sighed, in a scarcely intelligible
voice. She laid her head upon his knees, took his hand,
covered it with kisses, and remained thus without uttering
a word, and without looking at her father. Raphael's name
had produced the expected effect. She felt her father's hand
tremble beneath her lips; she heard his bitter reproaches;
his voice was harsh, and his ideas began to wander.

The poor girl's heart was nearly broken; her eyes filled
with tears, but she knew the sight of them would annoy her
father; and she also knew that absolute silence was the only
way to quiet him.

Mrs. Verboord fixed her eyes upon her husband, and
anxiously watched every movement of his face. When she

thought the violence of the shock had somewhat abated, she arose and approached him, smiling carelessly. She pretended not to notice his emotion, and not to attach any importance to what had happened.

" Do not mind Felicité's grief," she said. " You know, Verboord, how she sympathizes with other people's troubles. Raphael certainly did not behave very well towards you, or towards us; but a young man does not always know what he does; the love of travel, and the bad advice of friends, urge them to commit acts whose enormity they do not understand. It has no doubt been so with Raphael, as he is still grateful to you, and has come from America simply to obtain his pardon. God gives us an example of mercy. Felicité fears you may repel Raphael. It is not right for her to have so little confidence in her father's generosity. What an idea! That you should be more inexorable than God himself, and refuse to forgive the evils you have suffered, when the fault is acknowleged and your pity humbly entreated. Oh! Felicité, you do not know your father's heart. That you should think he, who is so very good and kind, would show such an implacable feeling to a poor suffering young man! Impossible! As Raphael is unhappy because he has offended his benefactor, and repents of his folly, let him believe in the kindness of your father. Be assured, my child, he will not leave here without being forgiven. Am I not right, Verboord; will you not show yourself as you are, kind and generous?"

The silence of Felicité, and her mother's words, were calculated to quiet the emotion of the old man, and to give him time to recover himself in some measure.

They had attained their object, contrary to their expectation; for the old man replied very quietly:

" You are right, Laurence; man must not cherish an old

bitterness in his heart, however justifiable his feelings may be. You say he regrets his fault? Let him come."

Felicité sprang up, joyfully, and kissed her father with renewed affection. She covered him with caresses and gave him every proof of love. Soon the old man's face became grave.

"I do not know," he said; "my heart beats violently. I am frightened. Will I be able to look at the ungrateful rascal?"

"He is grateful now, papa," said the girl, timidly. "His repentance and love for you have induced him to return from America to humble himself before you and beg your pardon."

"That pardon I will give him," stammered Mr. Verboord; "then he must go right away, immediately."

"As soon as you wish it, papa. Say a word, and he will leave, blessing you. Listen to him, if it be possible; he will tell you things which will make us happy, you, mamma, and myself."

An incredulous smile passed over the old man's face.

"He has deceived you with vain promises. You know, however, how quickly he breaks them."

"It is not that, papa. I beg you to let me tell you what Raphael intends proposing to you. Remain calm and quiet. Without your consent, I will not attempt to speak of it, nor Raphael either. At your first word, every one will be silent. Consequently, if the proposition does not suit you, you can silence us with a sign."

"Speak, my child," he said; "deceived or not, I will listen to you quietly."

"You see, papa, Raphael entered into business in America; he had favorable opportunities; he is worth half a million."

" Rich!" sneered Verboord. " God is just; the happiness of the wicked will vanish like smoke."

" Yes, papa, that is so; but Raphael regrets his mistake, and God is merciful. Although fortune has smiled on him, he has not forgotten what you had done for him. He constantly thought of his generous employer; and his sole object was to find means of proving his gratitude to you. He thinks he has found this means, at least, he hopes you will permit him to return your kindness. Be calm, papa; you are at perfect liberty to refuse his request. However laudable Raphael's intention may be, he will humbly submit to your decision."

Felicité knew by experience the best means to overcome her father's emotion. She spoke softly, without raising her voice; she went quietly to her end, and measured her words, to make the old man understand that no one wished to oppose him.

After a moment's silence, she sighed, and said:

" You would rather not know what he wishes to propose to you, papa; I will say no more."

" No, speak, my child."

" Well, if you wish it. Raphael, who desires to return to America, proposes to establish a large commercial house in Antwerp. He wishes you to assist him in it, to become his partner, and took the direction of the house in Antwerp. For that purpose, he will put three hundred thousand francs at your disposal."

The old man uttered a harsh cry, and his features moved convulsively. Felicité had foreseen this crisis; so she bowed her head and remained silent. Mrs. Verboord approached her husband, and said ·

" My friend, it is a simple proposition; reject it if you do not like it, and no one will say a word. Of course, there are reasons which make it difficult to accept such a proposition ; but there are others, which should warn us to examine it well before we positively reject it.   For instance, as the head of a large firm you will be able to make your great business knowledge available ; this mental employment will benefit your nerves more than the doctor's care. We will resume our social position in our native city ; and your fatherly heart, my dear Verboord, will have nothing to dread for the future of your only child."

"It is fearful!" murmured Verboord, gloomily.   "He has rendered my life bitter ; he has made me hate man as an ungrateful creature, and now he comes to present me with money to pay me for my griefs !   After four years of sorrow and trouble, can I receive a charity from my clerk ? Be quiet, be quiet ! I will die poor ; God wills it ; but I will hold up my head till I go to the tomb."

Felicité sighed, and tried to repress her sobs, while tears fell from her eyes, as she sat still.

After a few moments, her mother said :

"Certainly, Verboord, you are right,.we will bravely submit to our fate without blushing.   No one can trouble us.   But Felicité has not expressed it properly, or else you have not understood her.   Mr. Banks needs your assistance, and if you talk of a charity, it is he who comes to ask it of you.   He wishes to establish a house in Antwerp, and as he has to return to America, it is necessary to entrust all he has to some one who understands business.   His proposals are generous and liberal ; he will associate the head of the Antwerp house in all his profits.   Appreciating your vast knowledge, and your generosity, he has thought you might grant him this favor.   You cannot bear him any ill-will, he has too much confidence in your kindness.   Reject his offer, if you like ; but do not refuse to listen to him if

18

only for a few minutes. If he must cross the ocean again
without seeing you, he will be unhappy all his life; and
you, my friend, will perhaps regret this cruel moment."

Felicité had raised her head, and, as she gently caressed
his hand, looked at him beseechingly. He said, feebly:

"I would like to do what you wish. Will he really
leave at my first request? You say he will obey me. But,
alas! the thought alone that my eyes will behold him,
frightens me and excites all my nerves."

"Good heavens!" cried Felicité, in sudden alarm,
"there he is, there he is!"

She kissed her father, asked if Raphael might enter,
drew from him a doubtful consent, and ran across the room,
exclaiming:

"Mamma, mamma, strengthen my father in his good
resolution."

She ran to Raphael, took his hand, led him aside, and
said to him:

"Oh! Raphael! I am very happy. My father is
calmer than usual. Under other circumstances, he could
not have borne such excitement. He has consented to
receive you. If his reason does not desert him, he will
receive you kindly."

"Thank you, thank you, Felicité," replied Raphael.
"Since I saw you, my heart has been full of happiness;
everything is bright before my eyes. Your father will
receive me kindly. Your sweet hope will be realized. I
will be able to pay my mother's debt and mine. I will be
able to call my benefactor by a still dearer name. Come,
come, I am impatient to throw myself into my old employer's arms; come, I already feel his heart beating against
mine."

"No, Raphael, not yet; stay a moment longer. My

mother must have time to strengthen my father for the excitement of your visit. My joy deceives you. My father consenting to see you is such an unexpected happiness, that it has bewildered me. You must not show any emotion. You would throw yourself into his arms. Raphael, this would be sufficient to destroy all our hope. I have come out to warn you. My father is sick, and his nerves are extremely sensitive. Do not forget that violent emotion may effect his brain and disturb his mind. Your appearance alone will be a dangerous experiment for him; but if you will remain quiet till this first impression wears off, he will probably recover from the shock. Be prudent, Raphael, quiet and reserved, carefully watch my father' expression, to judge what you may say to him. To dispose him favorably to you, we have made him believe you have come to beg his pardon. In the beginning, do not speak of anything but that. Humble yourself, admit you are guilty to him, show your gratitude. Afterwards, if he does not order you to leave, speak to him by degrees of your plan, as if asking a favor from him. You have a sensitive heart; you will do your best to succeed. At first, let my father talk, and do not say much yourself. It is the only way to keep him from great excitement."

"It is all right, Felicité, I understand you," he replied, with a sigh. "Alas! is it thus I must meet my benefactor!"

"Do not lose courage," she said, "everything favors us; what we have already gained would have appeared to me this morning impossible. I admit I undertook it without hope; but God has heard my prayer. He will have pity on my poor father and on us, Raphael. Come now, come; who can tell but this day may be one of deliverance and intense joy?"

The young man was deeply agitated, and much pained; Felicité's words left him but little hope. As soon as he entered the room and saw his old master, he began to tremble. The sight of the old man's hair, as white as snow, and his hollow cheeks, pained him more deeply than the severe expression of his flashing eyes. Banks bowed his head upon his breast, and lowered his eyes. He remained thus silent, in the attitude of a man who admits his guilt, and begs for mercy. Felicité joined her hands in supplication. The old man trembled in every limb, and it was evident a bitter conflict was passing within his breast. However, he did not give way to his agitation; the humble attitude of Raphael seemed to give him unexpected strength. After keeping his eyes fixed for a moment upon his clerk, he said:

"Ah! here you are, sir! You are now aware you have treated me badly. Your conscience has reproached you, and certainly with good reason. I loved you as an only son, I wished for your happiness as if you had been my brother's child, yet you abandoned me the moment misfortune befell me, or you could aid and comfort me! Do not try to excuse yourself. They tell me you have repented of your ingratitude. You have come from America to ask my pardon. Well, I forgive you. Be at peace with your heart and conscience. Now leave this house; I am sick, and your presence excites my nerves, and does me harm."

"One word! grant me the privilege of speaking a word!" sighed Banks, who observed in alarm that the face of his old employer was very pale and his lips trembled.

"Speak briefly, then!" replied Verboord. "My patience is nearly exhausted."

"Oh, my kind master! You know that I have acted wrongly toward you, and you generously forgive me. May

God bless you! I will go away with my heart filled with gratitude and joy. But let me tell you, I have never ceased to respect and love the benefactor of my youth. If I had known that any misfortune had befallen you, if I had even imagined my presence would have been useful to you, danger of death would not even have kept me from you."

"Why then did you go away, after your promise?" interrupted the old man

This question embarrassed Raphael, he hesitated, and stammered some unintelligible words.

"Why, tell me why?" repeated Verboord, with feverish impatience.

"An irresistible desire to travel in distant countries, a kind of fever, or wandering of my brain."

"A desire to travel!" cried Verboord, sneeringly. "What nonsense, what folly. And for such a reason, you forgot my love for you. You abandoned me in misfortune, you left me in grief, without assistance or consolation, all to gratify a caprice. What you say is false. Leave me, leave me, your presence makes me ill. Begone! do not touch me, do not touch me, you would kill me!"

He fell back prostrate in his chair, his eyes glistened and turned frightfully beneath his half closed lids; a terrible emotion possessed him, the chair trembled beneath him. Raphael had fallen on his knees, and by his side, Felicité and her mother, all entreating for his forgiveness. But, Verboord, entirely out of his mind, arose, and with much excitement, extended his hand threateningly, and cried

"I ought to curse you; but I will not do it. God will punish you! Do not look at me with those false eyes, like a viper that is to throw forth its venom. The laughter on your lips is cowardly and deceitful. You offer me a charity,

18*

to insult me in my misery, you rejoice in the shame of your victim. Go, go! I beg and entreat of you have pity on my unhappy condition! Ah! I am giving way, I am dying, you have wounded me the second time."

And he fell backwards into his chair and lay there convulsed, panting, and helpless. The two ladies rushed to his assistance, and while Raphael stood in the middle of the room, his head upon his breast, almost annihilated, they took the old man, who was half fainting, by the arms, and led him to the chamber above. At the foot of the stair, the young girl made a sign to Raphael to leave the house.

"For the love of heaven, go away, sir," entreated her mother.

At the head of the stairs, he heard the trembling voice of the old man repeating:

"Go, go, or I will curse you, heartless murderer of my soul!"

But Raphael neither heard nor saw anything; his head reeled; and he felt as if he would lose his reason. He was suddenly aroused from his meditation by Mrs. Verboord's voice at his side, saying anxiously to him:

"Still here, Raphael! I beg you, go! Mr. Verboord may come down. In his moments of insanity, his ideas and wishes are constantly changing. Oh! if he should find you here!"

"Yes, I know it; he would curse me," replied Raphael. "He cannot see me any more; my presence torments him. I go, madam; but before I go I have something to say to you. Be kind enough to hear me; do me the favor to follow me to some place where we can talk in security. Only a few words."

Mrs. Verboord was silent and hesitated.

"Oh! I entreat you, do not refuse!" sighed the young man.

"Well! come, but do not detain me long. There is a little gate at the end of the garden. Come that way to the meadows."

She took a key and went out by the back door, Raphael following her.

"Mrs. Verboord," he said gravely, "you know why I so hastily left Antwerp. You even encouraged my departure, because you knew I was only obeying the voice of duty. I may therefore hope that you believe in my sincerity, and in my disinterested love for my poor master."

"Yes, Raphael, I know your heart, and have never ceased to love you."

"Thank you, madam; you give me courage to carry out my plan; you will assist me, will you not? Listen to what I have decided upon. I will leave here, not to return again till Mr. Verboord is cured; but, though absent, I will watch over him and you and Miss Felicité, as if God had imposed this duty upon me. Henceforth my life has but one object: to overcome my benefactor's terrible disease. I will go to Paris, London and Vienna, if necessary, to consult the most distinguished physicians. I will bring men to Brasschaet whose names are known throughout the world. Hope, therefore, madam; comfort and encourage Miss Felicité. Though far from here, I will be always with you, and I will find means of ascertaining Mr. Verboord's condition every day. Now, I have one thing more to speak to you about; I have a favor to ask of you; but I do not know how to express my wish without wounding you. Mr. Verboord ought to live more comfortably; his dwelling ought to be improved, his garden filled with flowers; in short, every-thing around him ought to be pleasing to his sight, to prevent his recalling the loss of his fortune. To accomplish this, money is necessary: I have ten thousand francs in my pocket-book, if you would—"

"Oh, do not speak of such things," sighed Mrs. Ver boord, a blush of shame upon her checks. "Let us at least preserve the pride of poverty in your eyes, Raphael!"

"I feared a refusal, and I will try to accomplish this part of my plan in another way. Now I will leave you. I am going to Paris, but will soon return Do not speak of me again to Mr. Verboord; do not let him hear my name. Be careful to spare him any excitement. Whatever else I may have to tell you, you will learn from others. Good-bye, Mrs. Verboord. I have commenced the struggle, and will continue it till I am conquered. There is no room in my heart for another thought. Before daybreak I will be in the capital of France. Let us trust in God's help."

He arose and walked towards the garden gate. Mrs. Verboord followed him, much affected, and, as he opened the door, said

"I bless you, Raphael, as wife and mother. God grant you may succeed in your generous plan; and may you return to us under happier circumstances."

"Yes, madam, you shall see me when my patron is cured."

Twelve days had passed since Raphael's visit. The violent scene which had occurred between him and the feeble old man had not had the expected effect upon the brain of the latter. The remembrance of that sad meeting had gradually faded away, and it might have been supposed that it had not left the slightest impression upon his mind, if he had not become more silent than ever, sometimes passing whole days without uttering a word. The last night, however, he seemed suddenly to grow worse. He talked much and rapidly; during the whole night he raved of business and money, and gritted his teeth as he uttered Banks' name. These were the usual signs of a violent nervous attack, and the only means of preventing it was to be perfectly quiet. Suddenly the old man gave a cry of joy, and struck his hand upon his desk.

"Ah! Ah, yes, that's it! I have found it. We wil be worth several millions. An angel from heaven has come to me, and given me the power to look into the future."

He rubbed his hands and laughed at the thought of his future fortune; then continued ·

"You think I am dreaming? I thought so too, but it is a mistake. What is easier than to amass a large amount of money, when we know before-hand what is going to happen in the world? In the course of the next month the price of coffee will rise higher than ever. It is inevitable; the reasons were revealed to me last night. I have calculated them, and traced them to their source. To-morrow I will begin to buy up all the coffee in Antwerp. I will send my orders to London, Amsterdam, Havre and Hamburg; yes, even across the sea to the country which produces it. Then when the price has risen to its highest, I will sell, and make two millions—three, four, many millions! Well, Laurence, what do you say to that, and you, my dear Felicité? To become so rich in a few months is nice, is it not?"

The two ladies tried to smile, but said nothing. The old man's thoughts took another direction, and his face clouded.

"To dare to offer me charity," he murmured. "Ungrateful scoundrel. He thinks we have become poor, and that I have neither sense nor strength to try my fortune again and regain what I have lost. He shall see! he shall see!"

After a few moments he smiled cheerfully, and said:

"To-morrow I will send for my master mason and hundreds of workmen of all kinds. The chateau will go up like magic. We will take the woods and fields behind our garden; we will dig, carry away, plant! In a few weeks we will have a beautiful park! My dear Felicité will marry the son of the richest merchant in Antwerp. The chateau will be her dower. For my dear Laurence I will build a house in the city, as large and beautiful as a palace. Yes, yes! my joy consists solely in working for the happiness of others; and I will do it with zeal, courage and love to the end of my life. I bless a merciful God for having left me sense and strength to do my duty as husband and father!"

He resumed his pen, and began to count with nervous energy. He gasped for breath, his teeth were clenched, and he seemed to be near fainting. Perhaps a ray of light crossed his mind. The poor old man suspected he was the victim of a delusion. He turned towards his companions, and cried:

"My paper? Where is to-day's *Precurseur?* Give it to me at once. I want it!"

"Dear papa, the postman will be here in an hour," replied Felicité. "He will bring the paper."

"Oh dear! How late he is!" sighed Verboord. "Our fortune, our happiness may depend upon his diligence!"

He struck his forehead like one who tries to resume a broken train of thought. After some moments of vain endeavor he said, despondingly:

"Laurence, all these mental efforts are for the happiness of yourself and our good Felicité. Leave me alone a little while, I beg of you."

Mrs. Verboord immediately went out by the back door, followed by Felicité.

They walked to the bank near the flower-garden, sat down, and resumed their work.

Tears were in Mrs. Verboord's eyes, while her breast heaved with bitter sighs.

Felicité overcame her own grief, and tried to comfort her mother, assuring her that Raphael would succeed in curing her father's malady; she described the pleasant and happy life the future had in reserve for them, and said, with a blush upon her cheeks:

"I also had a dream last night, and I have more right than my poor father to think an angel from heaven has revealed the future to me. I thought I entered a large church, with you and my father holding my hands. We passed between crowds of people; they praised my looks, they said I was beautiful, and·a wreath of orange flowers adorned my head. I was about to be married. The priest waited for us at the altar. Raphael was to be my husband, and you pressed him like a loving mother to your heart. My husband, the companion of my life, was also the saviour of my father! Noble and generous being! I cannot speak, mamma; my tears choke me."

"Good Banks," said Mrs. Verboord, after a short silence. "May the God of mercy bless him for his gratitude!"

"You see, mamma, sooner or later goodness has its reward."

"Ah, my child, your father was able to do very little for Raphael. We would have done the same for any other. So, Raphael does not owe us so much. Can we accept the sacrifice of his entire fortune?"

"Yes, mamma, accept Raphael's offer: his gifts are prompted by the purest feelings of the human soul—grati-tude and love. Oh! I would proudly accept it all: his favors, his fortune, his name, believing, mamma, that a refusal would render him unhappy."

"Are you quite sure of it, my child?"

"Why are you so incredulous, mamma? Be assured, Raphael will be a dutiful son to you. Do be hopeful, mamma. Good heavens, what is that frightful cry cf distress! It is papa! Alas! what has happened?"

They sprang up and rushed towards the house, pale and trembling. As they entered the room they perceived that Mr. Verboord had fallen back, with his head against the chair. He seemed to have fainted; around him, on the floor, were papers and letters, which had dropped from his lap as he fell back. Felicité took her father's hands, and called him by name. Her ineffectual efforts alarmed them extremely. Mrs. Verboord ran to the kitchen for water, and moistened his head and hands, while she said to her child:

"Do not be frightened, Felicité, my child. You see your father has fainted. It has happened before. He will, perhaps, escape a nervous attack. Do not weep. Help me: hold your father's hands in the basin, the fresh water will revive him."

For a long time their efforts were in vain; the old man remained stretched out like death. They soon became much alarmed. Seeing how her daughter trembled, Mrs. Verboord said to her, with assumed calmness:

"You are wrong, Felicité. Be reasonable. A fainting fit sometimes lasts a half hour; he will come to. If we could put him to bed it would soon be over; but we are not strong enough to lift him. Let us wait till he recovers. Take a chair, Felicité, and sit down. We can pray."

"Mamma, I will run for the doctor? Mr. Drooms is at home at this hour; he will come—"

"No, stay here; Mr. Drooms will bleed your father, and you know the city physician does not approve of it under any circumstances. Besides, your father dislikes Mr. Drooms, and to see him at his side when he awakes would be sufficient in itself to throw him into a nervous fever. Our situation is very sad, my child; but our duty is to submit patiently to our fate, in the assurance that God will not desert us in our trouble."

There was a long silence. For some time Mrs. Verboord continued her efforts to revive her husband; but at last, fatigued and discouraged, she suddenly took her daughter's hand and said:

"Felicité, go for the doctor; be quick, be quick, it is time!"

Felicité ran towards the door, but before she could reach it, a piercing cry, either of joy or fright, recalled her.

"Come back, come back," exclaimed her mother in a low voice. "Thank God, he revives! His hand has moved. Look at his cheeks; they are not so pale; sit down: do not let us make him angry; let us conceal our tears, that he may not observe our distress and alarm."

With beating hearts they went a few steps away from the sick man, and watched him closely.

There was a scarcely perceptible movement of the old man's fingers; the blood began to flow through his veins. The color gradually returned to his cheeks, and his breast began to heave; but his eyes still remained closed. After a moment, which seemed to them a century, the sick man opened his eyes, and looked silently at his wife and daughter. The latter had been unable to restrain a cry of anguish and alarm. She arose and looked at her father, as if something strange had happened.

In truth, her father's eyes, though very sad, had a different expression from what they had before. An unclouded light shone from the soul within. Her father stretched out his hands, and said feebly:

19

"Ah, there are my good angels, who never abandon me! Come to me, come."

They both went to him, and tenderly pressed his hands.

" My good Felicité, my dear Laurence," he said, " how glad I am to see you! What has happened to me? I feel as if I had come back from the grave!"

" Nothing, Verboord, excepting a fainting fit. It is over now. You feel better than before, do you not?"

"I have been asleep, have I not?" he asked, without noticing her words. " I have had a long and deep sleep. It seems to me I have been asleep for a year in this arm-chair. What strange dreams I have had! I thought I had lost my fortune, had become poor; but news came from America. What was it? Ah! I remember! The house of Ortado was going to pay its debts; I would recover all my fortune. I dreamed I became insane from joy. But no, no, it was not a dream! The mail did come! Speak, speak! is it not so? The mail brought me a letter—a letter from Charleston in America, via London—and money, a great amount of money? But where is the letter? Where is the money? Can it be a dream? Oh, relieve me from my doubts! Tell me, tell me—am I insane, or is it the truth? Look beside the desk; under the papers, perhaps."

He tried to rise, but fell back in his chair, holding out his hand, and pointing with his fingers to the papers which had fallen to the ground.

Mrs. Verboord tried to be calm. Felicité, to satisfy her father, picked up the papers.

" There it is, there it is," joyfully exclaimed Verboord; " the letter and the bank notes. Give it to me, give it to me, my child! Oh, thank God, I am not insane!"

He took the letter and money from his daughter, and pressed them to his heart.

"Peace, peace, I beg you. Let me breathe; leave me, my heart beats so violently. Ah, it was not a dream! The happiness of my wife! the future of my dear child!"

Tears fell from his eyes.

Mrs. Verboord was pale and silent; Felicité fell upon her knees. They still feared it might be a fancy, which would be followed by bitter disappointment; but the letter was there, and it was really notes, bank notes which Felicité had picked up.

"Come," said the sick man, after a long silence, "It is such great happiness, one might easily die of joy; but I feel quiet and calm. You look astonished. I understand. You cannot believe we have become rich, and you are impatient to know how it has happened. I had nearly forgotten it; but now my memory has returned. Listen, Laurence, listen, Felicité; all your doubts will vanish, and you' will thank God for such unexpected good fortune."

They drew near to him. as he opened the letter, and said:

"I was alone, I remember distinctly. The postman came and gave me a letter. The news it contained affected me so deeply that I became insensible. I will read the letter to you; you will then be satisfied of our good fortune. Listen; I was mistaken; the letter is from Antwerp; it is sent by Wulf, the banker, with whom I formerly kept my account. This is what he says:

"ANTWERP, July 15th, 1857.

Sir :—

"By order of the banking house of Stanhope & Co., London, I have the honor to inform you, that Henry Ortado, son of Christopher Ortado, of Charleston, has decided to pay the debts left by his late father. The amount due you, according to the books he left, is forty-three thousand dollars. If you do not consider this an exact calculation, I beg you to make out your account against the house of Ortado.

"Until there is a regular settlement, I enclose you herewith the sum of four thousand dollars, in Belgium notes, which Messrs. Stanhope requested me to send you immediately. The debts of the Ortado firm will be closed in ten payments, if possible, quarterly; but, under all circumstances you will receive during this year, at least, twelve thousand dollars on your account.

"I understand, sir, that you are indisposed. Do not take the trouble to come to the city. In a few days I will have the pleasure of calling on you myself. You can then give me your receipt, and we can speak more fully of this important matter. With every assurance of my sympathy,

"F. C. WULF."

Felicité threw herself on her father's neck and embraced him joyfully; but her mother gave her a sign to restrain her joy. It was not only the restoration of their money which filled Felicité with much delight, it was the hope, almost the certainty, she felt of her father's cure. Verboord continued:

"Do you understand, Laurence? It is a fortune of two hundred and twenty-one thousand francs, which is restored to us. Before the end of next year, we will possess the sum of sixty-five thousand francs! I am nearly overcome by my happiness. Not for myself; for you and our child. It was a cruel martyrdom to my heart to think that poverty would be your fate on earth; that the future of our only child was ruined forever! You do not seem pleased, my good Laurence?"

"Yes, I thank God, and am very happy," she replied; "but a man ought to be sensible, and keep as calm in prosperity as in misfortune."

"Misfortune, misfortune!" repeated Verboord, looking quietly around the room.

Mrs. Verboord said very sadly:

"My friend, grant me a favor."

"A favor, Laurence? You ask a favor? Command me and I will be delighted to obey."

" Well, I wish you to keep quiet. You have been very ill, Verboord, and although you appear cured, you ought not to excite yourself. Be calm, do not talk so much, it may do you harm. This fear alarms us, and we will be very grateful if you will grant us the favor we ask."

The old man looked at his wife in astonishment, and made some faint effort to overcome his feelings. Felicité and her mother watched his movements, and observed with anxiety that his expression became gradually more gloomy. At last he asked, as if talking to himself:

" What has happened to me? The letter is dated July 1857. Four years? Where are they? They have been to me but a single day! I have been sick. An astonishing sickness, to sleep four years! And I remember nothing whatever of what has happened. O, Laurence, what fearful sickness has afflicted me, to cause such a blank in my life?"

"A sickness which is not at all unusual," replied the lady; " you had a nervous fever; it is now cured; but you ought to be quiet, my dear Verboord."

He bowed his head and returned to his own thoughts, repeating in a low voice· " A nervous fever! a nervous fever!" He was then silent, becoming more deeply buried in thought.

Mrs. Verboord began to fear another attack would again obscure his restored reason; she took her husband's hand, and said:

" Verboord, do not refuse to follow the advice of your Laurence; take a little sleep; we will lead you to your room. When you are quite calm, we will talk of it, and rejoice over it without fear. Ah, I entreat you, my friend, grant my prayer."

" Thank you,. my good Laurence," he replied. " I do not

19*

know why it is, but I feel the need of silence and rest, more than I can tell you. Yes, let me collect my ideas, my thoughts. You may assist me," he murmured, with a smile, " as you doubtless have during these four sad years. So be it; but it is not necessary, I feel strong enough."

At the foot of the stairs, he stopped, and said:

" Is there not something which alarms you? I can guess what it is. Be hopeful. If you will leave me alone with my thoughts, I will get rid of the doubt which troubles me. Be quiet, both of you; your apprehension may vanish forever."

Assisted by the two ladies, he went up stairs. A few moments later they came down; but they had no sooner closed the door, than they threw themselves in each others arms, and burst into tears.

Felicité was the first to recover herself, and exclaimed:

" Papa will be cured! Papa will be cured! We are rich again! Oh! what will Raphael say when he learns this!"

But her mother put her hand on her mouth, and murmured:

" My child, my child, do not utter that name again. Your father may hear it. You know how the sound of it agitates him."

" Yes, yes," replied Felicité, " you are right, mamma. We ought to be careful how we speak till papa's cure is certain; but I cannot restrain my joy; I must speak, I must repeat our happiness, if only to these four walls."

" Felicité," said Mrs. Verboord, taking her hand, " let us not forget whence man receives all his benefits, all his happiness. Let us lift our hearts to Him who has granted our prayers."

" Oh, merciful God, may Thy name be blessed on earth," said Felicité.

The two ladies knelt down, and bowed their heads in silent, but heartfelt prayer.

CHAPTER XI.

FELICITÉ stood at the window which looked out upon the front gate. Her appearance was entirely changed. She wore an elegant silk dress, which had been carefully put away since the days of their prosperity, and her golden hair was wrapped about her head in heavy braids, a bright smile parted her lips, and her face was radiant with happiness. Her eyes shone with unwonted joy, while she gazed into space, as if dreaming of a happy future. A stout young peasant girl came out from the kitchen, and said, respectfully:

"I have finished cleaning, miss. Shall I begin to pick the chicken?"

"Yes, Marianne, if you have no other work. Mamma is coming down, and will tell you what you have to do."

"The cauliflower also ought to be prepared, if you would be kind enough to show me how I ought to do it."

"It is very simple, Marianne; I will show you if you wish; but you have plenty of time. My father is going to the city; we will not dine till three o'clock."

"You must excuse my awkwardness at first, miss," said the girl. "I have never lived with rich people, and I am afraid of not doing right."

"Do not be afraid," replied Felicité, with a pleasant smile. "I will assist you in the kitchen; besides my father will be tired and have a good appetite. The dinner to-day must be very nice. I want you to be praised for it. You seem a good girl; and we are going to live in the city."

The woman thanked her, and, at the same moment, Mrs. Verboord came down stairs.

"Well, mamma, how is papa?" asked Felicité.

"Still calm, with no symptoms of sickness. How happy I am! Since yesterday the world has seemed to me a paradise; everything is bright, and my heart is full of joy!"

"Papa is cured! Oh, if Raphael could know it!"

"He slept all night without the slightest movement, and probably without dreaming, for his breathing was perfectly regular."

The delighted girl threw her arms around her mother's neck, and exclaimed, as she kissed her:

"Thank God! Papa is cured, decidedly cured! You shake your head, mamma, do you still doubt? No, no, have faith in the future. There will not be happier people in the world than ourselves."

"Certainly, Felicite, we have reason to hope; but in one day we cannot abandon ourselves entirely to joy."

"But, my dear mamma, why worry yourself unnecessarily? Papa is cured, believe me. Yesterday afternoon and evening, he talked calmly and pleasantly with us, without the least excitement. Every word was rational; and although we had to tell him what had happened during his sickness, his mind seemed wonderfully clear."

"His strange resolve to go to the city troubles me, Felicité. You have not observed it, because your joy blinds you; but with the reasons which he gave for wishing to go to Antwerp, there was a reserve which made me doubt if he were really quite sane."

"You are mistaken, mamma," replied Felicité. "My father avowed his intention very naturally. From love for us, he wishes to make immediate use of the money which has been sent; but he does not wish to spend any of it till he has seen the banker and given him a receipt. My father was very exact in business and money matters, before he was ill. It is a proof that he is really cured."

Mrs. Verboord sighed deeply.

"Ah, mamma, you make me tremble," exclaimed Felicité. "Are you concealing the truth from me? Is papa not so well to-day."

"I tell you truly, he is better to-day than yesterday; but, notwithstanding my entreaties, he refuses to let me accompany him; that is one thing which does not appear natural. Besides, my child, do you not think it alarms me to have your father go alone to the city, exposed to all the sad and trying circumstances he may meet with there? Will he not return very much agitated? If he would only consent to take you with him, he would, at least, have some one to watch over him. But entirely alone!"

"I am dressed," said the young girl. "Suppose I ask him to let me go with him? Yesterday, I did not make much effort."

"No, my child, that would annoy him. You do not know how to control yourself. At the first cheerful word from your father you are carried away by your joy. See how imprudent you were yesterday evening! More than ten times you made some allusion to Raphael, apparently with the intention of bringing his name into the conversation. Fortunately, your father did not understand you; otherwise, you might have been the means of exciting very painful feelings."

"I beg your pardon, mamma," stammered the young

girl, with crimson cheeks. "You are right; yesterday, I was beside myself; to-day I will be calm, and will not say a word to trouble papa. Let me make the effort, at least. He will not refuse me; he is so kind to me!"

"Be it so, my child; make a last effort; but do not insist too much. I hear him coming down, be prudent."

Mr. Verboord appeared in the doorway, and kissed his daughter very tenderly.

The expression of the old man was gentle yet grave. A smile parted his lips, and his eye was bright, but there was something sad in his feeble movements.

"Well! Laurence," he asked, "have you sent the girl to the village? Will the carriage be ready?"

"The girl has been gone some time. I have no doubt you will find the horse at the gate."

"Good-bye, my dear children, till this afternoon!" said Mr. Verboord. "At two o'clock, perhaps earlier, I will return. After visiting Wulf, the banker, I will look at some houses to rent, and if I see any pleasantly situated, I will call on the owner. I had also thought of asking your former dressmaker to accompany me to Brasschaet, to talk to you about the wardrobe I wish to have prepared for you immediately, but I have changed my mind. I will arrange all business matters to-day with Mr. Wulf, and then I will have nothing else to think about, and to-morrow, we will go together to Antwerp, to buy all we need."

Felicité threw her arms around his neck, and murmured:

"Dear papa, you will not be angry if I ask a favor of you?"

"Certainly not, my child. If there is anything you wish, tell me unhesitatingly."

"Oh, papa! let me go with you to the city; I will be so grateful to you."

Without showing the slightest vexation, the old man smiled and said :

"You want something, I suppose, from the city. Is it a jewel or a dress? Whatever it may be, I will be happy to bring it to you."

"No, I want to go with you, papa."

"That is impossible. You may go to-morrow, my child."

"I submit, dear papa," said the young girl, sadly.

Mrs. Verboord looked beseechingly at her husband. The old man evidently understood the true reason of the wish to accompany him, for he looked from one to the other, took a hand of each, and said :

"You will not be unhappy and anxious during my absence, will you? Your love for me makes me uneasy. I know the idea of my going alone to the city alarms you, because you think my nerves are as sensitive as before. You are mistaken ; God has not given me a partial blessing, my disease has left me, and I am satisfied will not return."

Felicité gave an exclamation of delight.

"I understand," continued her father. "You are both doubtful of my cure, and wish to accompany me to watch me. I assure you it is no longer necessary. I have some affairs to arrange in the city, and must be alone. I cannot now tell you what it is, but on my return you shall know. Remain quiet and try to think during my absence of what we will buy to give us the comforts of which you have so long been deprived."

He again pressed their hands and went out.

"Well, well, mamma," cried Felicité, unable to restrain her joy, "do you still believe papa is not cured?"

"It is astonishing, he is certainly cured! Thank God for it!" murmurd Mrs. Verboord.

"He seems to be the same as before he was sick," exclaimed Felicité. "His thoughts are so clear, and he is so calm. How quickly he understood the cause of our anxiety. Ah! he no longer needs watching, he is entirely himself."

Mrs. Verboord sat down and remained a moment without speaking.

"Do you still doubt, mamma?" asked Felicité in surprise.

"No, my child, my apprehension is all gone. My emotion is caused by my joy. Let me recover myself. It is like a dream. On the same day your father is cured of his disease and our fortune is restored. Heaven seems to have loaded us with favors. How bright our future appears!"

"Yes, mamma, brighter than you think," exclaimed Felicité, joyfully. "Our happiness will be complete, nothing will be wanting. My father will become just and generous again, as God made him. He can no longer remain angry with Raphael; perhaps he may receive him with pleasure, for his reason will tell him he deserves his friendship and esteem. Then the last wish of our hearts will be accomplished. We will all live together, united by the truest affection. Raphael and I will make your life so happy that it will be an earthly paradise."

Mrs. Verboord dried her tears.

"I pray your hopes may be realized," she said. "You deserve it, and Raphael also. But, my child, do not speak so soon to your father of Raphael. It would be dangerous; we ought to give his reason time to grow strong."

"I will be prudent, mamma, and I will wait. But when the moment comes, I will frankly tell my father the truth. Of course, a young girl always hesitates to reveal the secrets of her heart; but I will not conceal my love, mother, and I will proudly tell my father I have loved Raphael from childhood."

"Your father will probably consent to anything which can make you happy, my child; but who knows? He was very angry at Raphael's unexpected departure before his mind was affected. Suppose this feeling should remain, notwithstanding his cure?"

"It is impossible, mamma, I will tell him why Raphael went away."

"Have patience, Felicité, and be prudent. It may yet be some time before we can venture to speak to your father of Raphael. I will help you, as a mother naturally would. Be hopeful, I do not doubt we will succeed."

"Dear mamma," said the young girl, "how Raphael will love you!"

"But, Felicité, suppose your father should have other plans for you? His fortune is restored. Perhaps he may remember that Raphael was his clerk."

Felicité remained silent a moment. She shook her head as if driving away an unpleasant thought, and exclaimed:

"Clerk? Could my father think of that, knowing what Raphael wished to do for him and us? I do not believe it, mamma. However, if a feeling of false pride should render my father unjust, I would oppose him for the first time in my life with courage and perseverance. I would beg, pray, and weep until I had overcome his opposition. Raphael, who was unjustly accused, has forgotten everything, excepting my father's kindness. He would sacrifice the fortune he has hardly gained to the cure of his old employer. Now we no longer need his assistance; his liberality will remain unrewarded, and he must remain unhappy forever because God has loaded us with blessings."

Mrs. Verboord took her daughter's hand.

"Be calm, my dear Felicité," she said, "you are too easily excited. Let me arrange it."

20

The conversation soon took another turn. The mother and daughter began to entertain more cheerful thoughts, to form plans for the future. They talked of everything, even of the house Felicité and Raphael would occupy when married, when suddenly the door opened quietly, and the young girl sprang from her chair, exclaiming:

" Raphael! Raphael! "

The young man stood before her smiling, but before he could speak, she seized both his hands, and cried, with sparkling eyes:

" Raphael, you do not know what has happened. We have become rich! "

" How is your father? " asked Banks, very gravely.

" My father is cured! "

" Entirely cured? "

" Yes, all of a sudden; a letter which restored his fortune, restored his health at the same time. O Raphael! my friend, you will no longer be able to accomplish your generous project; but I will not forget that you have devoted your life and fortune to my father's happiness."

" Then he is completely cured? " he again asked.

" Thoroughly; and I hope will have no return; his mind seems unusually clear."

Raphael raised his eyes to heaven, and cried:

" I thank Thee, oh my God, for blessing my efforts! my ruse has succeeded! "

" Your ruse! what do you mean? " asked the two ladies, in alarm.

" The letter and fortune were feigned. Ortado died insolvent in prison. But how sad this information makes you! Did you also believe it was true. Ah, I did not think of that. Forgive me; I could not do otherwise. To cure my benefactor was my supreme object, and I had not time to warn you. Perhaps I would not have done it; it might have prevented the fulfilment of my plans."

Mrs. Verboord and her daughter trembled, as they looked at him in silence. He took a chair, sat down, and continued ·

"I beg you to listen to me, I will explain all, and you will forgive me. As I told you, the evening I left you, I went to Paris. I was very unhappy and possessed by a feverish impatience. I began to think I had better go direct to London, where I could confer with the banker of our firm, and where a physician resides, who is celebrated all over the world for his treatment of diseases of the brain. Impelled, doubtless, by a secret inspiration, I left the railroad to Paris at Lille, and took the road to Calais, where I sailed in the first vessel for London. The physician I wished to consult was out of town. Four long days passed before I could see him. He questioned me for an hour on the character of the disease and the person affected. When, after reflection, he gave his opinion, I was in despair. According to him, a complete cure must be regarded as impossible, because the trouble had existed four years, and originated in a cause which could not be removed While I listened to his explanations, with bleeding heart, he made a remark which caused me to tremble with hope and joy. He said that a sudden event—something almost impossible—might offer a chance of curing him; that was to say, if his lost fortune was as suddenly restored to him as it was taken away, then perhaps——. My resolution was instantly taken, and I explained it to the doctor. He approved of it, and accompanied me to the banker's, who, after some hesitation, and after receiving security, permitted me to use his name in this humane act. I returned to Antwerp· The banker Wulf, who had been a friend of Mr. Verboord, also consented to assist me. The signature of the firm of Stanhope & Co., London, rendered the matter very easy, and I immediately placed in his hands the necessary sum. We wrote the letter, and trusted it to the mail to avoid suspicion. I had little hope. This morning, Mr. Wulf sent a message to Mr. Walput's house, requesting me to go to him immediately. I went, expecting news of the effect of the letter. Mr. Wulf informed me that Mr. Verboord had just left his office, and had given him a receipt for the amount sent. How deeply the banker's words moved me you may imagine. According to him, there was not the slightest trace of insanity either in Mr. Verboord's manner or language. On the contrary, he questioned Mr. Wulf with wonderful clearness of mind on the slightest circumstances connected with the unexpected restoration of his fortune, and he would have embarrassed the banker if we had not taken every precaution. Mr. Verboord told him that he would remain in town till twelve o'clock, at least. I knew, therefore, I would not find him here. Doubt and uncertainty made me miserable. I took a carriage and drove out to Brasschaet. You now tell me my old employer is decidedly cured. I have been able to save Felicité's father from the depth of madness! My object is accomplished. It is sufficient. I will bless God for this favor as long as I live.'

Mrs. Verboord kept her head bent down, while Felicité looked at the young man with tears in her eyes. She was pale, and appeared anxious.

"You are weeping, Felicité!" exclaimed Banks, in astonishment. "Not from joy, either. Is not your father's cure the greatest favor heaven could bestow upon you? Have you concealed anything from me?"

"No, no; it is not that," sobbed the young girl. "If

we must return to poverty, God's will be done; but when my father learns he has been deceived——."

"Alas! he will again lose his reason, and probably forever," sighed her mother.

"Oh, no, Mrs. Verboord," replied Raphael, "your fear is unfounded. Mr. Verboord cannot discover our ruse. Our precautions are too well taken. I understand that your delicacy of feeling revolts against the thought that this money, of which you must necessarily make free use, belongs to Raphael Banks. But is there not another tie between us besides my gratitude and my promise to my dying mother? Will not the sacred bond into which we wish to enter induce you to accept this fortune as the help of a friend or brother?"

"Noble-hearted Raphael!" said Mrs. Verboord, taking the young man's hands. "I bless you for your generosity. Yet, it may be impossible for us to show our gratitude for your favors. Suppose Mr. Verboord, not knowing what you are doing for him, should always continue to believe he has reason to be angry with you?"

A shudder ran through Raphael, and he trembled visibly.

"Oh, mamma, do not be so cruel to him," begged Felicité. "My father is no longer sick; he will become kind and just as he used to be."

"Certainly, madam," said Raphael, "my soul hopes for a reward, and I know my life will be one of sorrow, if the bright star which arose before my eyes should again disappear; but remember, I came from America with the intention of employing my fortune in returning the favors of my old employer. I then fully believed that Felicité's marriage had destroyed all hope for me. Suppose your fears correct; I would mourn the cruelty of fate; but I would still be grateful to God for permitting me to become

20*

the saviour of my benefactor, and to fulfil my mother's last prayer. My entire fortune is not too much to give for such a blessing."

"Do not despair, my noble friend," murmured Felicité. "If my father does not know what you are doing for him, I know it. Whatever the feeling may be which fills my heart, admiration, gratitude, or love, it will give me strength to fulfil my duty to my father's saviour."

Raphael looked lovingly at Felicité, and said:

"Mrs. Verboord, this money is a restitution; and if you and Mr. Verboord and Felicité all wish to refuse it, you cannot do so. Who can prevent my paying the debts of Ortado? If necessary, I will go to Charleston and give my whole fortune to Christopher Ortado's son, on condition that he pays his father's debts. Will you then refuse to receive what legitimately belongs to you?"

Felicité and her mother looked at him in admiration.

He raised his hands beseechingly, and said:

"Oh, Mrs. Verboord, be kind to me and accept the return of your favors to me, and the price of your love for my mother!"

Mrs. Verboord could no longer restrain her emotion. She arose, and threw her arms around the young man's neck, and kissed him affectionately, as she exclaimed:

"O Raphael! you love my poor husband more than if he were your father. Come to me, and be my son; I do indeed feel grateful. Let us hope a more sacred tie will soon unite us; but, be it as it may, command us and we will obey. We accept this fortune from you!"

Raphael trembled, he felt some one touch his hand softly with their lips, and bathe it with tears. He started back, and stammered in a scarcely intelligible voice:

'O, Felicité! what are you doing?"

There was a moment's silence, during which they all seemed disposed to yield to their emotions. Banks was the first to recover himself.

"Thank you, Mrs. Verboord," he said, "now I am happy. Let us sit down and talk calmly. I cannot remain here long, and it would be dangerous to let Mr. Verboord, on his return, suspect you have been so much excited. Listen, I pray you. The London doctor told me what was to be done if our efforts succeeded in whole or in part. Such a cure is not completed in a day; before the sick man's reason is strengthened, and there is danger of a relapse, you must endeavor to spare him any unpleasant feelings, and oppose him as little as possible. You must therefore permit him to have free use of the money he has received, and also of that which will be regularly sent to him, according to the promise in the letter. Above all, be cheerful, and never speak of anything which may induce serious reflection. You will, probably, not see me for a long time, and I will take care that Mr. Verboord shall not meet me. Do not be anxious about me. I will watch the progress of his cure as attentively as if I lived near him. Do not utter my name, and should he do so, pretend to be indifferent. When the time comes, I will find means of informing you. If you should have anything to communicate to me, Mr. Walput, with whom I am now staying, will receive your message. His wife, Lucy Spelt, who now knows, Felicité, that in your heart you have always been her friend, is impatient to again meet your mother and yourself."

A step was heard upon the porch; Mrs. Verboord looked towards the window.

"Oh dear, there is my husband," she exclaimed, in a low voice. "He looks sad, he is pale. What has happened?"

" Run, run," cried Felicité.

Banks hurried towards the door; but the young girl detained him, and pushed him into the kitchen, exclaiming:

" No, no, not that way, he will see you! Go into the garden! Quick, here he is! Oh, dear," she continued, "the little gate is closed. Go and sit down on the bank below, you cannot be seen from here. Wait till mamma brings you the key."

While Raphael hastened to the lower end of the garden, she returned and entered the room as her father opened the door.

The old man was very pale, and his face bore traces of great anxiety. Ilis wife and daughter looked at him, and trembled with fear; for they felt satisfied something unpleasant had happened. Perhaps his reason had again left him. He sank into a chair, as if overcome with fatigue, waited a moment to recover his breath, and said:

" Laurence, Felicité, a bitter disappointment has wounded my heart. I would gladly conceal from you the cause of my depression, but I cannot leave you under a false impression. Ah! I was so happy because I hoped to be able to reward your love and your long continued sorrows. I thought only of you and what I could do to render life pleasant and agreeable to you. This bright dream has vanished. Fortune has not been restored to me. I am as poor and helpless as before."

The two ladies were silent, rejoiced to find their apprehensions were without foundation.

" This fortune," he continued, " was a ruse, a stratagem to cure me. He who used it has gained his end. May God bless him for his generosity! But it is very sad for me to feel unable to raise you from poverty, to be unable to secure my child a comfortable future. Alas! what bright dreams my father's heart must renounce!"

Felicite kissed him.

" Oh, dear papa," she said, " do not be so unhappy.
It was not our humble life which made us sad. Your sickness alone caused us to suffer. You are cured, cured forever! All the riches in the world are not worth this
supreme happiness. Throw aside your sadness; have
courage; you shall see that mamma and I will always be
happy!"

" But, my friend, what about Mr. Wulf, the banker, and
the twenty thousand francs, which are there in the secre-
tary?" asked Mrs. Verboord.

" We will return the money to my saviour."

" To your saviour? Who is he?"

" I do not know."

" You are deceived by appearances, Verboord."

" No; judge for yourself, Laurence. I will explain how
I discovered the secret: Since yesterday evening I have
had some misgivings. The letter seemed strange; to send
such a large sum of money without any previous notice did
not appear natural. I believed my anxiety had no foundation; but I dared not, and did not, wish to use the money
until I had satisfied myself of the reality of the restitution.
The replies of Wulf to my questions were not such as satisfied me. I observed he was embarrassed, and endeavored
to avoid any reply to some of my objections. This increased
my anxiety and uncertainty. I determined to relieve myself of this distressing suspicion. Mr. Dorneval also lost a
large amount by the failure of Ortado; if the debts were
paid, he must necessarily know it. I went to see Dorneval.
He was astonished at what he called my credulity, and told
me Christopher Ortado had died insolvent in prison. Mr.
Dorneval's son went to Charleston, and learned positively
that there was no hope of any payment, however small, be-

cause Ortado left neither children nor relations who could make any sacrifices to restore his name. You see, therefore, that the letter and sending of the money were a stratagem to cure me. It was God himself who inspired the generous man with this plan, which he saw was the only way to restore the light to my troubled mind!"

"But do you not know who he is, papa?" asked Felicité, scarcely able to restrain her emotion.

"Who is he? I only have my suspicions. Dorneval, when I told him what had happened, suggested Raphael."

"Raphael Banks?" asked Felicité.

"Yes, my child, Raphael has made a large fortune in America, and has returned to Antwerp. If Mr. Dorneval's opinion is correct, I am indebted to Raphael for my cure. I thought I had reason to hate him. During my sickness his image appeared to me in my dreams like that of a traitor. Can he be my saviour? No, no, he abandoned me in misfortune; he is an ungrateful—"

Felicité put her hand over his mouth, and thus stopped the harsh words which were about to fall from his lips.

"Be quiet, be quiet, dear papa," she cried. "Raphael has blessed you! He has never ceased to love you. He would sacrifice his whole fortune, his life itself, to see us happy."

Frightened at her involuntary avowal, she fell! on her knees at his feet, and raised her hands beseechingly to him. Mrs. Verboord stood by, trembling from head to foot.

"Am I then really indebted to Raphael for the restoration of my reason?" stammered the old man, with extreme sadness.

"To Raphael, papa; he alone has saved you, in gratitude and love!"

"May God forgive me! He was willing to sacrifice himself for my happiness, and I have hated him, and may perhaps have cursed him, while out of my mind!"

"But now, now, papa?" asked Felicité.

"Now, my child, I bless him; now I admire his generosity; now I am happy to be able to love him again, he whom I cherished as a son."

"Suppose he should appear before you, papa?"

"I would press him to my heart."

The young girl, half wild with joy, sprang up, gave a cry of exultation, and ran out of the room. The old man followed her with his eyes, and turned to his wife.

"Where is Felicité going? What is the meaning of her sudden flight?" he asked in astonishment.

"She has gone to call Raphael."

"Is Raphael here?"

"Yes, Verboord, he came to learn the result of his efforts. Surprised by your appearance, and fearing that the sight of him might be disagreeable to you, he retired into the garden."

"Oh, let him come to me!"

Banks appeared at the door, hesitating and timid; but Mr. Verboord opened his arms and cried:

"Raphael, my friend, my saviour!"

He pressed the young man to his heart in a feverish embrace. Mrs. Verboord raised her hands to heaven, while Felicité wept. After the first excitement, Mr. Verboord said, gravely:

"My friend, you have restored to me my life and my reason. It is a kindness for which I will bless you as long as I live. I am glad to owe it to you, whose youth God permitted me to guide. You speak of fortune and riches. I know the sacrifices you are willing to make for your old employer; but I do not wish to take advantage of your generosity. No, no, do not insist. I could not endure the thought that I was robbing you of the fruit of your labors. We still possess this house; I will seek employment; I have friends; perhaps I may be able to find a place in some commercial house. Mr. Dorneval gave me hopes of it."

Raphael interrupted him.

"Oh, you were my benefactor," he said; "you assisted my mother in her last hours; give me the happiness of knowing that my fortune can render your life pleasant. Let me, at least, offer you the means of resuming the career which was closed to you by misfortune. Become my partner: accept as a loan a portion of what I possess. You can return it to me when fortune favors you. I entreat you, do not refuse! If I deserve a reward, then be generous to me!"

"It is impossible," said Mr. Verboord; "my conscience would condemn me as guilty. You wish to relieve my condition; and without knowing it, you would make me unhappy. Believe me, my greatest trial is that I am not able to reward your generous sacrifice."

"You can do it, sir!" cried Banks, with sudden decision of manner.

"By accepting your proposition?"

"No, sir, by a kindness of another kind: by granting me a still greater favor."

"Tell me what it is, my friend."

"Listen to me quietly and kindly, sir," continued Banks. "You may perhaps think my words presuming, and my hopes proud; but I beg you to forgive my frankness; you shall decide, and I will respectfully submit to your will, though it should condemn me for life to sorrow and despair. You do not know, sir, why I went to America, and left you, notwithstanding my promise Your daughter Felicité was about to be married; this marriage would have broken my heart, and rendered me unhappy for life. A secret love had taken possession of my soul, and overpowered me completely. I loved your daughter."

"You loved my daughter!" replied the father in amazement, looking from his wife to Felicité, who had bowed her head and dared not raise her eyes.

"I left my country," continued the young man, "thinking that a wild and active life, in a distant country, would cure the wound in my heart. During four years I struggled in vain with my grief. Her image was always before my eyes. It was a kind of hallucination which possessed me, for I believed Felicité was married. I entered into business and became rich. The remembrance of your kindness caused me to return to Antwerp. I intended to double your fortune, either openly or by strategy, and thus return what you did for my mother and myself. I found Miss Felicité still single, and my old patron sick. The first circumstance awakened my former hopes with new force, the second was a bitter disappointment to me. I resolved to devote my life and fortune to your cure. A voice within whispered: 'Save the father, and perhaps he will give you his daughter's hand as a reward!' Oh, sir, have mercy upon my long-continued sorrows! If your pride refuses the gifts of a stranger, accept the assistance of a son; grant the earnest desire of your dear child, your sweet and gentle Felicité!"

Mr. Verboord could hardly believe what he heard, and looked at his daughter in astonishment. She fell on her knees before him, raised her hands towards him, exclaiming:

"Papa, papa, forgive me! I love him, I have always loved him! He will never leave us; he will cheer and protect you in your old days. Ah! for my mother's sake, for your own, and for mine, be merciful and generous, like Raphael!"

The old man looked absently into the distance for a moment; but a bright smile soon parted his lips, and his face beamed with happiness. Trembling with emotion, he stretched forth his hands, stammering:

"Come to my heart, my children, come to my heart!" as he embraced them both affectionately.

"Raphael," he said, "there is the reward you ask! Make my Felicité happy. Yes, you shall be the support of my old age. Felicité will repay her father's debt by devoted and unlimited affection. Ah! how happy we will be! Nothing shall separate us. The bond which unites us is formed by the purest feelings of the human soul: love, gratitude, devotion, and generosity. Come, my dear Laurence, give your child's husband a maternal kiss!"

Mrs. Verboord drew near and embraced the young people.

The old man raised his eyes filled with tears to heaven, and addressed an earnest prayer to God.

THE END.